The Middle of the Air

The Middle of the Air

A Novel by
Kenneth Butcher

JOHN F. BLAIR, PUBLISHER
Winston-Salem, North Carolina

JOHN F. BLAIR
PUBLISHER
1406 Plaza Drive
Winston-Salem, North Carolina 27103
www.blairpub.com

Manufactured in the United States of America

The letter from Albert Einstein to Franklin Roosevelt on pages 142 - 143 is used by permission of the Franklin D. Roosevelt Presidential Library.

Library of Congress Cataloging-in-Publication Data

Butcher, Kenneth.
The middle of the air / by Kenneth Butcher.
p.   cm.
ISBN 978-089587-371-2 (alk. paper)
1. Radioactive wastes—Transportation—Fiction. 2. Terrorism—Prevention—Fiction. 3. Conspiracies—Fiction. 4. North Carolina—Fiction. 5. Tennessee—Fiction. I. Title.
PS3602.U855M53 2009
813'.6—dc22   2009020467

www.blairpub.com

BOOK DESIGN BY DEBRA LONG HAMPTON

To
Jen, Jonah, Sam, and Steve

Acknowledgments

I READ SOMEWHERE about the notion that the right teachers show up in our lives exactly when they are needed. Such has certainly been my experience with this book. One by one, they showed up, some new, some current, and some from my past—but show up they did.

For a start, I thank my family, who supported and encouraged me through the whole writing process.

I am most grateful for the encouragement and suggestions made by Charley Boyd, Norm Gayford, Gillian Coates, and Virginia Waratinsky, who read early versions of the manuscript and shared valuable insights. Special thanks goes to Marge Cotter, who undertook the daunting task of correcting spelling, grammar, and punctuation to the point that other people had a chance to make it through.

Finally, I extend my warmest thanks to Carolyn Sakowski, Steve Kirk, Kim Byerly, Debbie Hampton, and the rest of the staff at John F. Blair, Publisher, who magically, professionally, and carefully transformed a manuscript into the book you hold in your hands.

Prologue

THE FIRST TIME YOU DRIVE the stretch of interstate that runs between Asheville, North Carolina, and Knoxville, Tennessee, you might think it follows one of the most rugged and beautiful river gorges you have ever navigated. You might think its narrow and winding course is about the only place a road could be laid through that particular set of mountains. For the most part, the drive is just the road, the river, and the vertical cuts on either side. Looking at the cuts, you will not be pleased to hear about the rock slide that thundered down over the road a few years ago, closing the whole passage through the mountains for months. Now that place is marked by a barrier, a chain-link fence against the rockface like a paper doily stretched across the gate of a rhino pen.

On a good day, the sun comes off the water according to its moods. It glints off the surface where the bottom is smooth and sandy and not too deep. It dances off the parts where the ripples break the water into a thousand moving coins. It comes back like an emerald from the deep pools, then almost disappears in olive drab from the shadows underneath the rhododendron branches that reach out from the banks.

But even good days tend to begin and end with damp here. The mist in the valley is famous for its density, making this stretch of highway one of the most dangerous in the eastern United States. Throw in some rain and it feels like the moss is coming down off the hills and onto the road. At least that's what it seems like when you hit the brakes going into a curve.

This can get to even an experienced driver, which describes exactly what Jack Torre was. He had a late start from the Savannah River site— later than he wanted and later than the other trucks on the same run. He knew very well the difference between blowing by Pigeon Forge in the clear light of day and getting hung up there at dusk with fog, thunderstorms, and a bunch of tourists who didn't know how to deal with either one. But back at the plant, he had faced some kind of hold-up on the inspection, on the endless checking of load numbers versus numbers on paperwork versus numbers in the computer. Not that the bureaucracy on this particular project was bad. Quite the opposite. He had never seen one that was so secretive but at the same time so lax about security. They didn't even have escorts for the trucks.

So, following the late start, he had dragged up from South Carolina all afternoon, arriving in Asheville to make the turn onto the highway to the west just in time for the rush hour slowdown. Or, being Asheville, maybe it was the rush minute slowdown. In any case, he swung into the sun and popped in and out of gear for the next couple of miles as traffic jerked ahead.

He looked above the mess along the road, above the hotels and billboards and lumberyards, and followed the curve of the hills to the ridge tops. Up there, the cumulus clouds were starting to build to huge anvils against the blue sky.

By the time he reached Canton, the traffic was back to a continuous flow. The sun was no longer a problem because the thunderheads had merged into one black mass above him. The first fat raindrops flattened themselves against the windshield.

It stormed pretty much from there until he crossed the state line into Tennessee. The rain and headlights and steam rising off the pavement made for poor visibility. The storm dropped the temperature by ten degrees, which was ten degrees below the dew point, so after the storm moved on to the east the fog filled the open space. It was so thick and Jack was so tired that he didn't even play his usual game of looking for traces of the Appalachian Trail, which crossed the highway just at the border between the two states.

He pulled into one of the few places that could still legitimately be called a truck stop. He looked at the line of trucks parked and waiting and saw some that looked vaguely familiar, but no one from his company. They would all be unloading by now. Radios and cell phones didn't work so well in the river gorge, so he hadn't been in contact for some time. Climbing down, he felt every mile in his legs and thought one more time about maybe doing something else for a living. The fog had coated everything—the road, the rocks, the door to the diner—with a thin film of water.

He pushed on in, hit the rest room, and sat at the counter and ordered coffee. He wasn't the kind of trucker who craved conversation at such stops. He watched CNN on the TV for a little while, hearing the same stories that had been on the radio all day—congressional hearings, statements of legislators, the deteriorating situation of our latest escapades overseas. Nothing new. Twenty-four-hour news didn't mean there was anything to really talk about.

When he went out to the parking lot, the truck was gone. That's all there was to it. He went through the motions of looking around, but there was no point. He had no place to look.

Shit.

He searched his mind for the emergency procedures he had never before needed. He remembered the list of call-in numbers. He was to call this number in case of accident, another in case of spotting suspicious drivers, another for mechanical problems. He was to call dispatch for other things. The list also had a couple of other numbers if those didn't answer. Of course, all those numbers were in the truck.

He checked his cell phone. Still no signal, but he did have the dispatch number programmed in. He went back into the diner and called on the pay phone.

"Hey, this is Jack Torre."

"Where the hell are you, Jack?" said the voice on the other end.

"The truck's gone," he said, always one to get right to the point.

There followed a silence, but not for long.

"Where exactly are you?" asked the voice, now very dead and even.

Jack explained his location.

"Stay there. We'll send some guys to pick you up," said the voice. "Stay on the line a minute."

"Should I call the police or the highway patrol?" he asked, trying to think of something to do other than sitting passively in the diner.

After some muffled conversation, another voice broke in.

"Jack, listen to me. Under no circumstances are you to call the police, the highway patrol, your family, or anyone else. Is that clear?"

"Yes," Jack answered. He didn't have to know the person on the other end to sense the authority. He had dealt with the government long enough to recognize that.

"Are you calling from a cell phone or a landline?" asked the voice.

"Pay phone. I can't get a cell phone signal here."

"Sit tight and talk to no one," said the voice. This was followed by a click.

Thirty minutes later, a Humvee pulled up in front of the diner. A man in a dark suit emerged from the passenger door, and Jack left the diner before he had a chance to come in. The man did not speak, but simply opened the rear door and motioned him inside.

The belly of the beast, Jack thought as he climbed in.

Chapter 1

Beside the Lemur

THE ROOM WAS RICHLY POPULATED with parts of astronomical instruments and stuffed primates. On top of a long worktable, a
computer screen softly glowed. Green numbers and other characters
rearranged themselves from time to time in a slow, rhythmic pattern.
At the window, the curtains were parted only a few inches, admitting
little of the D.C. morning light into the darkness of the room.

The engineer Charles Colebrook was collapsed in a chair of unusual design. The padding was deep and pliant. The arms and back
formed a square box.

He wore a pair of navy-blue sweatpants and nothing on his feet
or upper body. He sank deeply into the cushions, his feet spread wide
and resting flat on a braided rug. His arms were motionless on the
chair arms, his head tilted back on the headrest.

His eyes were closed, his breathing slow and effortless. An expression of neutral calm was on his young face. He was a tall man with
thin limbs and wide, powerful shoulders. His features put him in his
mid-twenties, but his expression was without age.

A beautiful girl with straw-colored hair appeared in the doorway.

She was wrapped in a blue towel. Her hair formed spikes, still damp from a shower. She regarded the engineer for a second before deciding that he was not asleep.

"Charles, have you seen the address book?" she asked.

Without moving, he said, "Look beside the Madagascar lemur."

She regarded him a moment longer, not sure what to think of his economy of motion and response. She looked at the lemur with mild disgust. She never had cared for him, ringtail or no ringtail. She extracted the small leather-bound book from beside the primate, taking care not to touch his fur, then turned to leave.

Why do some things catch the eye? At the oddest moments, a singular detail can reach out and touch something inside a girl and grab her away from her course.

In this case, it was something about the line of the engineer's bare arm leading from his broad shoulder to his hand resting so poignantly on the padding of the chair. Something about that made the girl turn herself around and flush with ideas that had nothing to do with address books.

She paused for a moment, let the book drop to the floor, and stepped up to the seated figure. She sat and curled up sideways in his lap, leaning into him. Gently raising his face to hers with both hands, she settled into a deep kiss. He responded and moved his other hand behind her, drawing her closer still.

On the computer screen, the slow pulse of characters was interrupted. Two columns of red numbers advanced with building speed, followed by a flashing alarm bearing a message:

SIGNAL DETECTED

Meanwhile, on an ancient, timeless ridge top in the southern Appalachians, a black bear mother paused and pointed her snout into the air. It was more usual to hear humans well before smelling them, but not so this time.

The bear looked back over her shoulder in time to see a large brown-haired man appear over the crest of the ridge. Leon Colebrook, older brother to Charles, looked like a bear himself, an effect not diminished by his gait. His face was broad and handsome, his eyes the dark, shining brown of Turkish coffee. He was followed immediately by his wife, Sue, a lithe golden-haired woman. She was nearly his own height but elfin in form and motion. They both wore full hiking packs with an ease that suggested they had known many miles of these trails.

And there, between them, not seen at first, marched a much smaller human. A girl of perhaps five years, Audrey had hair yet more golden than her mother's, a striking contrast to the dark brown eyes she could have gotten only from her father. It was these eyes that saw the bear. She stopped as her mother stepped around her.

The bear felt connected eye to eye and heart to heart with the calm little girl who stood there looking back.* Neither made a move or a sound. There was none of the fear that usually accompanied such mutual sightings, not on the part of the bear or the girl. The woman and man stopped and looked back after three or four steps. They followed Audrey's gaze to the bear and stood quietly watching, too. They had seen the effect their daughter had on animals before.

After a few moments, the bear snorted herself out of reverie. She turned and lumbered away off the path.

The little girl looked at her mother and father and smiled, knowing they had seen the bear, too.

"This is close to the place we are looking for," she said, taking in the rock formations and the land around her.

"According to the map, a spring is located in the next ravine. Maybe that's the one," her father said. "You lead."

Without hesitation, the little girl stepped ahead of them and led the way down the path. She, too, carried a backpack, clearly

---

*Ironically, the work of a young biophysicist from Ecuador, Henrico Carr, a close friend of Leon's from grad school, would soon make it possible to translate bear thought patterns into human phrases. This technology would translate the bear word (or thought pattern, really) for human being into "skinny bear that buries its poop underground."

The idea of burying feces was quite foreign to bear instincts. Bears were actually rather proud of their poop, its odor reminding them of the things they have eaten to begin the alimentary process. If it were not for the quality and quantity of food that humans came up with, we would have been held in low esteem indeed. To bears, our food was no less than miraculous, and they held our hunting and gathering capabilities in the highest regard. Given the importance of food to bears, this counted for a great deal.

homemade to fit her size. The ridge top was fairly open and offered a good early-morning view to the west. The path began to descend, entering thicker woods and shadows as it swung to the west side of the mountain. They presently came to a depression where a small stream trickled across the trail.

The little girl stopped short of the stream and looked to the right to find the spring that was its source.

"I think this is it," she said.

They all turned from the trail and followed the stream uphill toward some moss-covered rocks. A pile of small rocks with a large slab of coarse marble partly covering it formed the pool of the spring. She ducked her head to see its underside, then jumped back with glee.

"This is it! This is the one I saw!"

She made way for the grownups to approach. They shrugged off the packs. The man reached into a small pocket at the top of his pack and removed a Petzl. He strapped it around his head and switched on the light as he got down on his knees and bent forward to see under the stone. He let out a barely audible "Wow!" as he bent closer still. Grasping the stone with one hand for balance, he dipped his other hand into the water of the spring and washed the underside of the slab for a better look.

He backed out and returned to the pack. Tearing open the main pocket, he rummaged until he found a book, which he pulled out and opened to a marked page. A torn dust cover bore the title *Treasures of the Ancient Mayans*. By this time, his wife had leaned under the rock herself. He put the opened book down next to her, and they both looked at the picture of an intricate carving of hieroglyphics.

"What do you think?" he said.

"That's it. Except there's more on this one," she said, slapping the rock with a wet hand.

The little girl by this time was looking for salamanders in the shallow creek. Without looking up, she said, "I told you."

ooooo

And later, in a campus apartment in Virginia, an engineering student, third brother in the family, Xavier Colebrook, came to life with a quick squirrel-like turn of the head. He rose to one elbow above a nest of blankets in an elevated bunk. His face was still sleepy, but his eyes, wide awake, darted around the room to see what had startled him from his sleep. He found a pair of wire-rim glasses and put them on.

An alarm sounded on his cell phone, located somewhere in the debris on his desk. The alarm indicated the receipt of a text message. At the same time, he heard a knock on his door, accompanied by an impatient shout.

"Hey, X-Man, someone is asking for you downstairs!"

"Oh, shit," said Xavier.

He jumped down from the bed with a soft thud, dressed only in boxer shorts. Though thin and not above average in height, he had wiry muscles and broad shoulders.

He found the cell phone, silenced the alarm, and punched up the text message:

IMPLEMENT EXIT PLAN

"Time to get out of here," said Xavier, struggling into a pair of canvas pants with cargo pockets. He pulled on a pair of running shoes, laces already tied. He picked up a maroon T-shirt from the floor, smelled it, and, apparently finding it acceptable, pulled that on, too. A blue work shirt and baseball cap completed the hasty outfit.

Looking around the room, he grabbed a backpack. He closed his laptop and threw it in, together with a few other objects from the desk and around the room.

"Later, Bleeksburg," he said, and ducked out the window onto the landing of a fire escape.

Chapter 2

Blue Hooded Sweatshirt

THE GIRL BEHIND THE WHEEL was wearing a navy-blue hooded sweatshirt, hood down in a bundle at the back of her neck. A brown ponytail emerged from the back of a matching watch cap.

She had told the group she could drive anything, though reflecting on her statement now, she was not sure what she had based that on. She was the new kid on the block, and this seemed like a great opportunity to prove herself. She was making a bit of a mess of the lower gears of the truck, but once she got going, she was okay.

She knew the route well. Bear right at the beginning of the entrance ramp instead of going onto the highway. At the bottom of the hill, turn left on the small road running back under the highway. Turn right at the road along the riverbank. All this was so well obscured by trees that it was almost invisible from the highway. After about a quarter-mile, she hung a hard left onto an old steel bridge across the river. There had been some discussion about this part during the planning. Questions had arisen about the ability of the bridge to hold the weight of the truck. Someone had checked out the nameplate on the bridge, which seemed to indicate it was adequate. The fact that the plate was almost rusted away did little to reassure her on that point.

An even bigger concern was negotiating the tight turn, but this she did without any unpleasant scraping sounds from the sides of the truck. She rumbled across and had little trouble turning left on the opposite bank, thanks to the wide gravel shoulder.

She drove slower now, breathing more easily. It was dark in the shadow of the mountain, the mist particularly dense by the river. The water was only a few feet below her. High on the bank to her right, she noticed a white rectangle painted on a tree trunk, the sign of the Appalachian Trail. Across the road, a small parking lot—not much more than a wide place on the side of the road—held several vehicles. These would have been left by hikers. She remembered years ago emerging at this point after the five-day stretch from Fontana Dam through the Great Smoky Mountains National Park. She had felt a lot more at ease then than she did now.

She covered less than a mile before she saw the lights of the power plant glowing through the darkness. The gate in the chain-link fence was open, and the parking lot was deserted except for a green Honda Civic and a couple of yellow service trucks with power company emblems on the doors. Yellow light radiated through the square glass panels set in the high bay doors of the main building. As she approached, two men swung them open. She rolled the truck into the opening, and the men pulled the doors shut again.

They had figured that, with luck, this would all be done before the theft of the truck was discovered.

They were right.

A third man walked out through the door as the truck rolled in. He looked at her face as they passed. He seemed amused at the concentration and relief he saw up there. The others had some doubts about her, but he had figured she would do fine.

The man was young—late twenties—and thin. He wore a bright yellow rain jacket that had seen a lot of wear, either on sailboats or troubleshooting electrical transmission equipment. Either activity seemed about equally probable.

He took out a pack of Camel filters and lit one with an old-fashioned flint-and-wheel lighter. He strolled over to the open gate and leaned against the post, dragging on the cigarette, exhaling clouds of smoke into the fog. He looked down the moist road and up across the river onto the highway above. He listened to the sounds of the river and the traffic up there on the highway, searching for anything that sounded out of place, any sound of panic on the night air. He looked for any red or blue flashing lights, or any speeding headlights heading down the small access road. Nothing.

The length of time it took to smoke the cigarette was enough to satisfy him that the truck had not been followed.

He turned and started walking back to the power plant. He had always liked the looks of the place at night. The building was somehow a little gothic, being built of stone and brick for the most part. Then there was the Jules Verne effect of the windows with small panes in the upper stories. Overlaid on that motif were the pinpoints of brilliance formed by the small halogen safety lights, which added a bit of mystery and excitement, like a Christmas tree lit up in a darkened room. Just behind the plant, the rockface was almost vertical. To the left, the river flowed in a wide, pebbly bed. In a way, the power plant looked as primeval as the river and mountain. Who said there was no art in this sort of thing?

Glancing once more over his shoulder, he entered the building by a smaller door.

Chapter 3

Philip and the Weiner Dog

PHILIP COLEBROOK, father of Leon, Charles, and Xavier, half-awakened and fed the dogs, who were delighted as always with their bowl of food in the morning. This day at work he did not look forward to. He never used to feel that way. Sometimes, he felt like water pouring over the edge of a bucket. Sometimes, he felt like a bucket with all its water poured out. Other times, he felt like some alternate metaphor that had nothing to do with either water or buckets.

He showered, which never failed to awaken his attention to the world. He made coffee and drank a cup while watching the morning news, then reluctantly headed out. To be able to sit and drink another cup—now, that would have been a great luxury.

A couple of months ago, he had finally agreed to sell the family business to a Swiss corporation. Now came the awkward transition period. The contract called for him to be there for two more years, though he knew they probably did not really want him around. From strictly a business point of view, this was the fulfillment of a dream, yet he could not bring himself to feel totally right about it. Nor did he know what he would do when he finally left the company behind.

He sailed into town without incident until he came upon the first of many traffic lights.

If I ever decide to leave this place, it will be to escape these freaking lights, he thought.

Indeed, the number and poor coordination of the town's traffic lights made driving as mind-numbing an experience as in a city many times its size. A story was told that anytime a traffic light became available in the state of North Carolina, it was sent to Hendersonville and hung in some random location.

He still felt half asleep when he stopped at the next light. He looked over as a brown Mercedes pulled up in the lane beside him. It was slightly forward of him, so that the back window was even with his face. And from that half-open back window protruded the face of a wiener dog. The wiener dog was beginning to show signs of age—a little gray on the muzzle, a little sagging around the eyes. The eyes had a liquid quality about them, although they were not pleading like some dog eyes. In fact, they were more or less without expression, staring directly and frankly into Philip's. Man and dog sat that way until the Mercedes jogged forward with the changing of the light, leaving Philip sitting alone.

In that moment, Philip felt a profound connection to the wiener dog. He remembered hearing on a PBS special that 90 percent of the DNA of all mammals was identical. The seemingly vast differences among the species were all coded in the remaining 10 percent. Just as he shared much of the same DNA with the wiener dog, he speculated that their souls, too, were made of much the same material. What they had in common dwarfed the differences.

I am the wiener dog, and the wiener dog is me, he said to himself. *I am one with the wiener dog.**

A horn broke his reverie. He glided forward and checked the

---

* Shortly, the Ecuadorian biophysicist Henrico Carr would be able to confirm Philip's sentiments—or to confirm that the sentiments were shared by the wiener dog, at least. Several of Carr's best friends happened to own wiener dogs. Carr discovered, among other things, that the wiener dog felt itself to be much closer to humans than to many other breeds of dogs.

rearview mirror. As he suspected, the car behind him was piloted by an overly aggressive red-faced retiree, one whose ass he would dearly have loved to kick.

He proceeded to the Athenaeum parking lot and found it about three-quarters full, a result of the Swiss "rearrangement" of personnel. As was his custom, he stopped first by his secretary's office to check for messages, mail, and the general office news. She looked up with a strange expression on her face, and he followed her gaze to a picture leaning against the wall, facing inward.

"They took it down this morning," she said, still looking at him, as if to gauge his reaction.

He knew what it was, but he dropped his briefcase on a chair and picked it up anyway. It was a painting that had hung in the entryway for years. He could not look at it without a smile.

"It won't be the same around here without it," the secretary said.

"Not progressive enough," Philip said. "Not in the spirit of the new organization," he added, using a quote he had heard often in the past few weeks.

The painting did not reflect the usual style or subject matter of the artist's work. It showed a fat boy nine or ten years of age bouncing on a trampoline. At the moment captured in the painting, the youth was suspended in midair, a small white clapboard house and a tobacco field in the background. The body language and the face both expressed pure joy. Philip's father, James Colebrook, better know as Pipo, had painted the picture to cheer up Philip and Lilly when their first son, Leon, had moved out to go to college. The picture was entitled *The Middle of the Air*.

"I remember him using that expression all the time," the secretary said. "I didn't always understand what he meant."

"Well, you're in good company there," Philip said with a grin. "Usually, he meant the place where ideas come from, like when you're designing something or solving a problem. You look at all the information and maybe what has been done before, but then eventually you have to make something up from nothing, like grabbing it from the middle of the air."

"I guess they won't be needing that much anymore," said the secretary.

Philip looked at her with amusement. Every now and then, she still surprised him.

"No, I guess they won't."

He tucked the painting under his arm and moved on to his office.

Chapter 4

A Second Finding

AS THEY DESCENDED FROM THE RIDGE, Leon and Sue continued to discuss the rock and the symbols and what they might imply. They were also thinking about what to do next. Whom should they involve? If they didn't do this right, they would have hundreds of people tramping around one of their favorite places, probably messing up the site from an archaeological point of view, to say nothing of the natural beauty of the place.

As usual, Audrey was living much more in the moment, taking in everything around her. So it was that she spotted the wreckage in the limbs of a red oak tree. She stopped and took it in for a moment before speaking.

At first, she could make no sense of the odd shape in the branches. The delta wing was the first part that grabbed her attention, although its dull gray-black color blended in surprisingly well with the forest background. Though somewhat crumpled, the craft appeared to have a wingspan of about eight feet. The engine was like a hump on the back of the fuselage. The propeller was gone.

"It's a toy airplane!" she said.

Leon and Sue came up behind her, and all three stood looking into the tree. After some discussion about how to get it down, Leon threw a length of rope over the branch. Using exaggerated motions, he swung the branch up and down until the craft nudged loose and finally fell to the ground.

"What kind of a plane is that?" asked the girl.

"It looks like what they call an autonomous aircraft. They used to call them drones. See, that looks like a little TV camera, and that's the engine, and I think that's the battery pack down there."

"Can we take it home?" she asked.

"I think we need to take it to your uncle Xavier. He'll know what to do with it."

"It looks kind of creepy," Audrey said.

"You know what I think makes it look creepy?" said Sue. "It doesn't have any markings."

She was right. The plane bore no letters, no numbers, no markings of any kind whatsoever.

"How are we going to carry that thing out of here?" she asked.

She had a point. Although the entire craft weighed probably less than thirty pounds, it was unwieldy because of its size and shape.

"We'll take it apart and just bring the engine and controls," Leon said.

This was easier said than done, given that he had only camping tools with him. It wasn't pretty either. He hacked and tore at the composite material, which proved to be surprisingly tough. However, he finished the job at length, and they strode off, Leon balancing the fuselage across his right shoulder like a World War II soldier with a bazooka.

As they left, an odd sound caused the little girl to look back over her shoulder. Just as she did, she thought she heard the sound again. But seeing nothing, she marched on without a word.

ooooo

The United States Army Ranger trainees could not have been better camouflaged, their faces painted green and black, sprigs of foliage in the netting of their helmets, fatigues of olive drab and brown. It was part of their exercise to remain silent and unseen, observing hikers as they passed. This time of year, hikers were plentiful, so the Rangers were getting good at the game. As time went by, the objective was to get closer and closer to the trail and still remain invisible.

This day, they got a bonus. The hikers had actually discovered something interesting. After the sergeant in charge of the maneuver gave the hand signal to converge on the trail, they moved quickly to the spot where the plane had been crudely dismantled. Although he had never seen anything like it, the sergeant identified it as military in nature, and so he was disposed to feel somewhat possessive of it, since he thought of himself and his captain as the only military authorities in that part of the forest.

He instructed the trainees to pick up the wings and any other pieces of the craft and head back to their wilderness camp.

Chapter 5

I ra Hudson

IRA HUDSON WAS A NERVOUS MAN in a roomful of nervous men. Gray was the predominant color. Outside the meeting room, gray metal desks bore stacks of papers and forms. Outside the window were gray skies, gray streets, and gray buildings on a standard Washington rainy day: fifty degrees and overcast.

Ira Hudson wanted information, and he wanted a cigarette. A truck and its six tons of fuel-grade radioactive material were missing. That wasn't supposed to happen. Ever. Details on the driver, the route, the time of departure, and the estimated time of arrival were missing. The radio check-in log was missing. The director of transport, the only competent one of the bunch, was on vacation—and so, effectively, missing.

All the safeguards—the checking, the double-checking, the foolproof redundant measures—were proving useless. The second line of defense, satellite tracking, provided only a confusing, unreadable map of the southeastern United States that meant nothing to him or anyone else he could put his hands on. The unmanned low-level surveillance plane, not responding to commands, was also missing.

Of course, the safety measures were a drastic abbreviation of the normal crap the government required. Streamlining, getting rid of all the unnecessary steps that had held up progress in the past, was part of the plan.

This plan was perhaps the purest application of the philosophy that the current administration summarized with the catch phrase "Government Without Shame," or G.W.S. for short. According to G.W.S., decisions were to be guided more by principle and strategy than by details of implementation. Replacing people of high technical competence with those who understood and endorsed the administration's goals resulted in much less internal strife. Becoming bogged down in the analysis of outcomes was a mistake that the administration was going to avoid at all costs.

In less than thirty minutes, Hudson was going to have to start notifying people that the truck and materials were gone and that he had absolutely no idea what was going on.

A secretary stuck her head in the room.

"It's a phone call for you, Mr. Hudson. Oak Ridge. Line three," she said.

He looked at the phone in the conference room and decided he didn't want to take the call there. He asked the secretary for a private place. She escorted him to an empty office a few doors down the hall.

He returned to the meeting room a few minutes later. The others looked at him in expectation.

"Nothing," he said. "They brought the driver in but haven't gotten anything useful out of him yet. They'll keep him there and go over everything some more, but it doesn't sound like he knows anything. He got going late, didn't make particularly good time, stopped for some coffee, and the truck was gone when he came out. Didn't see anything or anyone."

He exchanged glances with an older man at the table, then turned to the rest of the group.

"Listen, you guys follow up on the material we discussed and meet back here in one hour," he said.

All but the older man got up immediately.

"What assets do we have in place to work this?" the older man asked when the team had left.

"So far, not much. We sent an autonomous flier over western Virginia and south over the area. But it's down now, or at least not responding."

"You think that's part of this?" the older man asked.

"I don't know. I don't know how reliable those things are right now," said Ira.

"Because if we are dealing with someone who could detect one of those things and bring it down, then that's different from a missing truck. That's a whole different thing," he said.

Ira Hudson had thought about the same thing.

"So what else?" the older man asked.

"We've got someone in Savannah River. He's checking on that end. Like, why did the guy leave late? What was holding him up?" said Hudson.

"Can he do that without stirring up a lot of shit down there?" asked the older man.

"He knows what he has to do," said Hudson. "Damn it, this is exactly the kind of thing they assured us could not happen."

"They being everyone you didn't fire after firing everyone who actually knew anything about this kind of operation," the older man said.

"That was part of G.W.S., as you may recall. Those people were simply not on board with the program."

The older man understood it was not the time for such a conversation. He got up and walked to a map on the wall showing East Tennessee and western North Carolina, with the tips of Georgia and South Carolina peeking in at the bottom. It was dense with topographical lines, elevation numbers, roads, and waterways.

"What is this?" he asked, pointing to a thin red dashed line coming up from northern Georgia, passing through western North Carolina, then following the border of North Carolina and Tennessee until it disappeared off the map into Virginia.

"They tell me that's the A.T.—the Appalachian Trial," Hudson said.

The older man followed it south to north with his finger. Using his other hand, he traced Interstate 40 east to west, bringing his two index fingers together precisely where the truck was stolen. He looked at Ira and raised his eyebrows. Neither was in any mood to believe in coincidence.

The older man lifted a finger and used it to circle the area where the A.T. crossed the border between Georgia and North Carolina.

"So, this Appalachian Trail," said the older man. "Can you drive a truck on it?"

"Not hardly," said Hudson. "At least from what I've heard about it. For the most part, it's just a narrow footpath through the woods."

"Still," said the older man, "I guess you could move people and maybe equipment over it."

They both paused and thought for a minute.

"I seem to remember that this area is used for Ranger training," said the older man.

"The last I knew, the Rangers did most of their training in northern Georgia. That's not too far away," said Ira. "I know someone there. I know the captain in charge of training and selection."

"Find out where he is and if he has any guys out there now," the older man said. "Don't tell him what's going on, but tell him we need some eyes and ears out there."

"Better yet," said Hudson, "I can say we need him to look for the downed plane. I can ask him to cover the trail, look for suspicious people, find out if anything unusual is going on."

"Let's get on it," said the older man.

He got up and left.

Sitting in Washington looking at a map of the southern Appalachians, it was not hard to observe that northern Georgia was close to the Great Smoky Mountains National Park, which lay just south of where I-40 crossed the Appalachian Trail. However, as many a prospective thru-hiker on the A.T. could attest, a lot of rough country and not many roads were between the two points. Of the three to four thousand people who set out from Springer Mountain, the southern end of the Appalachian Trail, each spring, fewer than half made it through their first week and reached the southern border of North Carolina. Fewer than 15 percent made it through the Great Smoky Mountains National Park and ended up crossing the highway where the truck disappeared.

Those who did make it that far often told stories of seeing Rangers doing wilderness training exercises along the trail. The army called them "snake eaters." Hikers who saw these men in their silent stalking and eluding exercises described it as a spooky, surreal experience. The mountain maneuvers were part of Hell Week for the men. They were deprived of sleep and food, as if moving through rugged terrain day and night was not enough of a challenge. One hiker told the story of climbing a trail in the early morning and being startled by fifteen to twenty men on either side holding machine guns. The general rule was that no contact should exist between hikers and Rangers. They each just sort of pretended the other didn't exist. Sometimes, though, hikers took pity on the starving men and slipped them candy bars or trail mix. God only knew what would happen to a trainee if caught in that kind of exchange.

Captain Watts got the call from Washington in the early evening in the relative luxury of camp. (He actually had a tent and was eating hot food from the campfire.) He had mixed emotions about the request. On one hand, anything that interfered with the carefully orchestrated drama of Hell Week could break a longstanding tradition. On the other hand, he knew that the Rangers were far enough in that he had lost everyone he was going to lose. The ones remaining were so far past taking any feedback from their normal senses that they would do anything they were told to do, to the point of dropping dead. Anyway, the training was getting a little old by now, and a real assignment—especially one that called upon the special talents of the Rangers—was welcome.

What he received took the form of a request, not an order through normal channels. He was pretty much given free rein during the training phase, so he owned his guys for about another month.

Chapter 6

Continuous Improvement with No Change

PHILIP SIPPED COFFEE and looked out his office window into the parking lot of the Athenaeum Company. He watched as two maintenance men unfurled a banner bearing the letters *C.I.N.C.* This stood for the new company motto, Continuous Improvement with No Change. The men studied the front of the building, trying to figure out how they would hang the banner over the bronze letters of the company name.

C.I.N.C. was invented by a British economics professor. According to the C.I.N.C. philosophy, decisions should be guided more by principle and strategy than by details of products and service. Replacing people of high technical competence with those who endorsed the corporate philosophy resulted in much less strife within the company. Becoming bogged down in the analysis of actual results was a mistake the new management group intended to avoid.

Looking to his left, Philip noted the arrival of a goldfinch at the bird feeder near the lunch room. He assumed it was the same goldfinch he had been watching for some years. *It really isn't gold,* he thought. *Should be the banana finch or maybe the lemon finch. But definitely not the goldfinch.*[*]

The bird abruptly fled as a car rammed into the nearest parking place. It was the BMW company car of Michael Palance, the CEO installed by the new Swiss owners. Both the driver's and passenger's doors swung open in perfect unison, Judy Gold emerging from the shotgun position. Judy was a middle-aged woman whom the new owners had put in charge of quality assurance. Since then, she had spent most of her time off-site at training seminars. Predictably, she had become an expert at the mechanics of the discipline while developing no understanding of its underlying purpose.

Philip watched as Michael and Judy stepped toward the front of the car and exchanged a few words, looking back and forth between the bird feeder and the car. He knew that Michael was worried about birds pooping on his hood, despite assurances that the placement of the feeder left a sufficient buffer zone. The pair then walked to the back of the car, opened the trunk, and removed two wooden boxes with handles. They seemed pleased and excited.

Philip wondered again if Judy and Michael were sleeping together and immediately berated himself for having such an unkind and ungenerous thought, and for inflicting upon his own mind a physically revolting picture.

He savored his coffee a few more minutes, then glanced at his watch and concluded he could no longer put off the inevitable. After grabbing a notebook to head toward the conference room, he stuck his head into his secretary's office.

"I'm headed to a C.I.N.C. meeting in the conference room," he said.

---

[*] A graduate student working under Professor Henrico Carr was just then studying goldfinch thought patterns using Carr's new technology. In the bird world, the color yellow was associated with high religious stature. In its particular sphere, the goldfinch was held in a position similar to that of a Buddhist monk in human culture. Among goldfinches, most human activities and products were considered dangerous and spiritually insignificant. One exception was the yellow school bus, worshiped as a manifestation of God on earth.

She looked at him for a moment, then said, "I know," and gave a small smile of irony that acknowledged his pain without offering any support or pity for it. "The usual instructions?" she asked.

"Yes," he said, and pulled back out into the hall.

"No problem," she said without removing her eyes from her computer screen.

The usual instructions were as follows: If the meeting did not end promptly in one hour as it was supposed to, she was to throw open the door and shoot him in the face. He had often assured her that being shot in the face would be infinitely preferable to spending more than an hour in such a meeting. Although she had failed to carry out these instructions any number of times, she always agreed that she would be happy to do so this time.

"By the way," she whispered, "Leon phoned before you came in. He said to have you call when you're alone and away from the company."

To this he gave a nod and a frown of curiosity. Why had his oldest son, Leon, chosen not to leave a voice mail, and why did he need to phone when he was away from the company?

He took his few last steps down the hall and entered the conference room, which he found distasteful on several levels: furniture, lighting, wall hangings, sickly vibe emanating from the group assembled there.

Apparently the last to arrive, he took his usual seat, the one closest to the door.

Without preamble, Judy began. "This is going to be a special meeting. We will continue to develop some tools to deal with conflict at the workplace and to imagine how our attitudes and actions affect those around us."

Judy and Michael had just returned from still another training course, and rumors were circulating. She moved to the end of the table opposite Philip and near the pair of boxes. Michael was already standing behind one of the boxes with a clever smile on his face.

"Today, we will work with a tool borrowed from an ancient tradition," Judy said, placing her hand on the lid of the other box.

Michael and Judy both opened their box lids by a fraction, stuck their hands inside, and seemed to grope around a little, presently finding what they were looking for.

"Today," she said, looking at Michael to confirm that he was ready, "we will learn to work with puppets!"

With this, Judy and Michael flung open the lids and produced with a flourish two of the most morbid and grotesque wooden figures Philip had ever set eyes upon. Pleased with the theatricality of the stunt, Michael and Judy beamed with pride. They were greeted with dead silence from the rest of the room.

Philip balanced on the knife edge between revulsion and ribald laughter. He most especially did not want to give in to laughter, as this would be material evidence that he was not taking the game seriously, not "supporting the goals of the transition," as described in the legal contract. He also knew from experience that once he got started on that type of laughter, he had no means of stopping it and might require as much as an hour before he could do anything useful.

He glanced around the table at the other team members.

Sheila was a hands-on detail worker in the plant who had been with the company for years. Though deeply religious and generally quiet, she was touchy on certain subjects. Philip had never been able to predict those subjects in advance and always found himself surprised when her temper flared.

Sheila's face was a mask of horror.

Buddy was a resourceful maintenance man known for solving problems that stumped others, and also for the occasional cutting one-liner.

Buddy's jaw had dropped so low it threatened to come out of joint. The last time Philip had seen that look on Buddy's face was when one of the junior guys hooked up the wrong regulator to the paint booth and blew up a canister full of yellow paint.

Buddy was also known for the use of what Philip called a "universal simile." Specifically, Buddy compared everything to a son of a bitch. For instance, it could be hot as a son of a bitch. It could be cold as a son of a bitch. The simile could also be used to suggest that a thing was good or bad. For instance, you could ask, "Buddy, how did that experimental run of parts go?" Buddy would say, "Oh, those parts? They ran like a son of a bitch." Those who knew Buddy could read from the inflection of his voice and by the look on his face whether the run had gone well or poorly. Shades of gray were more difficult to read, this being a shortcoming of the universal simile. The new owners had a lot of trouble understanding Buddy at all.

Judy and Michael were trying their best to read the reaction, which was clearly not what they were looking for.

"I don't sink dey know vat to make of us," Judy said, or rather Judy made her puppet say.

The embarrassment and confusion of the moment were amplified by Judy's limited skill as a puppet master, as shown for example by the poor coordination between her words and the movement of the puppet's jaw. In addition, Judy's adopted accent could not be linked to any known nationality or ethnic group. It seemed to be a composite of several foreign accents.

"Waal, Aya thank y'all just need ta tell um wot we're up to," replied Michael's puppet.

Philip and the other team members glanced at each other, searching for some clue as to how they were supposed to react to this scene.

It took a moment to sink in that Michael was attempting to make his puppet produce a Southern accent. Of the many such attempts Philip had heard from non-Southerners, this was clearly the worst. Philip found it especially infuriating that people like Michael could not understand the proper use of *y'all*. The contraction was simply the second person plural! Nothing else! It wasn't that difficult.

Philip saw that the others were beginning to take offense.

Sheila raised her hand, and Judy's puppet nodded at her.

"Are we going to have to put our hands into those things?" Sheila addressed Michael and Judy, refusing to lock eyes with the puppets being shoved in her direction.

"Vell, jew see, Sheila, zometimes ve puppets can zay sings dat real people can't zay," said Judy's puppet.

"Y'all got that rought," Michael's puppet chimed in. "Don't nobody gets mad at a puppet, no madder whot they says."

"I just don't want to stick my hand up inside of a body," said Sheila.

Once again, Philip had not seen this coming. Of all the possible objections, he could never have predicted that Shelia would come up with this. However, once she brought the issue to light, sticking a hand inside a body did seem revolting to Philip as well.

"Vell, Sheila, jew don't hove to use zeez puppets, jew con make jor own," said Judy's puppet, its accent deteriorating with every word spoken.

"How about a hand puppet?" said Carl, the suck-ass accounting clerk.

Everyone looked at him, mostly in confusion.

"You know," he said. "A hand puppet."

Carl was eager to be seen as a company man and proactive problem solver. He jumped up and snatched a red marker from the conference-room board. Then, making a loose fist, he drew two eyes and a pair of lips on the knuckles of his index finger and thumb. He held his hand up proudly and demonstrated the opening and closing of the mouth by moving his thumb up and down.

"I'm not sure that qualifies as a puppet," said Lewis, the quality technician. True to form, the more remote a detail was from the central issue, the more interested Lewis grew, and the more tenaciously he would grapple with it until he was satisfied that correctness had been achieved.

"It is a puppet," Carl said. "You know, the name is *hand puppet*. Why would everyone call it a hand puppet if it's not considered a puppet?"

"Just because everyone calls something by some name doesn't mean it's right. Like everyone calling a tomato a vegetable when it's really a fruit. Or the fact that a sunflower is not a real flower," said Lewis.

"Excuse me, Lewis. I'm pretty sure a sunflower really is a flower." This came from one of the foundry technicians. "Although I do acknowledge that a tomato is not a vegetable."

Philip sat back and rubbed his eyes. It never ceased to amaze him how quickly a group of people could follow a downward spiral, all joining hands and heading straight for hell. He looked over at Buddy, who seemed to be having similar thoughts.

For his part, Michael Palance had promised himself that he would not under any circumstance lose his patience with the group this week. Dropping the puppet voice for the moment, he returned to his normal authoritative tone and said, "I think we can leave the discussion of fruits and flowers for another time and refocus on the purpose of the meeting."

"Do you want me to get a dictionary and look up the word *puppet*?" Lewis offered.

Michael looked down at the table to regain his composure.

Judy jumped in. Or rather her puppet did. "Ve sink it's okay to do za hand puppet. Za point is to eggspress jorselve, not to forry about if it is correct. Jew con make any kind of puppet jew vant."

This seemed to bring the meeting right back to where it had been a few moments ago. Sheila made a fist and seemed to try to visualize a face on it, but she had trouble moving her thumb enough to make the mouth work.

In the fullness of the awkward moment, Buddy slipped a small pair of vice-grip pliers out of his back pocket and made an adjustment on the knob. He held the pliers up and began to manipulate the handles, making the jaws open and close.

"Hi, I'm Bobo the dinosaur," said the pliers.

Michael and Judy were delighted to see this sign that the team was finally joining in the spirit of the meeting.

"Hi, Bobo!" said their two puppets in unison, accents suddenly dropped.

"Bobo, how are y'all feeling today?" asked Michael's puppet, remembering its accent.

"Waal, I'm a-feeling mighty good. Just like a big old dinosaur should," said Bobo.

The others looked on in fascination. Buddy really made those vice-grip pliers come to life.

"Bobo, how do y'all like a-working at this here company?" said

Michael's puppet. Michael seemed a little unsure where to take the conversation, now that he had it going.

"Waal, I likes it just fine. Just fine. But rought now, I gots myself a little bit of a problem," said the pliers.

Michael and Judy were really getting somewhere. This was exactly what puppet therapy was all about.

"Tell us, Bobo, what kind of a problem do y'all have today?" said Michael's puppet.

"Waal, Mr. Southern Boy, Ah'm feeling hongry. Mighty, mighty hongry," said Bobo the pliers dinosaur puppet.

"Waal, Bobo, what do y'all feel lak a-eatin' on today?" said Michael's puppet.

"Y'all knows Ah likes my Vienna sausages," said Bobo.

With that, Buddy reached across the conference table and clamped the pliers to the crotch of Michael's puppet.

"Now, remember," he said. "Don't nobody gets mad at a puppet."

Buddy shoved his chair back and left the room.

Philip chose a small inkblot on the edge of his notebook to focus upon. Only by achieving the concentration of a Zen master could he avoid the laughing fit held just beneath the surface. After a moment, he was able to look up to see Michael, Judy, and their two puppets staring at him, as if he had set the whole scene up. The pliers still dangled limply from the male puppet's crotch.

"Maybe I should go have a talk with Buddy," Philip managed to get out.

Four heads nodded at him.

As he left the room, Sheila cast him a look of desperation. *Don't leave me alone with these things*, her eyes seemed to be saying.

Michael began fiddling with the pliers, not understanding how to release the clamping mechanism. He looked as if they were clamped to his crotch instead of the puppet's.

"We will discuss this later," Michael said.

"Have your puppet make an appointment with my teddy bear," Philip said from the hallway.

Chapter 7

A Covert Launch

THE ADVANTAGES OF UNMANNED AIRCRAFT were well documented in the country's latest adventures in foreign lands.

Ira Hudson, working closer to home, had discovered still more advantages in his particular line of work. They all revolved around the number of people who needed to know about any given flight, and especially the documentation that was created by such an operation. For a conventional flight, the pilot—or, more generally, the pilot and other crew members—had to be considered. The records of takeoffs and landings at either military or civilian airports were factors. Then came the fact that the data acquired passed through several hands before it got to him.

Unmanned aircraft—or, as the tech guys preferred, autonomous aircraft—could be launched from various places. In this case, the little plane would go up from a private airstrip in Virginia that was home to only the small start-up company and a local club of model aircraft builders. Hudson communicated the desired coordinates to his men on the ground there. The data could be uplinked to a satellite, but in this case he instructed them to just make a recording with no further transmission. No one else needed to see what they saw. Pretty clean.

The hangar at the far side of the runway served as workshop, assembly area, and control center for the start-up company, which built and flew the latest autonomous aircraft. The windows of the rusty metal structure had been spray-painted a light color that let in a little light but left the interior unobservable from the outside. Its large overhead doors in the front and two small doors, one in front and one in back, were all kept scrupulously locked. Inside, the main bay held several small airplanes in various stages of assembly or disassembly, plus a small, mean-looking helicopter that was intended for God knew what. Scattered about were several red tool chests with multiple drawers, a workbench with a vise, a drill press, a lathe, and a solid old Bridgeport mill. Various forms and molds used to lay up composite body parts lined one wall. The office area was marked as such by only a couple of worn-out couches and a worktable holding two computers. Between the couches was a piece of carpet that completed the area designed for human comfort.

The day started well enough. They received orders about when to launch and details of the destination and search parameters. The route there and back was up to them.

Leeman and Jones, the technicians, went through the vehicle checklist they had developed. Knowing that the round trip Hudson had prescribed was going to push the limits of their machine, they changed out some of the battery packs to maximize the energy stored on board. They added the monitoring device that had arrived by special dispatch from Washington the evening before. They also removed some of the other components, making more room for extra batteries and fuel. They figured the little plane had a good shot at completing the round trip—depending, as always, on the winds and weather.

Their older coworker, Lines, spent the early morning reviewing code and running a testing protocol to make sure the latest changes did not screw up something else in the programming or operation.

Once all was ready, the launch itself was almost anticlimactic. The little plane took off into an insignificant headwind. It cruised slowly at first while Lines went through the diagnostic sequence to confirm everything was working well. Then they put the spurs to it and headed down to the target area, a flight that took just under two hours from their location.

In order to save power, they did not transmit video signal the whole trip. They followed the position of the craft using the GPS system on board, transmitting a burst every forty-five seconds. The position—together with altitude, airspeed, and certain diagnostic data—was displayed on a map feature on one of the wide-screen monitors. To this data, standard for all their flights, they had added a readout on the level of the special sensor they had installed.

Not being clear about the engineering units represented, the output was simply shown as a percent-of-scale number.

Leeman was on duty in the late afternoon. Since the operation had reached a routine stage, they decided that one guy watching the screen was plenty until the plane reached the target area. The sensor reading pretty much flat-lined until the plane crossed Interstate 40 near Asheville, North Carolina. There, Leeman noticed the reading jump to nearly 70 percent of scale in one data burst, then recede to about 15 percent forty-five seconds later in the next burst. That was still well above background.

"We got something," he said.

"What's up?" Lines asked, approaching the screen.

Leeman tapped some keys, and the numbers were replaced by line graphs showing the last several readings. The spike in the sensor level was obvious. They watched as the next reading came up around 20 percent.

After some discussion, they decided to switch the video to continuous and increase the frequency of data collection to every fifteen seconds. Noting their proximity to a major road, they decided to break into the preprogrammed flight plan, come around, and fly over the highway for a while.

"Westbound or eastbound?" Leeman asked.

They thought for a moment before choosing westbound because of the direction of the turn they had made.

Before long, they could easily make out the road beside the river following the narrow gorge in the mountains.

"This camera is fantastic," said Jones. He had joined the others at the monitor. He had been told numerous times in the past two weeks that he and the camera should get a room, but the fact was, he was right. It was a fantastic camera, especially when its size and weight were taken into account.

They could easily make out the cars and trucks on the highway. Jones began playing with the zoom of the lens.

"See if you can read a license plate," said Leeman.

The answer was yes. Jones zoomed in on the back of a pickup truck. The image was clear enough to read but was bouncing around too much. With a keystroke, Jones captured and froze one frame and moved it to the upper right-hand corner of the screen.

"This guy's a long way from Minnesota," he said. Indeed, even the state name was easily readable on the frozen screen.

Judging from the movement of the cars, the plane was going a little bit faster than the posted speed on the highway. After playing around to slow the plane down, they spotted two girls in a convertible. Their vantage didn't give them a very good view, the most exciting event occurring when the passenger girl uncrossed and recrossed her legs. They accelerated and moved up the line of traffic, looking for anything else of interest.

"Whoa!" Lines yelled, glancing back and forth between the functional monitor and the larger one with the video image. He was the only one with the presence of mind to pay attention to the output of the special sensor during the "aircraft test activity," as it would be logged in their account of the flight.

Since they had swung the plane back over the road, the response had bounced around between 20 and 25 percent. Shortly after the plane flew past the girls in the convertible, the needle spiked to the 90s.

On the video was a tanker truck of unusual design. They zoomed in and matched speed.

"I'm guessing that's not the local milk truck," Leeman said.

They watched it for another minute, noting the absence of markings—at least any that they could see.

Sensing that they might be getting into one of those areas where it does not pay a prudent government-funded observer to tread, Lines straightened up.

"Let's get back on task here," he said to the others. He glanced at his watch. "Christ, we've been dicking around with this for half an hour."

They all knew they didn't have that kind of time or power to throw away.

"At least we're not far from the target zone," he said, glancing at the map.

Jones punched in a few keystrokes, and they watched as the plane veered up and banked left away from the highway, crossing a river. They found themselves looking down at an almost unbroken canopy of forest dominated by poplars, oaks, and white pines. The terrain was extremely rugged, a series of knife ridges and steep walls. Here and there, the green was broken by a rock outcropping or the glint of a stream.

After a while, the plane reached a series of mountaintops covered with grass and broken rock.

"Those are balds," Leeman said. He had done some hiking a little north of there. He was referring to the mountains in the southern Appalachians that supported alpine meadows rather than the dense deciduous forest their neighbors wore. No one knew exactly why this happened.

"There," said Leeman. "Looks like a trail."

When Jones zoomed in closer, they clearly saw a worn footpath bisecting one of the balds. He put the plane in manual control and took it to a lower altitude for a better look. They passed what appeared to be a campsite with a fire ring but saw no hikers or animals.

The path began to descend and disappeared under the leaves again. Just before they lost sight of it, they saw a post with a square white mark painted on the side.

"Just what I thought," said Leeman. "That's the Appalachian Trail, the A.T. Let me see if I can follow it."

In view of his hiking experience, he felt he had some chance of predicting where the trailblazers would have taken the A.T. In fact, in this area, the route could well have dated back to an Indian path. As it happened, a few clearings were located in the area in addition to the balds, so for a time, thanks to observation and intuition and some backseat driving from Jones, he did actually manage to follow the trail. However, as it descended, the cover became thicker. Any evidence of the trail or anything else made by mankind vanished beneath shades of green.

When they checked the coordinates against their maps, they found that this diversion had taken them almost to the target zone. They gained some altitude and set the program back to self-directed. The little plane hardly changed course, continuing generally south-southeast.

Within minutes, the dot on the map representing the target and the dot representing the airplane became one. They glanced from map to video screen and saw nothing but more of the same: trees and steep mountainsides. They reduced altitude to go in for a closer look.

"There it is again," said Jones. He was looking at a footpath emerging from the trees into a small clearing.

"That's a path, all right," said Leeman. "But I don't think it's the A.T. It might be some side trail."

He was about to go on, but as the plane passed the clearing and the trail began to dip off the rise, Lines preempted him.

"Heads up!" he called. Lines was watching the sensor response, which had abruptly gone full scale.

Leeman switched to manual control, banked the plane slightly right, and descended, instinctively guessing the direction of the trail. In a few seconds, they could see where it crossed a small stream.

"We're still at full response," said Lines, glancing between the two screens.

Leeman continued to hold the plane in a gentle bank, following the curve of the hillside, as he guessed the path would do also.

As the plane rounded the hill, Lines said, "Okay, we're losing response now." After another moment, he added, "Okay, now it's gone." The indicator was back to the background level.

"What do you want to do now?" Leeman said.

Once the plane rounded the hillside, he had lost any sense of where the trail might lead. Since they had also lost the sensor reading, he had nothing to go by now.

The others were equally confused. While they didn't know exactly what they were looking for, this seemed of little interest to anyone but Nature Channel viewers. As far as they could see, no roads were anywhere near this place.

"Take it up and circle," Lines said. "Let's get a high-level view of this situation and see if anything interesting is nearby."

Leeman nodded and typed in the appropriate command. It sounded like as good a plan as any.

As the plane circled and gained altitude, they regained the signal from the sensor, which indicated they were in the vicinity of the source again, and were not blocked out by the hillsides. When they began losing the sensor reading again, they decided to circle back and try to pinpoint the source. The sensor was not tied to the control loop—they hadn't been given time to install and debug that—so they worked by old-fashioned iteration. Though the source seemed to be near where the path crossed the stream, they saw nothing of interest there, other than a pile of large rocks just upstream from the crossing.

"Take a lower pass," Lines said. "This is what we're supposed to be checking out. The order says locate and ID the source, and get usable photographs of any personnel in the area."

Leeman brought the plane around again and dropped the altitude. Jones took over the camera control and panned the creek area as they went by at minimum altitude and speed.

In fact, given the terrain, Leeman took the plane very low indeed, low enough to scare Jones when he looked away from the camera screen and saw the altitude indicator.

"Christ! Get that thing up!" he yelled. "You're at forty-five hundred feet. Some of these peaks are over five thousand."

Leeman muttered something under his breath but did as Jones suggested.

"Not much to photograph," said Lines. "Whatever it is we're looking for, I don't see us finding it anywhere close to here." Apart from a group crossing one of the balds many miles back on the A.T., they had seen no evidence of humans.

Leeman brought the plane up, and Jones backed off on the camera zoom to take in as much area as possible. They were all thinking the same thing. They wanted to locate some people, since reporting back and saying they had found none would sound like failure. It would be hard to explain to the wonks in Washington that only a few hours away were wilderness places that saw no people for months at a time or even longer.

Leeman began a search pattern that consisted of a slow outward spiral. This time, they all watched the video screen. It was Lines who caught the first sign of movement. Jones manipulated the camera in the direction that Lines indicated just in time to see two hikers disappear into the woods. They were now at least a mile from the "point source," as they had begun to call it.

"Now what?" Leeman asked.

"Now we jump ahead of them on the path, circle over the next clearing, and get some quality video when they come by," Lines answered.

It did seem the best strategy. Moreover, Leeman thought he remembered a clearing a little way back that would make a perfect ambush point. He was amazed how the human mind could start to form a map of an area given only a few data points and the odd perspective of looking through the lens of a little plane hundreds of miles away.

The plane gained altitude and flew as directed. Presently, they found the clearing Leeman remembered, although slightly farther along than expected. There, he put the plane into a left-hand bank and spiraled in on the meadow.

Then things started to go wrong. First came a major jarring of the picture they were all watching. Leeman and Jones switched their attention to the function screen, which showed they were losing altitude, and fast. Their degree of panic was no different from what they would have felt had they been physically on the plane themselves. The bank indicator told them they were still in a left-hand downward spiral, only steeper and picking up speed.

"Try leveling out," Jones suggested, almost under his breath.

"Nothing doing," Leeman said. He had tried but was getting no response from his controls.

They looked back to the video screen and recoiled when the plane hit, spun around once, and came to rest.

But the weird thing was that they were still getting a picture, and not a closeup of blades of grass either.

"What the hell?" Jones said.

They looked for a moment more. What they had was a still life of a clearing in the woods, dense forest on the other side. Leeman tried the zoom function and lost the camera feed for a second. Then the picture came back on unchanged. He stepped back from the controls. The picture oscillated in a slow, unsettling way, like a ship bobbing on a gentle sea. Not quite a still life after all.

"We're in a tree branch," Lines said.

The others could see he was right. Everything made sense if you strapped on that perspective.

Leeman experimented with the controls, trying to zoom and move the camera direction. He got no response, so they sat and watched.

Lines was just thinking how he found this strangely relaxing, forgetting for the moment his concerns about losing a six-hundred-thousand-dollar piece of equipment and having to explain it to certain people in Washington, when they saw movement on the far right side of the screen.

Two hikers with large packs, a man and a woman, were walking side by side, not single file, which was unusual for a trail. And then behind them a third figure appeared—a little girl, also with a pack, who seemed to be studying a flower she held in her hand. She looked like she was ambling along, in no hurry whatsoever. Then she looked up in their direction.

The movement of her head was so sudden and direct that it made Leeman wonder if she had heard some sound the plane was making. She put down the flower and headed off the trail directly for the plane. She raised her finger and pointed and moved her mouth, yelling something to alert her parents.

Then she just walked toward the plane, looking at it with curiosity. Actually, it seemed she was peering right through the camera lens at them. She approached close to the lens, tilting her head to one side with curiosity. Then the image suddenly froze on the screen.

Though they could do nothing at this point, they tried everything they could think of anyway. None of them was in a hurry to place a phone call to Washington.

ooooo

An hour later, Leeman was asleep on one of the couches. Lines sat at the table working at one of the computers, while Jones went from toolbox to toolbox looking for some missing implement and cursing under his breath.

The phone rang several times before any of them altered his behavior in any way. Leeman finally stirred on the couch. Seeing he was closest to the portable phone, he grabbed it and brought it to his ear.

"Hello, Leeman here," he said. He glared at his coworkers, who took absolutely no notice.

"We don't know what happened. We lost signal a little while ago, just before dark," he said in answer to a question.

"Um, yes, we do have video from the flight," he said after another pause.

At the word *video*, the older man at the computer looked up.

As Leeman continued to listen, he got up from the couch and began to pace and grimace. He looked at Lines, searching for some sign as to how to deal with the caller.

"You want the last thirty minutes of transmission?" he said, to let the others know what was up.

Jones threw a wrench into a toolbox drawer and joined the others in the office area.

Leeman stopped pacing and straightened almost to attention, taking orders from the person on the other end.

"Okay," he said quietly, and hung up.

The others watched him.

"They're sending someone down to pick up the last thirty minutes of video," he said.

They all looked at the computer screen, where the image of Audrey Colebrook looked right back at them. They were in unspoken agreement that sending that image to the reptiles who funded this project just did not feel right.

Chapter 8
Breakfast in the Power Plant

THE BROWN-HAIRED GIRL ROSE to the smells of bacon and coffee, just about the best way in the world to wake up. After delivering the truck as per plan, she had spent the night in the loft of the power plant, and the morning sun was filtering through the clerestory windows, white as winter light because of the fog in the valley.

She pulled on a sweatshirt and a pair of shorts and descended barefoot the steps to the second floor, where the kitchen was located.

The others were already in various stages of preparing and eating breakfast. One of her co-conspirators had the morning paper open in front of a used plate at the long table. The plate bore traces of egg yolk and toast crumbs swirling outward from the center like the Milky Way galaxy.

Their leader, at the stove as usual, called to her, "Eggs and bacon?"

"Oh, yeah," she said without hesitation. She headed for the coffee maker and found an unused cup.

Most of the others were watching the local news on a small TV.

"Anything about the truck?" she asked.

A couple of head shakes told her no. Their eyes never left the screen.

"There's not going to be any news about this," said the young plant manager.

He was holding a bottle of V8 juice and standing at the window, which gave him a view of the parking lot and the road beyond. The rain of the night before had given way to a morning of light fog. By ten o'clock, the fog would lift and the day would be clear and beautiful. A black sedan drove past the gates and on up the road. She had joined him there and saw it, too.

"That's the third one in the last half-hour," he said.

"Nobody's stopped here yet?" she asked.

"I don't think they're going to," he said. "Power stations are so big they become part of the background, not objects in the field of vision."

As they watched, a sheriff's van made its way along the road, negotiated the turn, and proceeded up the hill. On the side was "K9 Division."

"Calling out the dogs, are they?" she said.

"Serving and protecting," he said. "I'll go down to the diner for lunch and see what the buzz is with the deputies later on."

"Be interesting to hear what they told the local police," she said.

She couldn't resist the temptation to descend the next flight of stairs to the truck. Halfway down, she saw it there in all its glory. Two guys and a girl were working around it. She did a quick mental count, adding these three to the group upstairs. She worried again about the number of people and what it meant for the probability of keeping the operation a secret.

The three down on the ground level were busy. One was arranging spotlights while another set up an expensive-looking camera on a tripod. The third, a girl with red hair, struggled with a tape measure. She was attempting to line up the free end with features on the truck and read the numbers on the other end, a process made awkward because she was simultaneously trying to clamp a notebook under one arm.

An older man stepped from behind the truck and asked, "Did you get the wheelbase yet?"

Jeez, the brown-haired girl thought, *somebody else in on this.*

The red-haired girl, a little exasperated with her shortage of hands, said, "Here, hold this."

She handed the older man the free end of the tape and nodded to the front wheel. He clamped a sketchbook under his arm, took the tape, and laid the end on the ground opposite the center of the front hubcap.

"Let's go center to center," he said.

The red-haired girl obliged.

The plant manager began descending the steps, too, stopping just above the brown-haired girl to check on the progress.

"Who are these people?" she whispered.

"That's our sculptor," he said, nodding toward the older man. "And his assistants."

"Sculptor?" she asked.

"Yeah, he's cool. He teaches some classes at the college and does some work on his own and for a couple of companies in the area," he said. "I'll tell you about phase two of our little operation in a little while. It involves making a scale model of the truck."

"Like half-size?" she asked.

"No, more like about three feet long. They're taking measurements to get the proportions true to life."

"I need to be getting back to work pretty soon," she said. She checked her watch and then said, "Actually, I need to get going right now."

"Another day in the fudge mines?" he asked.

"Sweetest job I ever had," she said, and turned to go back up to collect her things.

"Listen," he said. "Check in with South Carolina if you don't hear from them by the end of the day."

Chapter 9

Back on the Campus

NEAR THE CENTER OF CAMPUS in Blacksburg, Virginia, Xavier leaned out the window of his Toyota and swiped a badge over a sensor. A tall garage door rattled up in the building in front of him. When the door came to an uncertain and quivering stop, he pulled into the work bay of the special projects building.

"Easier than finding a parking place," he said to his brother, and laughed, head tilted back slightly, mouth open, eyes squinted almost shut. The laughter exploded out. To be in the presence of this laugh and not succumb to its charm was pretty much impossible. So his older brother Leon laughed, too.

They popped the trunk. Leon pulled out a long cylindrical shape wrapped in a wool blanket and followed Xavier down a hallway lined with offices and work rooms on one side and work bays divided by chain-link fencing on the other.

"Are these all different teams?" asked Leon, indicating the cagelike areas formed by the fencing.

They were, in fact, in a building the university reserved for teams devoted to various engineering challenge competitions. In one cage, a small racecar took center stage. This was a Baja-style vehicle with a high and springy suspension and a seat protected by a sturdy roll cage. Its medium-sized motorcycle engine was connected by a drive chain to a complex transmission that was currently open and under some kind of alteration.

In another cage, a sleek craft sat on an elevated platform. About twelve feet long and covered with iridescent paint that changed color as they walked by, it looked like a rocket ship from the cover of an old science fiction magazine. The sign over the gate read, "Human-Powered Submarine Team."

Leon leaned in and saw bicycle pedals inside the fiberglass hull.

"Someone gets into that thing in the water?" he asked Xavier.

It did look like a tight fit.

"Yeah, they go down with scuba gear and button the guy up and close the hatch. He has a small air bottle inside that he uses when they're going for the time trials. The main problem they're having is with the controls. I guess it's pretty hard to pedal and steer at the same time. Harder than you'd think, anyway."

In all, about a dozen teams were preparing to enter various engineering competitions. Each had its own cage, in which workbenches, tools, and laptop computers were scattered everywhere. Also prevalent were signs from sponsors who footed the bills for all the stuff.

"The university provides the building and faculty advisers. The rest all comes from private sponsors," Xavier explained.

Nearly all the cages were jumping with activity. The sight of two men walking by with what looked like the end of a small ICBM sticking out of a rolled-up blanket aroused no special attention. Leon supposed that strange objects were transported in and out pretty much around the clock here.

They came to the end of the hallway without seeing the workspace for Xavier's team.

Leon was about to ask when Xavier pulled out the security card again and swiped it on an ID pad by a steel door. The door buzzed, and they pushed it open and entered.

The other work areas had not prepared Leon for what he saw here. First of all, this was a room, not a caged area like the others. It had at least four times the floor space, apparently spanning the entire width of the building. The ceiling was at least twenty feet high. A bank of windows covered most of the opposite side down to the level of a workbench that ran the length of the wall. To the left was a small but well-equipped machine shop with a lathe, a CNC mill, a drill press, and a variety of saws and welding equipment. On the workbench were electronic test equipment, computers, and several electromechanical assemblies whose purpose Leon could only guess.

Hanging from the ceiling on wires was the most impressive sight in the room, an oddly shaped airplane with a wingspan of perhaps twelve feet.

Xavier watched Leon look up.

"The Simian Bat," he said by way of introduction.

"Damn!" said Leon.

It did indeed look somehow simian and batlike at the same time. For one thing, it was painted black. Then there were the wings, which were slanted slightly forward where they protruded from the body, then raked backward near the tips. Very batlike. The instrument pod on the fuselage was nearly round. Two discs protruded from its sides. They did resemble monkey ears, although they actually housed tiny TV cameras.

Leon had of course heard stories about the Simian Bat. The Simian Bat was the autonomous aircraft the team had built last year and with which it had won the national competition. Rumors circulated that many features from the Simian Bat had found their way into a design that the team's adviser, Dr. Lines, had built for the CIA. Of course, the team members didn't know that for sure, but that was the story.

The fact that all the funding for the team came from a single company known to supply the government probably helped fuel the rumors. That and the fact that the team did its work behind closed (and locked) doors out of sight of the public.

Leon looked around, taking the whole room in again.

"You guys do rate, don't you?" he said.

Xavier's only answer was another of his patented laughs.

He proceeded to the center portion of the bench and cleared away some electronic parts and a CD player.

"Put the patient up here, and let's see what we've got," he said.

Leon plopped the package down and spread back the blanket, revealing the recovered fuselage. Xavier looked at the rough, broken metal mesh and polymer composite where the wings had been removed.

"What did you do, chew them off?" he asked.

"Just about," said Leon. "We didn't exactly have a lot of tools with us."

Xavier quickly examined the fuselage. He located a metal ring just behind the nose cone assembly and found some flat-headed bolts with hex indentations. He reached for a plastic folding container that opened to a set of hex wrenches. Leon reflected on the fact that Xavier was one of the few people in his experience who could actually keep a set of hex wrenches complete. Many people had complete sets of socket wrenches. A few even had complete sets of drill bits. But rarely outside the confines of a hardware store did one see a complete set of hex wrenches.

Xavier loosened and removed half a dozen brass-colored set screws and then, giving the nose cone a slight twist, confirmed that it was free to move. He withdrew the nose cone slowly from the fuselage, occasionally giving it a gentle turn if he felt resistance. The nose cone came free quickly, trailing a mass of fine wires and circuit boards mounted on a light, open framework of metal. The process reminded Leon of cracking a lobster claw and withdrawing the meat. (This, though, may have been influenced by the fact that Leon was hungry.)

"Very interesting," said Xavier.

He bent close to the assembly, craning his neck and poking around with a Phillips screwdriver, moving wire bundles aside for a better look at the components.

"These are the batteries," he said, pointing to a plastic pouch with two wires coming out.

"They look awfully small for something this size," said Leon.

"They're not for the propulsion, just the instrument package," Xavier explained. Pointing to two small holes in the underside of the nose cone, he said, "These are the TV cameras. This thing probably runs on binocular vision to estimate the distance to objects, maybe even navigate toward objects. I'm not sure. We tried something like that, but we had the cameras way out on the wingtips to make the triangle bigger for more accuracy. Trouble was, the wings flexed too much and got our cameras out of line anyway. We never got back to the idea."

"So who do you think made this?" asked Leon.

"Not that many people could," Xavier said, still poking around. "I'll tell you one thing. It's not cheap."

He started naming components and estimating their costs.

"Damn, this is a nice camera," he said. He appeared to be thinking he just might have to scavenge it.

"What would something like this be used for?" Leon asked.

"Surveillance, mostly," Xavier answered. "You could use it anywhere it might be dangerous for a manned airplane to fly. I said that stuff is expensive, but it's still cheap compared to a real airplane. If it gets shot down or crashes, no one gets killed, so it really doesn't cost that much. Or you could use it if you wanted stealth, if you didn't want to draw attention to the surveillance. It could also be used to deliver weapons, but I don't see anything like that here."

He continued his examination of the craft's innards while Leon poked around the shell of the fuselage.

"The only thing I don't understand is what this is," Xavier said, indicating a device with a small lenslike protuberance set in the bottom of the nose cone. On the inside, it was connected to a metal cylinder, from which four wires ran to the rest of the assembly. Xavier disconnected the device from the nose cone by compressing a clip ring and pushing the lens through to the inside. He then disconnected the four wires and was able to withdraw the whole device and hold it in his hand. He held it up to the window for better light. It had some numbers on the side, but they made no particular sense to him.

"Let's see if there's any life in this thing," he said, taking it to one of the electronic test areas. "By the way it was mounted, I would assume it's some kind of sensor. These are almost certainly the power supply wires." He indicated the white and black wires. "I'm not sure what voltage it wants, so I'll start low and then kick it up if we don't see anything."

Using two wires with alligator clips, he hooked the device to a power supply and adjusted it to 7.2 volts DC. He then connected the two other wires to a complicated electronics rig.

"This is a data acquisition board that's hooked up to this computer," he said, touching the keyboard, then using a mouse to click on an icon that looked like an old oscilloscope. The screen changed to show a panel with various electrical measurements and a round circle with a flat line crossing the center. The readings showed only a few millivolts and nearly no current. Xavier pointed the device at the window, then covered it with his hand. The readings showed almost no change.

"Doesn't look like it responds to light," he observed.

He then laid the device on the bench and walked over to the work area. He produced a propane torch from one of the drawers and lit it with a striker. Approaching the device, he watched the screen as he moved the torch closer to the sensor head. Again, almost no change in the readings occurred.

Leon came over to join the experiment.

"It doesn't seem to be sensitive to heat or light," said Xavier.

When Leon reached out to pick up the device, the screen went crazy. The voltage reading jumped from millivolts to several volts, and the signal indictor in the center of the circle showed several blips. This was accompanied by a clicking sound from the computer speakers. The commotion startled Leon so much that he pulled back his hand like he had touched a hot stove.

The two brothers looked at each other and simultaneously said, "Whoa!"

"Do that again," said Xavier.

More slowly this time, Leon reached his left hand toward the device. The readings once again began to jump. He withdrew it, and the readings declined. He then moved his hand back and forth a couple of times and watched the readings rise and fall accordingly.

"Let me see your watch," said Xavier.

Leon slid the watch over his hand and gave it to his brother. It was an old rectangular watch with a gold spandex band. Pipo, their grandfather, had given it to him. ·

Xavier held it up to the device, and the screen went crazy.

"It's the radium in the dial," he said. "These old watches used radium to make the hands glow in the dark. This is a radiation detector."

They both stood for a moment looking at the device, sorting out the implications. Leon took the watch back and snapped it onto his wrist. He moved his arm back and forth in front of the detector, watching the screen light up with numbers and peaks each time the watch approached.

"Interesting," said Xavier.

He unclipped the leads and picked up the device to look at it again. It was about an inch in diameter and four inches long and had a little weight to it. He slipped it into his pocket and turned back to the rest of the wreck. Leon looked around the lab while Xavier poked and prodded at various pieces without saying much.

"Let's get something to eat," Leon said, partly because he hadn't eaten since he left North Carolina and partly in acknowledgment that they were pretty much out of ideas for the time being.

Unseen, a security camera followed their movements as they left, Xavier giving the door a pull to check that it was locked. Another camera followed their exit down the corridor.

They ate at a favorite Cajun place nearby. Leon decided to make the drive home that night. They agreed that Xavier would show the plane to his adviser to see what, if anything, he could learn.

"There's a high probability he'll know but won't be able to tell," Xavier warned as they parted company.

"If we hadn't found the thing so close to our site, I wouldn't care so much," said Leon.

Chapter 10

P ictures from the Middle of the Air

BACK IN WASHINGTON, D.C., Charles Colebrook stopped to check e-mail messages before heading home. He scanned the names quickly and decided he could answer most the next day. He smiled when he saw his brother Leon's screen name appear.

Must be off the trail, Charles thought. He read quickly.

The message described a particular location near the Appalachian Trail in the western part of North Carolina not far from where they had grown up. It said that Audrey had found something "interesting." The word *interesting* was shorthand that only Charles and a very few other people in the world might come close to understanding. It had to do, no doubt, with the special project Leon had been working on for the better part of a year. The message further asked if Charles could "help out."

This referred to a conversation they had in North Carolina last Christmas, during one of those incredible warm spells that come from time to time to the southern Appalachians even in the middle of winter. The family had eaten yet another in a series of holiday feasts and decided to walk it off with a hike and a subsequent soak in the hot springs just off the trail. That they would have an interesting and memorable conversation while partially submerged in water was a natural event for this group of people. The youngest brother, Xavier, claimed to have a distinct memory of learning some basic principles of algebra while floating near a reef off the coast of Jamaica with their father, Philip.

In any case, on that particular December day, bobbing in the natural hot springs just north of Asheville, Leon described the kinds of things he was looking for, and what the difficulties might be in locating them, and what the impact might be on archaeology if he could locate them. Leon was beginning to suspect some links between the region and Central America at much earlier dates than previously considered.

This brought to mind for Charles the capabilities of a satellite he had a small part in outfitting about a year previously. The most unusual feature of the satellite was its ability to scan and analyze bundled frequencies of infrared light. This, as he explained, made it extremely sensitive in distinguishing objects of different temperatures. Sometimes, it could detect objects otherwise hidden by vegetation or some other cover. For instance, a large metal object like a tank would heat and cool at a different rate than the surrounding landscape. Even if it were covered by camouflage netting, its rectangular outline might light up during periods of rapid heating or cooling, such as near sunrise or sunset. The same principle might apply to the ancient structures Leon was looking for, although it would take some doing to pick out the kind of patterns involved.

Charles had not thought much about it since that conversation. He knew Leon had spent the winter on other tasks and on research for his special project. But lately, since the weather turned, Leon and family had been back out on the trail doing fieldwork and must have come across something.

He turned to a second computer screen on his desk and scrolled down a list of active satellites until he found the entry he was looking for. He clicked on Geostat IV, and a map of the world replaced the list. A Mercator projection with a sine wave displayed the orbital path of the Geostat IV satellite, a blinking light showing its present position.

A few more keystrokes produced a second blinking light over the eastern United States and a time of day—06:08 hours, just a little after sunrise the following morning. That was pretty close to perfect for his purposes.

He picked up the phone and was relieved but not surprised to find his friend still in.

"Hey, it's Charles," he said when he heard the technician's voice.

"Hey, Charles, what's up?" said the technician. The tone of his voice showed sincere pleasure in hearing from Charles. Charles tended to stay on the good side of these guys, since the success of his projects often depended on their willingness and ability to do their jobs right. He stayed on their good side by doing excellent work and by supplying quantities of chocolate from his mother's business back in North Carolina.

"How's Geostat doing?" Charles asked.

"It's doing good, man. We're getting some killer resolution lately. We're learning some things about the frame timing and angles, but mostly it's in the analysis software," the technician said.

Charles jumped in, sensing this could turn into a long conversation if he let it.

"How's the load?" he asked. The load on the satellite referred to the work load, or how much time it was booked for its primary mission.

"Not too bad. We still have a good chunk of time scheduled for diagnostics and development, so we haven't opened it up all the way to users yet," the technician said.

This was good news, since it meant his friend still had some time at his discretion.

"Could you take a couple of pictures for me?" Charles asked.

He went on to describe the time frame and location he was looking for.

"I can get you some images, but you're going to have to talk to the girls down in Enhancement about the computer work on them if you don't see what you're looking for," said the technician.

Charles did a quick mental calculation. This was going to cost him at minimum a plate of pasta at Cafe Luna, a prospect he did not really mind.

Charles thought no more about the request for satellite images the next day. His group was busy with a design review meeting. However, on the drive home, he did wonder what Leon had come up with.

Could be pretty exciting, he thought.

Chapter 11
S atellite Map

ON THE SCREEN, AN IMAGE BEGAN TO FORM, first of obscure gray patterns, which presently refined themselves into some detail of topography. Bands of roads and highways became visible. Along one of them, a number of tiny luminescent dots were visible.

"What are we looking at?" Ira Hudson growled.

"Let me find something to hang the map grid on," the military technician said, squinting at the screen. He moved the cursor and typed a few keystrokes, and a grid pattern appeared. He was working with the latest satellite data they had collected.

"That should be the state line there," he said. "That's the line between North Carolina and Tennessee at that point, if I have it right. It should pretty well follow the main ridge line of the mountains." He was consulting a topo map on the desk beside the monitor. "I should be able to find a mountain peak or something distinct to confirm."

"How about that one?" said Ira Hudson. He struck the map with his finger, then leaned in to read the name. "Wesser Bald."

"Yeah, that's it," said the technician. "See those two other peaks almost in line? That's it, all right."

"So the dots are the trucks on the interstate highway?" Hudson asked.

"I guess so," said the technician, looking at the map again. "Yes, Interstates 40 and 26."

"Then what's that?" Hudson asked. He was looking at a slightly larger dot some distance south of what they had determined to be the highway leading to Oak Ridge.

"That's a good question," said the technician.

"What's down there?" Hudson asked.

They both turned to the map again.

"That's the Great Smoky Mountains National Park. So maybe a few forest service roads, but no towns, no houses or farms or anything like that," said the technician.

Hudson took out his cell phone, flipped it open, and punched in a speed-dial number.

"Captain Watts, I have more information for you," he said. He noticed the technician looking up at him and removed himself to the hall, closing the door behind him.

Hudson listened to the voice on the other end, then returned to the technician and got coordinates, which he relayed into the phone.

Then, in answer to a short question, he said, "No, only to me. This is not a chain-of-command kind of thing," And then he hung up.

Chapter 12

B ody Language

LILLY COLEBROOK—mother of Leon, Charles, and Xavier, wife of Philip—was a lady of few indulgences. One of the few was Body Language 101.

Body Language 101 was a course offered by the Psychology Department at the university in Asheville. It was popular among the regular degree-seeking student body of almost all disciplines. The appeal to psychology students was obvious. The theater arts people took it for insights into facial expressions and body movements, so as to add depth and realism to their performances. Visual arts students employed elements learned in the class in portraits for added subliminal impact. Political science majors took it to analyze speeches and to learn how to "control the message." It also attracted interest from local business, law enforcement, and educational folks. Accordingly, it was generally offered as a night course to allow the university to attract the working population, thereby increasing its outreach and income.

For Lilly, it started as a stimulating diversion and a good reason to get together twice a week with a few friends from her eco group, the Sisterhood of the Ancient Mountains. Like the other students, she soon became completely engrossed. The classes were a rich blend of lectures, multimedia, exercises, games, and active assignments.

For a textbook, the students used a draft of a book still under development by their professor. The title of this draft, like the book's contents, was subject to frequent changes. In previous semesters, it had been "A Brief History of Lying," "Modern Developments in Lying," "Lying: A Practical Guide," and "So You Want to Be a Liar." Currently, it was called "Beyond Lying."

A major theme of the text was a phenomenon that seemed to have come to a head in the 1980s—that is, an acceptance on the part of the American public of things known to be untrue, or at least known to not be what they were presented to be. The book included chapters on professional wrestling and tabloid newspapers, both of which saw their popularity skyrocket in the eighties. It also contained several chapters on political trends and manners of speech, culminating with the presidency of Ronald Reagan.

As a frightening illustration of her point, the professor cited the results of a poll taken in 1985 concerning Reagan's personal history. When asked about his college background, a large percentage of the voting public responded that he attended Notre Dame and was a star on its football team. When asked about his service in World War II, many people answered that he was a bomber pilot.

So there began, according to the textbook, the collapsing of popular fiction into reality, or at least the melding of people's perceptions of the two. There began, in effect, the loss of the ability—or perhaps the will—to distinguish between what was real and what was on TV or in the movies. Perhaps the difference between the two was just no longer deemed important.

What were the implications for a society in which truth and integrity meant less than appearance? Just how far could this be taken in the realms of politics, business, and personal relationships? These were the questions addressed by the text.

And yet, according to the professor, there still lurked in each of us the innate ability to distinguish one from another. This built-in lie detector might be atrophied from disuse. It might need to be retrained, or just reconnected to our conscious minds, but it was still there. The object of Body Language 101 was to reawaken it as a tool of survival. This was one of the themes that resonated most strongly with Lilly and her friends.

The students first learned some of the basic mechanics. They focused on avoidance moves—covering the mouth, looking away, looking down, and so on.

Once they understood the basics, they began examining tapes of White House press conferences, which lately featured the smarmiest character anyone had seen in years, even by the degenerate standards of the day. The class first watched the tapes with no sound. This allowed students to study the expressions and gestures of the press secretary without the distraction of words, and also occasionally to observe the effect his evasive and disingenuous nonreplies had on the press corps.

This guy was beautiful. He began displaying the classic lying signs even as he approached the podium. He displayed them as he gave his opening statement and kept on displaying them right through the question-and-answer period. As a matter of fact, his face froze into a permanent lying mask.

Later, the students listened as the tapes were played back with sound. This allowed the professor to point out features of sentence structure engineered by the image experts in the administration to serve, in a legalistic sort of way, as a scaffolding to support the nonlies/nontruths.

Equally interesting was the level of acceptance among the press corps. They listened and asked questions in a resigned sort of way, straining to hear any piece of honest information that might by some remote chance filter through the whole bizarre act taking place in front of them. It seemed they were living in a desert and had to look for any trace of water whatsoever.

This particular evening, they watched a press conference taped earlier that day. The press secretary made no opening comments but went directly to questions from the assembled reporters. Lilly always wondered what that meant. Did he really have nothing to say? Was nothing going on? Or was so much crap going on that no subject could be safely mentioned?

The opening salvo concerned the current war being conducted in a Third World country. It was pretty boring stuff, the replies heavy on the same prepackaged phrases they had been hearing for weeks.

Golden oldies like "We need to fight them there so we don't have to fight them here."

Various forms of "This administration will continue to support our troops."

Lip service paid to "reaching out to the international community," by which everyone understood him to mean that we were doing exactly what we wanted to do and condemning any other nation or group that did not fully support us.

This was all good stuff but nothing new, and the class picked up on the usual signs with no problem.

Just when the daily drama began to lose what little energy it had in the first place, a new reporter in the back row actually asked a question on a different topic.

"What is the White House position on the congressional investigation into what is called Teraplex Building?"

The pause after the question was the first thing that caught Lilly's attention. She looked around and saw that her friends from the Sisterhood had picked up on it, too, as had the professor and most of the other students. For some reason, even though this had been a minor news story for a couple of weeks, it seemed to catch the press secretary off balance. And then, in delivering his nonanswer, the secretary displayed some truly fine nonverbal stuff.

"We have no comment on that, since it is an ongoing investigation," he mumbled.

"Oh, Jeez," groaned the woman beside Lilly, the proprietor of one of the B&Bs in town. "Don't give us the old 'ongoing investigation' line."

On the screen, the press secretary seemed to regain his usual nauseating composure.

"And we only hope that Congress can move past it with a minimum of political grandstanding and get back to the serious issues that are really on the minds of the American public," he said.

Most members of the press corps stopped writing in their notepads and actually looked up and listened to what the man had to say. However, true to form, the spark failed to light a fire. No one had any follow-up questions, and so the press conference wound down.

Lilly looked at a couple of the Sisterhood, and they all rolled their eyes.

Chapter 13
Submarine Sandwich

A YOUNG MAN IN A WHITE SHIRT and tie sat at a computer console in a typical office in D.C. He was removing a submarine sandwich from a bag and arranging a napkin on the margin of desk in front of his keyboard. Though at the moment the sandwich was of higher priority than the keyboard, he could eat and look at the screen at the same time. The young man was into correlations.* He was into comparing different databases one to another. He was good at writing programs that looked at patterns and trends and coincidences. He did not really believe in the latter.

The thing that made him stop chewing his first bite of sandwich was not so subtle that it took his special talents. Even the most amateur analysis would have picked it up.

---

* Saying he was into correlations is an understatement. The young man actually published some of the most advanced correlation software on the planet. This went largely unnoticed by his peers but was not lost on Ecuadorian biophysicist Henrico Carr. It proved a key tool in his decoding of certain thought patterns in animals. To his credit, Carr fully acknowledged the young man's contribution.

He finished chewing the bite and took a drink of soda to wash it down, then put the sandwich to the side in favor of the keyboard and mouse. He scrolled up to recheck the results, then referenced the original databases directly. He had just received another list of several thousand people, which he arranged alphabetically by last name. Without then rerunning the correlation program, he scrolled down and saw the name he was looking for.

He grabbed his windbreaker, jumped up from his desk, and started down the hall. Then, thinking better of it, he turned back and took another bite of sandwich.

On the street, the rain had stopped, at least for the moment. He took out his cell phone and rang the familiar number.

"Hudson," said the voice on the other end.

"Mr. Hudson, it's Jim," he said. "I found something you should see."

"You have a name?"

"Names," said the young man. "That is, one last name and two brothers."

"Well?"

"Colebrook," said the young man.

"What lists? Fill me in," said Hudson.

"Some of the ones we're not necessarily supposed to have," said the young man, looking around.

Hudson paused on the other end of the line.

"Okay. You're not calling me from the office, right?" he said.

"No, I'm on the street," said the young man.

"Okay. Keep up the good work. And keep our contacts like this. We don't need any written reports at this point," Hudson said.

"Do you want me to expand the search under the new parameters?" the young man asked.

"Sure, expand it any which way you think you should," Hudson said.

He liked this kid. Finally, someone who could get him results.

Chapter 14

Local FBI

WHEN AGENTS WERE SENT from Washington to the local FBI office, it almost always meant something big was up. This, the local agents felt, was bogus because they were the ones who knew the terrain and people, which was why they were there in the first place. Never mind that most of the local work was dead boring, contrary to what people thought when you told them you were with the FBI.

A lot of it was background checks. If someone applied for most any job with most any government agency, they filled out a form with about fifty questions—where they worked, where they lived, with whom they lived, what organizations they belonged to.

Let's say someone was applying to be a librarian at one of the national labs. The applicant had to list the names and phone numbers of references. Someone had to call up at least a few of those people and make appointments to go out and meet with them. At any such meeting, the agent asked a few questions about the prospective librarian. Did the person know her? When did the person know her? In what capacity did the person know her? To the best of the person's knowledge, did she use drugs, associate with questionable sorts of people, or belong to any communist, terrorist, or anti-American organizations? Furthermore, had anything made the person question her moral integrity or made them think, in any way, that she should not be trusted with the position for which she was applying, or should not be trusted with material that might come into her possession as a result of that position?

The folks at the local FBI office went out and asked those questions. They tended to spend a lot more time on this than on dusting for fingerprints and sitting in dark vans on midnight stakeouts.

This time, when they got the call that an agent named Tomblyn would be flying in accompanied by a "technical specialist," they were a little surprised to hear that the services of at least one of the local staff might be required. The two visitors would be arriving in forty minutes on a business jet at the Asheville Regional Airport. A local agent should pick them up personally so he could be briefed on the case and on what assistance was needed. This was a little dramatic even for people who had a tendency to be dramatic.

Agent Paul Tomblyn turned out to be an extremely young-looking man. Meyers, of the local office, made him to be no more than twenty-six, and the very image of a young, upwardly mobile agency man, complete with crisp business suit and slim briefcase. A folding garment bag hanging from a shoulder strap told Meyers that this might be a prolonged visit.

Tomblyn was followed by an older man, maybe fifty-five or so, who was no less properly dressed but definitely higher mileage. Meyers had not been given his name.

Meyers watched as they picked up their bags and made the short walk across the tarmac from the plane to the receiving lounge.

Agent Tomblyn spotted Meyers right away and came forward with hand outstretched.

"Hello, Agent Meyers. I'm Paul Tomblyn, and this is Joe Haven. Joe is helping us with some technical aspects of this case."

Haven nodded and walked past them into the heart of the lounge. He was brought up short by a large mural hanging above the central receiving desk. He looked up in silence while the other two walked up behind him.

"Local artist," said Meyers by way of explanation. "Specializes in that sort of thing."

"Is that who I think it is?" asked Haven.

"The Wright brothers," said Meyers, trying to gauge his reaction.

Of reactions, Meyers had seen several. Some serious-minded people found the depiction demeaning or even disrespectful or insulting. Others found it simply funny, regarding it for a moment, then walking away with a laugh. A few studied it awhile for deeper meaning, even finding themselves moved at the quality of the artwork. Many took photographs of it, or had their photos taken standing in front of it.

Alas, most people walked by without noticing the painting at all, allowing it to blend in with the other unnoticed, unheeded messages that surrounded their lives. To them, it was incidental background to the missions they were on at that particular moment.

Even for people who walked around with blinders on 99 percent of their lives, this painting was a particularly loud cry for attention. The colors alone should have been enough to catch the eye.

The painting did in fact show Orville and Wilbur Wright, but not the usual sepia images of serious young men in tweed. These Wright brothers, dressed in full racing livery, were leading two thoroughbred horses onto a track in front of several other horses and riders. Orville was on the viewer's left, a short step ahead of Wilbur. Some thoughtful observers had suggested that this symbolized the fact that Orville took the first history-making ride. Orville was wearing bright red silks with white piping. Wilbur was in saffron yellow silks with dark blue piping. Their horses, side by side and almost touching, were adorned with warmups that matched the riders. The grandstand in the background was full and colorful. The sky was blue, and all seemed ready for a breathtaking day at the races.

Almost unnoticed, a bookie in front of the stands was posting odds on a chalkboard. A viewer who approached the painting close-ly and squinted could just make out that the odds were not in the Wrights' favor.

This was a striking scene. To a keen observer, the expressions on the faces of the brothers were the most remarkable feature. They seemed to gaze directly at the observer in a calm, open manner—the look of men who simply saw the success of their future endeavor as though it were a *fait accompli*. The expressions showed a simple frankness—no display of ego, but a recognition that they were on a track to the inevi-table fulfillment of their vision.

After a while, Haven turned and headed toward the door. Meyers scooted ahead of him to hold it while his two visitors walked through. Haven could not resist a last glance back over his shoulder.

They headed to a black Ford Taurus parked at the curb. Agent Tomblyn stopped to study the view before getting in the shotgun po-sition. It was late morning, and the early mist had cleared to reveal a beautiful mountain day. The airport was situated on a high plateau at an elevation of about two thousand feet. The plateau was surrounded by mountains, so the agent had to make a full 360-degree turn to take them all in.

Without comment, he ducked into the car. Then, turning to Mey-ers he said, "We need to learn about a certain family here."

The Ford pulled quickly away.

"We're looking at a family named Colebrook," said Tomblyn.

"Colebrook?" said Meyers.

"You know them?" asked Tomblyn.

"Well, if you mean the artist, that was one of his paintings you were just looking at," said Meyers.

This got Haven's attention from the backseat.

"Colebrook is an artist?" he asked.

"The old man is an artist. James Colebrook. People call him Pipo. Painting is pretty much all he does now. He used to run a company here that built fountains and things like that. I think his son runs it now," Meyers said.

"You have a file on him?" asked Tomblyn.

"I'll have to see. I remember some trouble years ago, or at least some controversy. A few church people protested a couple of paintings he did," said Meyers, trying to bring the incident into focus. "We didn't end up getting much involved, but at the time we were asked to keep an eye on it in case something bigger developed."

"What about the son?" asked Tomblyn.

"I don't know much about him. I think his name is Philip. He's an engineer. He runs the company. But now that I think about it, I believe I heard the company was being sold," Meyers said.

"So, no next generation?" asked Tomblyn.

"Yeah, I think he has some sons. They're engineers or scientists or something. But I don't think they wanted to run the business, so they're off doing other things now."

Agent Tomblyn let this sink in for a few minutes as the scenery drifted by. He had in fact read a brief account of some trouble over the senior Colebrook's paintings. He couldn't tell if religious fanatics were involved or if the old man was a real asshole looking for trouble.

Chapter 15

Congressional Hearing

THE SENATOR FROM NORTH CAROLINA sometimes felt guilty about how much he had grown to love Washington. In some ways, he loved it more than the state he represented. He had found so many things here that he could never explain to the folks back home. But at least most of his constituents would appreciate the aesthetics and the sense of history he felt every day when he walked from his apartment house on 4th Street.

Emerging from the front door, he walked down the half-flight of stone and brick stairs and through the intricate gate in the black ironwork fence. This was truly a pleasure every morning, one that he was very conscious of. He never complained about the weather, unlike almost everyone he knew. He felt blessed by each and every mood of nature in this place.

He walked down the street past the other narrow townhouses built in seemingly endless variations of the same basic style. They possessed a feeling of strength and mass, a sense of craftsmanship and lasting quality that was missing in most modern buildings.

On rare occasions, he stopped for coffee at a shop on the corner, thinking the robustness of the drink the perfect complement to the city. He liked to watch the variety of people coming in and out of the shop, people involved with all levels of government, most seeming to be in some great hurry but like him taking a few moments for a restorative cup.

As soon as the Capitol came into view, his sense of history kicked in as well. He thought every day about the things that had happened there—different times, different people, but all on the same stage. It made him conscious of his particular part in the drama. He was clear about this. Though he did not imagine his to be a lead role, he understood the things he was here to do and knew that he was exactly the right person at the right time to do them. Since arriving in Washington more than twenty-five years ago, he had become much more of a history scholar than he had ever been in school or during his years of law practice. He had begun to feel that maybe he knew the men who had come to this place before him better than he knew the voters back home.

These things he thought about every morning, no matter how focused he would become later on the matters at hand. He suspected this was the main difference between himself and the others in the elected bodies.

All these feelings grew stronger as he entered the Senate Office Building, though they moved under the flow of his conscious mind. He nodded and spoke to several staffers and other officials as he walked down the ample hallway. *Here*, he thought, *is a good example of architectural decline.* They would never design buildings nowadays with hallways as wide and as high as these. It would be considered wasted space and resources. No value was placed on the feelings invoked or the messages sent to the ages.

On this morning, he bypassed the elevator that would have taken him to his office and proceeded directly to one of the main hearing rooms. He had been asked to sit on this committee hearing as a voice of reason, to keep things from getting out of control. His party had bigger fish to fry just now, but the issue of Teraplex Building had reached a level of rumor that could no longer be ignored.

The hearing room had a long, curved table at the front. Seated at that table were several fairly old men. A number of younger and more attractive aides stood or sat against the wall behind them. In front of the table was a short empty space that the senator thought of as the demilitarized zone. On the other side of the DMZ, looking distinctly smaller, perhaps because it was on a lower level, was the table for the witness.

Around the senators' table, aides leaned over and spoke and various people shuffled papers and got themselves organized. Presently, the gavel came down and the chairman called the hearing to order. He explained that this was a nonjudicial hearing being held for no other reason than fact-finding. After asking the other committee members if they had any opening remarks before they called their first witness, he deferred to the senator on his far left.

That senator cleared his throat, lifted some papers, and began to speak without ever raising his eyes from the pages.

"Thank you, Mr. Chairman. I want to start by saying that the hearings today are not a witch hunt or part of a witch hunt or anything remotely resembling a witch hunt."

The senator from North Carolina thought, *Translation: This is a witch hunt.*

The other senator continued, "This committee is charged with the oversight of nuclear materials and their use and accounting and disposition. We simply owe it to the American people to do this as part of that oversight function. The American people need to know that these materials are handled properly, and in light of the recent rumors and news stories, we owe it to them to get to the bottom of this situation."

The senator from North Carolina formed the opinion that the other senator had some juicy tidbit of information he could not wait to dump on the hearing.

The other senator continued in this vein for a few minutes, then yielded the floor. A couple of other senators spoke equally empty and useless remarks designed to set up their positions or to make excuses to some part of their constituencies for being there at all. The senator from North Carolina chose not to speak. That was one of the things that endeared him to the more grounded people back home—speaking only when he had something significant to say.

At length, it came time to call the first witness. Three men entered the hearing room and paused by the door for a quick conference. The oldest of the three grasped the youngest by the sleeve of his coat and said something in a low voice.

Perhaps it was the abruptness of this gesture that caught the eye of the senator from North Carolina. Then again, something was familiar about the man—his profile and the way he moved. With the slightest move of his finger, the senator motioned an aide forward and whispered something in his ear.

The older man in question sat in the back as the two others proceeded to the witness table. The younger man was well dressed and of average build and looked to be in his early to mid-forties. The third man was presumably his lawyer, judging from his briefcase and his air of confidence.

The younger man calmly surveyed the Senate table as he was sworn in.

"Please state your name for the committee," said the chairman.

"My name is Earl Cascon," he said.

"And where are you currently employed?" asked the chairman.

"I am currently employed at the Office of Land Acquisition for the U.S. Department of Transportation," Cascon said.

Some confusion arose over this. The DOT? Why were they having some bureaucrat from the DOT testify?

The chairman shuffled some papers, then asked, "Mr. Cascon, can you tell the committee if you were an employee of the U.S. Department of Energy between the dates of August 10, 1989, and the early part of April of this year?"

At this point, a profound change came over the witness. He began squirming in his seat. Beads of sweat formed on his forehead. He suddenly felt the need to loosen his tie, as if he were being hanged by it.

Cascon leaned unnecessarily close to the microphone and answered, "Yes, senator."

"And can you tell us in what capacity you were employed there?" asked the chairman.

Cascon conferred with his lawyer. This was clearly not going to be a smooth information-sharing session.

"I was hired as a technical specialist and later became program director for some exploratory technologies," he finally answered.

"And what was the nature of your technical specialty?" the chairman asked.

"You could probably say certain aspects of deriving energy from nuclear reactions," Cascon said.

"To clarify your background, let me ask you this," the chairman said. "Directly prior to joining the Department of Energy, where were you employed?"

"I worked for the navy," Cascon answered.

Showing no sign of impatience, the chairman asked, "In what capacity were you employed at the navy?"

"I worked in alternative propulsion systems," Cascon answered.

"And by alternative propulsion systems, you mean small nuclear power plants capable of producing heat and electricity," the chairman said, reading from a document in front of him.

"That would describe part of what I worked on, yes," Cascon said.

The senator from North Carolina noted that once Earl Cascon settled into the rhythm of the questions and answers, he seemed to regain his composure.

"Mr. Cascon, during your tenure at the Department of Energy, were you involved with a program called Teraplex Building?" the chairman asked.

"I have no specific recollection of that program," Cascon answered immediately.

He was waiting for that one, thought the senator from North Carolina.

The answer clearly surprised several of the committee members, who looked up from their notes. One of them beckoned an aide and whispered something in her ear as she bent to confer with him.

The chairman looked as perplexed as anyone. He studied Cascon for a moment.

"Mr. Cascon, I want to be very clear about this point. Do I understand you to say that you were not involved with a project known as Teraplex Building?" he said.

"I do not specifically recall any program with the official name Teraplex Building," Cascon answered. He had about him the air of a man walking carefully though a minefield, or at least a lawn littered with dog shit.

"Do you recall working on a program involving new nuclear technology that had not gone through the official steps before being approved for deployment?" the chairman asked.

"During my time at the navy as well as my time at the Department of Energy, I did work on several projects having to do with nuclear technology. I have been advised by counsel that it would not be appropriate to discuss the details of those projects for reasons of confidentiality and national security," Cascon said. He seemed pleased with himself for delivering his longest speech so far without screwing up.

The senator from North Carolina listened to this exchange, glancing from time to time at the man in the back row who had attracted his attention earlier. He prided himself on knowing everybody, and it was driving him crazy that he could not remember this guy or how he recognized him. At a pause in the proceedings after the last outlandish answer, the senator's aide handed him a slip of paper. The senator discreetly unfolded it and read the name: Ira Hudson.

The kind of satisfaction associated with tumblers clicking into place showed on the senator's face, followed quickly by a furrowing of the brow. He remembered Ira Hudson from a meeting with the vice president. Hudson was on the VP's staff in some capacity that had never been made crystal-clear. At the time, the senator had assumed he was one of those guys the VP kept around to help him get into whatever kind of mischief he chose to get into.

This would definitely take some investigation. And it gave the senator a whole new level of interest in the committee proceedings.

Before this, he had figured that the whispers about some secret program were just rumors, and that this hearing had been concocted by his esteemed colleagues to get themselves some airtime on TV. But now, the specter of Ira Hudson skulking in the back row of a low-level committee hearing shone a different light on the whole thing.

The senator left with the question of the day on his mind: *What is an aide to the vice president doing at a hearing about misuse of nuclear materials?*

Chapter 16
Charles is Out

A COUPLE OF DAYS AFTER requesting the satellite data, Charles showed up at work near the southernmost tip of D.C. He held his security badge up to the sensor. Instead of the normal sound of a small animal being electrocuted and a pop of the latch, he heard nothing. The badges got messed up sometimes, so he took it to the central security office, peeved with the delay.

As usual for that hour of the morning, vendors and contractors were lined up trying to arrange access to the lab, so he ran into a further delay before he could even get to one of the clerks. When he did reach the desk, the bored attendant communicated by every possible form of facial expression and body language that she would rather be anywhere else, and that whatever issue he had was an inconvenience to her.

"I've got some kind of problem with my badge," Charles said. "It's not letting me in this morning."

She answered by holding out her hand and looking sideways. He passed her the badge. She pulled it roughly off the lanyard, then slammed the lanyard down on the counter in front of Charles.

She swiped the badge in a sensor by her computer and typed in a few keystrokes at high speed. Something came up on the screen that wiped the bored expression off her face. She glanced up at Charles. Turning her back to him, she picked up a phone and whispered something into the receiver.

Charles was growing concerned.

"Is there some problem?" he asked.

"Please take a seat over there," she said, indicating a row of chairs against the wall.

Charles stood and looked at her a moment, trying to read some clue in her expression, which had assumed a not-sharing-anything poker face. His mind was racing, trying to make sense of what was going on. He backed up to the chairs without turning and sat down, still watching the clerk. She seemed to be overly careful not to glance in his direction.

He jumped when his cell phone went off.

"Don't come in today," a voice whispered when he answered. It was the secretary from the lab.

"What are you talking about?" he whispered, looking around.

"Some security guys are here, and they impounded your computer," she said.

He didn't know what to say.

"I've got to go," the secretary said, and hung up.

Charles snapped the phone shut, turned, and walked slowly out of the building.

He did not become a fugitive right away. He went back to his apartment and tried to open his e-mail account but found his access denied. After talking it over with his girlfriend, he decided to leave a message for his boss to the effect that he was taking a couple of weeks of the copious vacation time he had piled up. He knew that for some reason, one of the security agencies had become interested in him. His first instinct was to go in and confront the thing, but he knew that could backfire. The fact was that a huge gap existed between suspecting someone and actually taking legal action against them. Security people lived in that gap. He decided to not make it easy on them. If they wanted him, they would have to come and get him.

He packed up and headed south.

Chapter 17

The Boarding House

NEAR THE END OF THEIR FIRST DAY in North Carolina, Agents Tomblyn and Haven headed to their hostelry.

At the request of Haven, Meyers's secretary canceled the rooms at the modern motel on the outskirts of town in favor of something more intimate and traditional. More to the point, Haven wanted a place in the middle of town where they might get a better feel for the place and perhaps pick up some gossip. Tomblyn immediately saw the value of this, although it did arouse some degree of discomfort in breaking his well-honed travel routine. It took him outside the world of brick and cement rooms with totally interchangeable looks—two queen-sized beds; television; phone on the bedside table; bathroom with glaring white fluorescent lights, two bath towels, two washcloths, two face towels, and a tub/shower combination with exactly 32 psi water pressure and nonconfusing tap arrangements. This was a world Tomblyn found highly reassuring.

As they pulled up to the large clapboard B&B with two giant syca-more trees in the front yard, he could not suppress his misgivings about the tradeoffs between quaintness and functionality. He also could not put together a mental image of what his room might look like.

Haven, at a different point in the parabolic trajectory of his career, was much better pleased.

"Perfect," he said, looking up at the wide front porch.

To his left up a small rise, he saw that they were only a few blocks from Main Street. To his right was a small park with six tennis courts, and across the street from that the athletic fields and gray granite building of the high school. Beside the tennis courts, for no apparent reason, stood a large fiberglass bear, mouth open in a growl, paws raised to rend flesh. The effect was more comical than scary.

They carried their small travel bags up the stairs to the porch, passing along the way the traditional rocking chairs, a few of which were occupied. In the nearest sat a thin woman working on a crossword puzzle. She looked up and smiled as they approached. Beside her, a small hound, part beagle and part blue tick, jumped to attention and wagged his tail.

"Settle down, Mikey," she said.

The dog looked back at her and sighed.*

The men walked through the large painted doors to the small lobby. There, above the fireplace, they encountered their second remarkable piece of artwork that day. The painting was about three by five feet, framed with a heavy, deeply carved dark wood. The painting depicted a farm pond in summer. The surface of the pond was mesmerizing, going from a dark green suggesting a deep pool to the shimmering silver of the sky reflected on the ripples of the surface. The bank was lush green grass, neat but not newly cut or manicured. Farther along the bank, cattails grew from the shallow water, together with a single white water lily in full bloom. Farther still was a willow tree, its outermost branches hanging over the water. A martin house sat on a pole and showed sights of habitation.

---

* The hound found the name Mikey disrespectful. If Henrico Carr's technology had been available to allow the thoughts of the other animals in the neighborhood to be translated into human speech, it would have shown the hound to be held in the highest possible regard in spite of his size. It also would have shown his name to be best translated as Don Miguel.

In the foreground, a man held up a catfish he had just caught on a piece of piano wire. He was wearing a white shirt with the sleeves rolled up above the elbows. His khaki slacks were rolled nearly to his knees, and his feet were bare and wet. His skin was a smooth light brown, contrasting with the bright white of the shirt. The look on his face conveyed as pure a joy as Haven had ever seen in a painting, or in real life, for that matter. It was as if this were the only fish caught in the history of mankind. An openness in the features and especially the eyes invited the viewer into the scene and perhaps into knowing the fisherman himself. The man was clearly Mahatma Gandhi.

"It's by a local artist," said a middle-aged woman from behind the desk, as if Tomblyn and Haven had any doubt about who had painted it.

"A friend of yours?" asked Haven, turning away from the painting to regard the woman. He was thinking that his strategy was paying off already.

"Well, I guess you could say Mr. Colebrook is a friend of the family," she said. "He gave that to my father about ten years ago. He and Daddy used to go hiking and fishing together, and Daddy did some work for him when he needed extra help."

"Did your father have some particular connection to India or Gandhi?" asked Agent Tomblyn.

"Not hardly. You don't always know exactly why Mr. Colebrook does what he does or paints what he paints," she said. Now, she, too, was looking at the painting. "He used to call Daddy his spiritual adviser. Maybe that had something to do with it."

"Does your father still work for Mr. Colebrook?" Haven asked.

"Oh, no, Daddy died two years ago," she said. "I brought that painting in here after that, and it reminds me of him every day."

"What about the rest of the Colebrook family?" asked Tomblyn.

This seemed to snap the woman out of her reverie. She regarded Tomblyn with a look poised between curiosity and suspicion.

"Sure, I know the whole family," she said. "Are you friends of theirs?"

The flow of the conversation had been destroyed. Haven tried not to show his annoyance with the heavy-handed intrusion from his colleague.

They all regarded the painting for a moment more, then turned to the desk for the business of checking in. The proprietor seemed comfortable with a somewhat open-ended stay. After the usual formalities, she showed her visitors to two rooms side by side on the second floor. Agent Tomblyn seemed relieved that the room had at least most of the features to which he had grown accustomed. Haven was particularly pleased with the view of the shady street out his windows.

After a little time to settle in and clean up, they decided to take a stroll. They went onto the front porch, took a deep breath of mountain air just losing the heat of the day, strode down the front steps, and hung a right toward downtown.

Like many towns in America, this one had survived a near-death experience in the sixties and seventies, when business moved to the shopping malls. It now seemed well on its way to a complete revival. Storefronts that only a few years ago had been abandoned, run down, or both were looking downright trendy. The junk stores had been replaced with real antique shops that were clean and well organized. The couple of diners and home-cooking restaurants had been supplanted by more upscale eating establishments and even a small microbrewery. Some of the older, more robust businesses still survived, among them a men's clothing store complete with a little old Jewish tailor and a combination that dealt in real estate and gold jewelry. The old newsstand had been replaced by a well-ordered bookstore. Over all this, several bank buildings kept watch.

The sidewalks bore a moderate amount of traffic for a small-town weeknight. As they approached the north end of Main Street, they began to notice with increasing frequency people licking and nibbling on ice-cream cones. They did not have to call upon their advanced techniques as professional intelligence operatives to discover the source. For one thing, they saw a group of people with cones congregating around some benches and raised planters outside a particularly well-lit shop. Secondly, they noticed a couple of bright blue-and-yellow ice-cream flags blowing in the breeze above the windows. If this were not enough, they were overtaken upon their approach by an incredible aroma emanating from the store.

This became their destination, with no discussion needed.

The inside of the shop looked as good as the outside smelled. To the left of the entrance was a pair of waffle irons, the source of the fragrant steam that carried out to the street. A teenage girl opened the irons and deftly pulled up the soft brown waffle. She positioned this in an oddly shaped steel holder and inserted a heavy metal cone that looked a little like a medieval weapon used for piercing armor. As she rotated the weapon carefully, the waffle was rolled up between it and the holder to form a perfect cone. She then poured a fresh cup of batter onto the hot irons and closed them, starting the process again. In the meantime, the first waffle cone had cooled and hardened. She removed it from the forming die to reveal a perfect cone ready to receive ice cream.

On the other side of the aisle behind a white fence was a candy kitchen. A young man in a brown apron was using a wooden paddle to stir something in a twenty-gallon copper pot while he joked with some girls leaning toward him over the fence. Tomblyn tipped up his head to get a better look into the pot. The smooth and glossy brown mixture was just coming to a rolling boil. Although he paid plenty of attention to the girls, the cook did not neglect his mixture. He kept the paddle in vigorous motion, glancing at the mixture frequently. As the steam rose, an unbelievable chocolate aroma filled the area. The young man switched on a fan in a hood above the pot. The agents noticed that the pipe from this exhaust hood led directly onto the street. They could appreciate the effectiveness of this advertising ploy, which bypassed other parts of the brain to connect directly to the innocent pedestrian's lust for sweets.

From a rack on the wall, the cook picked up a two-foot-long thermometer and hung it from a hook over the pot so that the business end of the instrument was submerged four or five inches into the boiling chocolate magma. He wiped the steam away from the calibrations and bent over to bring his eye level with the mercury, stirring the while. After a few moments of intense focus, he flicked off a switch with his

foot and reached for a block of butter the size of a paving brick. This
he dropped into the pot and stirred vigorously for a few minutes until he was satisfied the temperature was dropping. He then resumed
a slower stirring while the butter shrank and eventually disappeared
into the pool of brown, shiny glass.

And then, bidden by some unspoken sign, the cook was joined by
another worker. Together, they hoisted the pot by its handles, walked
it carefully to a table with a six-inch-thick monolith of marble for a
top, and poured the dark mixture onto the stone.

On the marble surface, four steel bars had been arranged in a rectangle that kept the dark liquid from flowing onto the floor. Tomblyn
and Haven watched in fascination as the cooks withdrew the pot, leaving the smooth, brown, glassy surface cooling on the slab. Just when
they thought it could not smell any better, the cook approached again
and drizzled a spoonful of vanilla onto the surface, where it hissed and
vaporized and mixed its sweet down-home smell with the chocolate
vapors already filling the shop.

After a few minutes, the cook tested the sheet of fudge on the
table and apparently decided it had cooled enough. He removed the
steel bars one by one, then took down a long-handled scraper from a
rack on the wall. Holding this tool at an angle to the table, he plowed
through the fudge, folded it over on top of itself, and dragged the
blade back. This he did down one side of the table and, switching ends,
back up the other side. The movements of the cook and the flowing
of the glossy chocolate mixture were hypnotic. Tomblyn and Haven
were joined by others in watching the dance around the table. A few
asked questions, but mostly they watched in silence. The crowd let out
a collective groan when a tool missed a thin stream of liquid fudge and
a small brown drop hit the floor.

With each pass of the cook around the table, the fudge cooled and
flowed less freely. Presently, it began to lose the glossy sheen and take
on a more dull appearance. This seemed to be the signal for the cook to
put down his large tool and pick up a much smaller hand implement.
Using pushing and lifting motions, the cook began to pile the fudge
into a long loaf. At first, the fudge flowed back almost to its original

form, but as he worked his way around the table, the mixture began to stiffen and retain its shape. One final pass formed the fudge into a long, smooth loaf. The cook raised his tool above the table and looked for any irregularities. Seeing none, he put the tool down and looked up, at which the audience promptly clapped for the performance.

Turning to the heart of the store, Tomblyn and Haven found people milling around, eating ice-cream cones, and bending over the glass cases. Agent Tomblyn decided to check out the cases, too.

On the left close to the entrance were loaves of fudge, for which he now had a greater understanding and interest. A young girl behind the case was passing out samples, weighing slabs, and packaging them for customers.

To the right were two more cases. One was filled with fancy creams and truffles of every description. The other contained more whimsical selections also made on the premises. Among them were a variety of objects dipped in chocolate: potato chips dipped in chocolate, dried fruit dipped in chocolate, pretzels dipped in chocolate, and, as if they did not already contain enough chocolate, Oreo cookies dipped in chocolate. Moreover, customers could choose among milk, dark, and white chocolate. He even saw dog bones dipped in white chocolate. They were labeled, "For Your K9 Friends."

At the back of the store were two large ice-cream cases. These seemed to invite the closest study of all. The shop offered thirty-two flavors, and most customers needed to sample at least two or three before progressing to the buying stage. Then came the decision about the type of cone, of which several selections were available as well.

Haven took note of the lovely dark-haired salesgirl behind the counter. She wore a hooded sweatshirt, presumably to fend off the coolness of the ice-cream cases, and had a somewhat mysterious, patient, and bemused look on her face. He then noticed an interesting phenomenon among the people perusing the ice-cream landscape. One person in each group would generally emerge to act as interpreter and spokesman. Other members would study the ice-cream possibilities, whispering occasionally to the spokesman. Finally, sensing that the group was approaching a decision point, the spokesman would make eye contact with the salesgirl. The conversation followed a definite pattern.

Salesgirl: "May I help you?"

Spokesmen to member of his group: "John, what kind do you want?"

John to spokesman: "What's in the Carolina Mud?"

Spokesman to salesgirl, before salesgirl could answer the question directly: "What's in the Carolina Mud?"

Salesgirl to John, attempting to bypass the spokesman: "It's vanilla ice cream with caramel and flecks of chocolate."

Spokesman to John, apparently fearing that John did not speak the same dialect of English as the salesgirl: "Vanilla, caramel, and chocolate."

John to spokesman: "I'll have the rum raisin."

Spokesman to salesgirl: "One rum raisin."

Salesgirl to spokesman, giving up on the idea of direct communication and gesturing to the display rack directly in front of the spokesman's face: "What kind of cone would you like that in?"

Spokesman to John, taking him by the shoulders and positioning him directly in front of the cone display: "What kind of cone?"

John, after a few moments of confusion, during which he seemed to have trouble focusing on the display: "A regular cone."

Salesgirl, pointing to one on the rack, since none was labeled *regular*: "Would you like this one?"

John would then mumble something inaudible to the spokesman.

Spokesman to salesgirl: "Yeah."

The salesgirl would pick up a metal scoop from a water well, deftly scoop a gleaming sphere of rum raisin ice cream, and place it on a cake cone. This she would hand to John with a smile and ask, "Can I help the next person?"

At this point, the process started again. Working through the spokesman one by one, flavor by flavor, each member of the group was hooked up with the combination of his or her choice. They then began to slurp at the cones, eyes rolling back in ecstasy.

When the time came for the spokesman to get a cone for himself, none of the information transmitted through him to the other group members seemed to be accessible for his own use. Indeed, the very thought that he might get an ice-cream cone himself seemed completely novel.

"What do *I* want? Let me see."

The spokesman would walk the entire length of the case, seeing the flavors as if for the first time. Nor, upon eventually selecting a flavor, would the spokesman volunteer any information about what type of cone he desired.

Undaunted, the salesgirl would say, "Do you want that in a waffle cone?"

The spokesman, surprised by this question, would dig himself out of his hole by carefully studying the cone display one more time and finally selecting a dish.

Haven finally had all he could take. He approached the ice-cream case at the next open interval.

"Chocolate peanut butter in a waffle cone," he said to the girl, taking some pride in reducing the ordering ritual to the minimum possible number of words.

"Same," said Agent Tomblyn, stepping up behind him.

The two men received their cones and dug in. The flavor was amazing, and for a moment they stood transfixed. Then, having no other agenda, they began once again to look around the store.

Tomblyn noticed a little blond-haired girl of perhaps five years sitting on a high wooden stool. Her legs were folded so that her stocking feet rested on the topmost rungs. The stool faced a high oak table that paralleled the fence into the kitchen area. The little girl, bent over some project on the table, seemed to be engaged in an intermittent conversation with the cook, who was now in the process of cleaning the utensils he had used to make the batch of fudge.

Tomblyn moved closer so he could look over her shoulder, expecting perhaps some coloring book or word puzzle. What he saw made him forget the chocolate peanut butter ice cream.

The girl was intently focused on a scroll of light brown paper, the center of which was flattened on the tabletop. With her right hand, she held a large tarot card in position while she traced around it with a reddish pencil grasped in her left. That done, she slid the card aside and regarded the rectangular frame her tracing had formed. As though seeking some reference, she unrolled part of the top half of the scroll, which proved to have several similar rectangular frames drawn in neat rows. Within each of the frames was the drawing of an angel, each in a different pose. Just above the empty frame was an angel reaching up to trim a vine growing on a curved arbor. Next to that, a frame contained an angel playing cards. Next to that, an angel pointed skyward with a serene look on her face. Or maybe it was *his* face, for all the angels were fairly androgynous.

"What angel are you going to draw next, Audrey?" asked the cook. As he said it, he looked at Tomblyn, perhaps making sure the man was okay, and letting him know he was paying attention to the little girl.

Tomblyn stood transfixed by both the subject matter and the precision and detail of the drawings. Both seemed far beyond the years of the child artist.

She did not answer the cook right away but sat looking at the empty frame and the other drawings. She unfurled the scroll a little more, as if to remind herself of angels already accounted for.

"Maybe it's time to draw the angel that makes candy," she said. By the tone of her voice, it was not clear if she was serious or if she was teasing the cook.

"Is he the candy-making angel?" Tomblyn asked with a grin, indicating the cook. He felt compelled to somehow learn more about this remarkable child.

Audrey turned her head to see who had approached but showed little surprise. Her hair was a golden blond and her eyes a deep nut-brown color, an unusual combination, and quite striking. She regarded him for a moment, seemingly taking in the details of his presence in an open and nonjudgmental pass.

"He's a human being." This she said in a matter-of-fact way. Her response held no particular edge, being just a straightforward answer to a reasonable question.

If it was Tomblyn's intention to strike up a conversation, the question did not have the desired effect.

"Those are very good drawings," said Tomblyn.

"Thank you," replied Audrey.

"Who taught you to draw like that?" he asked.

"My Pipo taught me to draw, but he said everyone draws in their own way," Audrey said, still not looking up from the scroll. She was making faint strokes of the pencil. Tomblyn thought she was probably starting to form an outline of the next drawing on the scroll, but he could not as yet tell what the figure might be.

Hearing the little voice say the nickname Pipo, Haven snapped his attention away from the two camp counselors at the ice-cream case. He walked up and looked over the little girl's other shoulder. He, too, stood transfixed by the drawings on the unusual scroll as the identity of the little girl sank in. He and Tomblyn straightened up and exchanged a glance behind her back, then looked around the store with a renewed and more professional interest.

Out of the back came a thin lady of middle years dressed in an apron bearing the name of the shop. She closed the distance with a few quick, purposeful strides, handed the cook a bowl of walnuts, gave the fudge he had just completed an appraising look, and examined the rest of the kitchen area. She seemed to find all in order with the exception of a set of measuring spoons, which she picked up from the table and hung from a hook on the wall. Then, turning to the high table, she saw Audrey with the two strangers standing close behind her. Her quick look of concern was replaced by a professional smile.

"How is your ice cream?" she asked Haven and Tomblyn.

They looked at each other before Tomblyn answered, "Oh, it's fine. It's good."

She smiled again, then bent her head close to Audrey.

"Honey, why don't you come in the back with Grandma and get some supper?"

Tomblyn and Meyers backed up a step to give the girl room to climb down from the stool.

"Can I take my work with me, Grandma Lilly?" she asked.

"Grandma will bring it back for you, sweetheart," she said as she carefully gathered up the scroll.

She took the little girl's hand and led her to the back of the store, glancing at the two strangers as she and her granddaughter disappeared into the inner sanctum.

Haven and Tomblyn watched them go, then headed out onto the street.

A moment later, the grandmother came out the door of the shop and looked up and down the street until she saw the pair walking toward their boardinghouse. She studied them for a moment as if committing their appearances to memory, after which she turned back inside.

Chapter 18

Root Beer Deprivation

XAVIER SUSPECTED SOMETHING WAS UP when he returned to the robotics lab the next morning and found the fuselage of the plane missing. He was more peeved than anything. He cursed one of his teammates who was a neat freak and always cleaned things up. This was not the first time that some interesting but junky stuff had fallen victim to a "quality cleanup."

The second clue came when he went to buy a can of root beer from a vending machine and found that his all-purpose university card—a cross between an ID and a credit card, used at the school for everything from purchasing snacks to accessing records to opening doors—would not work. This proved to be an emotional blow far beyond the immediate root beer deprivation. He had been conditioned over the past few years to depend on that card.

He retuned to his apartment and tried to access his e-mail account, only to find a message reading, "Account suspended due to code 1023 violation."

A code 1023 violation, as he learned from a friend who worked in the bursar's office, indicated that the student's status was under review for "serious or potentially felonious violations of the university ethics code."

"What exactly did you do?" his friend asked.

"Nothing. I mean, I don't know. How serious is this anyway?" he asked.

"It usually ends badly for the student," she said.

"Define *badly*," Xavier said.

"Suspension without credit or refund of tuition and remanding of records to law enforcement authorities," she said, lapsing into official dialect.

"Define *usually*," Xavier said, looking for some ray of hope in this mess.

"Always," she said.

"Your recommendation?" he asked.

"Get out of Dodge and try to straighten this thing out," she said.

The expression on his face collapsed, which was most unusual for a young man normally so buoyant.

"Sometimes you feel like a motherless child," she said, giving him a hug.

"A motherless child without root beer or e-mail," he said, and gave her one of his laughs to let her know he was already on his way back up.

Chapter 19

A rt History for Lawmen

In Washington, the FBI had, if nothing else, a great data system and plenty of people who knew how to use it. Tomblyn had a search done there and sent to his attention.

He took the resulting file out of a folder from his briefcase and handed it to Meyers.

Meyers read,

FBI File 27094

Subject: Colebrook, James R., a.k.a. Pipo
Civil/Political Disturbance

Incident Summary—A coalition of church groups staged a protest outside the Charlotte Museum of Art. The focal point was a series of paintings by James R. Colebrook that they found "offensive, irreverent, and sacrilegious." The paintings were part of an exhibition of North Carolina artists that was due to be the subject of national reviews and possibly a PBS television program. The church people were especially sensitive to this, as they were afraid of the image this would paint of their state, otherwise viewed as the buckle on the Bible Belt. The church groups demanded that the museum withdraw Colebrook's paintings from the exhibition and replace them with "works more representative of sentiments of the people of our region, works that reflect the beauty of creation and God's plan for us here."

Colebrook is well known regionally as a painter and business owner and for occasionally becoming politically active on certain specific projects.

Colebrook refused interviews with the papers and television.

"Yeah, I remember this," Meyers said. "It was about ten or twelve years ago. Most people around here were okay with the paintings, especially the people who knew him or had worked with him. I think they knew he didn't mean anything by them. But the group down in Charlotte, the fundamentalists, they were pissed. They took it as a protest to their put-religion-back-in-the-schools movement."

Later articles traced the progress of the protest over several months. The museum director refused to remove the paintings, as he regarded them as artistically superior to anything else in the exhibit. He was also not one to be pushed around by a crowd.

The protesters moved on to the city council, which was pretty much split on how to deal with the situation, eventually voting by a slim margin to back the museum director, whom it had appointed.

The protesters then moved on to their state representatives, who were only too happy to get involved, since it was far simpler to meddle in a local high-profile issue than to work at the complicated matters they had been elected to deal with. Ultimately, a local bill was passed that formed a citizens' committee to review all works of art put on public display.

"So how did Colebrook take all of this?" Haven asked.

"As I recall, he declined any public comment on the matter," Meyers said. "His attitude was that a painting is like anything else—it is what it is, no use talking about it. Actually, he doesn't talk about anything—I mean, not in a literal sense. He doesn't talk at all. That's another quirky thing about him that I remember. He decided to take a vow of silence several years ago."

"That's weird. But this report left out the most interesting part," said Tomblyn. "What were the paintings that got everyone so upset?"

"It's probably better to show them to you than to try to describe them," said Meyers.

He could not suppress a laugh as he thought about them. Tomblyn gave him a sideways look, wondering not for the first time if Meyers was enjoying this a little too much.

"What about this?" said Tomblyn, pushing over another report, this one several pages in length.

"What is this, a whole media scan?" asked Meyers.

"I think they just put in the family name Colebrook, and western North Carolina, and that's what they came up with."

Meyers scanned the first page, then began leafing. He saw names and events he knew and ones he did not.

"Interesting family," he said.

"Maybe a little too interesting for their own good," said Tomblyn.

The clippings, arranged roughly in chronological order, covered some installations of artwork and fountains.

Then came one about the establishment of Athenaeum. As described in the article, the company was in the business of designing, building, and installing fountains and other public works of art. A quote from its founder, James Colebrook, described it as the "engineering side of the art world. You want the artists to design and sculpt things, but you also want the fountains to actually work, and you want the big bronze statues to not fall on people and to survive little kids climbing on them."

Other articles treated Athenaeum as it expanded. Among them were announcements of various contracts all over the world, as well as coverage of the addition of the foundry, which in addition to making bronze castings of artworks began creating other objects as well—anything from pump parts to replicas of ancient cannons to church bells to commemorative plaques.

Next came the inclusion of James's son, Philip, in the business. Apparently, Athenaeum had expanded rapidly with Philip's help. Stories from this period covered exciting project announcements and contracts, as the company was able to take on increasingly ambitious work. The business became an active part of the community, making frequent donations to charities and sponsoring various school events and internships.

The articles included no formal announcement of James's retirement, but his name appeared less frequently in the news items, and Philip was listed as the "company head."

Later, articles began to appear about Philip's three sons—mostly the usual stuff about athletics and academic accomplishments typical in small-town newspapers. They were all swimmers. They were all admitted to engineering programs. The oldest two appeared on lists of graduates. The youngest was still in school, by Tomblyn's calculation.

After graduation, the oldest son, Leon, largely dropped out of the news, reappearing about six years later in a wedding announcement, the ceremony to be performed by a waterfall in Pisgah National Forest. Meyers made a mental note to look into what Leon had been doing in the ensuing years. The bride was Sue Castallini, a local girl. Her picture was traditional except for a crown and matching necklace crafted from silver and displaying the Celtic cross as the prominent motif. The wedding piece was followed a couple of years later by a birth announcement of a daughter, Audrey. Leon also appeared in an article about local people who had hiked the entire Appalachian Trail.

Some clippings covered the college swimming career of the second son, Charles. After graduation, he appeared in a couple of NASA publications as a member and then leader of some of the design teams for various spacecraft, especially satellites with unusual missions. He was also listed as a team member in the Washington, D.C., Adult Kickball League.

"Did I read that right?" asked Meyers. "Adult kickball?"

"Oh, yeah, very big in Washington," said Tomblyn.

This piece of information did little to elevate Meyers's view of our nation's capital and the people who lived and worked there.

The youngest son, Xavier, appeared first for touring Europe with a band while still in high school. Also included were some amazing photographs he had taken of supersonic bullets piercing various objects: balloons, pieces of wood, playing cards, even stale brownies. By using special techniques, he was able to photograph the shock waves propagating off the bullets and bouncing back from the objects they were aimed at. Some of the photos had been published in a textbook on high-speed photography. The amazing thing was that this was one of his high-school science projects. Dated shortly thereafter was a story about his getting a full scholarship to an engineering school in a neighboring state.

And their mother was in there, too. It seemed she had dealt with empty nest syndrome by opening a chocolate and ice-cream shop, the Chocolate Moose. This had grown and prospered and become a principal downtown destination, as Haven and Tomblyn could now attest.

"You have got to check out the caramel apples at that place," Meyers said.

"Yeah, we've done some surveillance at the Chocolate Moose already," Haven said, a bit wishfully.

"At least one person in the family seems normal," Tomblyn observed.

"So what's your interest in the Colebrooks?" asked Meyers.

"As you may have gathered, we have a problem," said Tomblyn. "As of right now, we are not at liberty to say exactly what that problem is, for reasons of national security."

Meyers tried his best not to take this personally, but that was a little difficult. He was, after all, Tomblyn's senior in more ways than just the number of years they had logged on the planet. And then there was the perception that the world was divided into two types of people: those who were from Washington and those who were from some lesser place.

Tomblyn looked over to see how Meyers was taking all this, but Meyers didn't give him the satisfaction.

"Anyway, I guess it's fair to say we are missing something that certain people want back very badly," Tomblyn said. "As we begin to check on who else seems to be interested, or who had access to certain assets, or who was in the wrong place at the wrong time, we keep tripping over these names. One person in this family after another. I'm not real big on coincidences, and our bosses back in Washington are sure as hell not believers. On the other hand, we don't really see why these people would have any interest in the . . . the thing that's missing. So for right now, our job is to check them out, find out a little more about them, find out who they're connected with, and see what happens next. If all these things are coincidences, fine. I'm willing to become a believer. If not, we're on the scene."

Meyers was left to wonder that much more. The Colebrooks were an interesting family, to be sure, but one that kept pretty much on its own track. And that track did not seem to be one that should come to the attention of the government crowd, unless you counted the installation of a public fountain or statue here and there.

Haven found himself growing more and more interested in James Colebrook's paintings.

"When can we see those paintings?" he asked Meyers.

"I think they're in a private collection now, but I believe I saw them in a book on local art. We could stop by the bookstore and have a look," Meyers said.

"That's okay. We'll walk downtown after dinner tonight," Haven said.

That the three agents did. After locating the large book they were looking for, they flipped to the full-page images of the paintings in question, referred to as "the Religious Series."

The first painting was set in a gilded frame, the design of which was similar to the religious icons painted for churches in the Byzantine era. It had straight sides and an arched top. The frame was deeply sculpted in a geometric pattern and appeared to be covered in a veneer of pressed gold leaf. In the arched portion of the painting was the oval head of the Madonna, her eyes raised skyward. A golden halo surrounded the head, its rays of light spreading wide. All was set against a sky of china blue.

The Madonna was clothed richly in heavy, colorful robes. Out of a central pocket in the abdominal area peeked the head of a tiny infant. He, too, had a halo. His open and steady gaze seemed to fix the viewer squarely in the eye.

Hovering in the air above mother and child were numerous winged figures. These might at first be seen as angels, but upon closer examination they proved to be kangaroos with wings. A larger kangaroo stood behind the Madonna, whispering in her ear—what message, the viewer was left to speculate upon.

A plaque beneath the frame revealed the work to be entitled *Marsupial Madonna*.

Apparently, part of the controversy concerned whether *marsupial* referred just to the angelic kangaroos or whether the Madonna herself was intended to be a marsupial, complete with pouch. As usual with Colebrook paintings, much was left to the imagination of the viewer.

Little wonder that this painting was objectionable to traditional Catholics in the area.

The second painting, however, managed to offend all Christian denominations pretty much equally.

Its official title was *Seven Iron or a Strong 8*. However, the newspapers had referred to it as "Crucifixion on the 13th Green." The painting was on a square canvas in a plain pine frame with a rather rough finish. It showed a Jesus-like figure flanked by two thieves, all of them dressed as modern-day golfers. Their three crosses had been erected on an elevated putting green. The point of view appeared to be the tee box looking across a water hazard. It was clear that an errant shot either short or to the right would be big trouble. In the foreground, a marker advised the viewer that it was a 153-yard par-three hole. On the left across the water but short of the green was a white circle in the grass suggesting a drop zone, the golfer's equivalent of purgatory.

The three figures were shown in classic crucifixion poses. The head of the central one was inclined to the side. His crown of thorns included a sun visor.

"Wow!" said Haven. "You think he was a little frustrated with religion back then?"

"More likely frustrated with golf," said a man who had walked into the store unnoticed while the agents were engrossed in the book.

Haven and Tomblyn looked up at him, startled.

"You've seen these paintings before?" Tomblyn asked.

"Oh, yeah, I've seen quite a lot of those paintings," the man said.

"I hear they made quite a stir around here," said Meyers. He was thinking the man looked somehow familiar.

"You have no idea," the man said, then laughed as he turned toward the sales clerk and paid for a magazine he had just picked up. "Check out the one on page 123. It's my favorite," he said as he walked out the door.

The agents looked at each other. Tomblyn began flipping pages.

"Was that guy some kind of authority on Colebrook?" Haven asked the clerk.

"I guess if anyone is, he would be," the clerk said. "That was Philip Colebrook. His dad made those paintings you're looking at."

All three looked at the empty door.

On page 123, Tomblyn read aloud the title, *Adoration of the Magi.*

The *Adoration*, according to the book, was mounted in a gilded frame about three feet square. At first glance, it appeared to be a pretty typical manger scene. The Star of the East shone down upon the vaulted thatch roof of an open stable, where various animals were arranged around the central figures.

However, upon closer examination, the three wise men turned out to be the Marx Brothers.

Groucho, kneeling beside the baby, had his head turned toward the viewer. His eyes were pointed heavenward. In his grinning mouth was a smoldering cigar. He was holding forth a box of Havanas to the babe, as if in invitation to join him in an after-dinner smoke.

Harpo looked especially at home wearing robes of the period. Needless to say, a number of horns with rubber bulbs were wedged under his belt. His face held its customary look of angelic delight as he nuzzled against the neck of a donkey.

Chico held the bridle of a camel. Both were shown in profile looking intently at the babe. Both he and the camel were smoking cigarettes.

Mary seemed more than a little startled by the appearance of these three. The artist had not gone so far as to cast Margaret Dumont in this role. However, upon reflection, the face of the camel did bear a strong resemblance to the hefty actress.

"Hard to get too mad at the Marx Brothers," Haven said.

Meyers just smiled, turned the page, and pointed to the first paragraph on the next page, part of a newspaper article that described the objection of some local groups to the painting. The Reverend Ten Ferrell was quoted as saying, "Jewish people have no place in a picture about our Lord."

That was the closest the book ever came to editorial comment.

There remained plenty that the file did not say, and that the FBI agents would have to glean from further investigation and questioning.

The old man, James, was known to virtually everyone as Pipo, a name given to him by his son presumably because he was seldom seen without a pipe in his mouth. He still smoked frequently, especially when painting or walking—which indeed accounted for most of his waking hours.

That he had little hair left on his head was of minor consequence, since he nearly always wore a cap of one sort or another. In cold weather, it would likely be a beret of ancient origin. In warmer times, an endless parade of ball caps made their appearance. His beard was full but trimmed short, ranging from gray to white in color. His skin never paled, owing to his frequent walks in the mountains. His deep-set brown eyes rarely failed to connect on some fundamental level with the people he encountered. They were at once searching and filled with a grand amusement, giving his companions the feeling he would rather be nowhere else and with no one else.

These feelings almost always emerged in spite of his most remarkable and best-known attribute: he did not speak. He had in fact abandoned the use of verbal communication at the age of fifty-eight. He had announced his intention to do so because, with few exceptions, he was not fond of hearing old people talk. He most often found their remarks tiresome and tedious and the inflection of their voices equally unpleasant. Above all, he did not wish to fall even occasionally into that category. Secondly, he theorized that giving up speaking would increase the power and scope of his nonverbal communication skills. No doubt, this was true.

He had run the fountain company for many years and was still responsible for some of its more whimsical designs. However, he now channeled most of his creative energy into his painting. He often depicted his subjects dressed in clothing from other periods of time. Indeed, he was best known for painting historical figures drastically— some would say grotesquely—displaced in time and space.

If he had any problems with Philip's selling Athenaeum, he kept them to himself. He had moved on, something Philip was clearly still struggling with.

Chapter 20

The Sad Spanish Song

BELIEVING THE SAD SPANISH SONG was about her, the aged yellow Labrador raised her nose to the sky and closed her eyes.

So sad, she said to herself. *So tragic. That a life lived with utter fidelity and passion should come to this. Neglected, overlooked, misunderstood. So few walks. So little food.**

These sentiments were based on nothing more than the Labrador's tendency to experience such sentiments. She was in fact fed twice daily and enjoyed many Milk Bone treats. Likewise, her walks were frequent, at least by the standards of most dogs—short walks at least once a day and lengthy hikes in the national park several times a week. Add to that a pond right by the house for swimming. But then the Labrador lived in a very Labrador-centric universe, so it was not surprising that she failed to achieve a more realistic perspective.

---

* Labrador retrievers were among the first subjects of experimentation when Ecuadorian biophysicist Henrico Carr began developing his technology to translate the thought patterns of animals into human speech. He discovered that Labrador thoughts were especially well focused and linear, even if self-absorbed.

A column of smoke rose from the other side of the drawing board. Pipo considered his painting and glanced around the board at the dog. Seeing the pose, he thought, *Give me a freaking break.* No stranger to the mood swings of such creatures, he was not about to be sucked into her self-indulgent morass.

And yet he was distracted from the work in front of him. Sometimes his painting flowed, and sometimes it didn't. Sometimes, if he managed to stick with it, it began to flow again, and sometimes the hill just got steeper.

After another moment, he pulled a tarp over the canvas and went to clean his brushes. The portrait of James Joyce at the wheel of a Boston Whaler would wait for another time. He had not in any case decided who would be water-skiing behind it.

About the time he finished the last brush, he heard tires on the gravel driveway. He was delighted to see the black Toyota pickup with two blond heads and one bearlike brown one in the cab.

The instant the truck crunched to a stop and did a little bob from the parking brake, the passenger door flew open and a small figure flew out and into his arms, hardly touching the ground in between. The Labrador joined the excitement with a few barks and a lot of tail wagging.

"Are you painting, Pipo?" asked Audrey.

He answered with a shrug. They understood this to mean that yes, he was probably working on something, but no, he did not know if it was going anywhere, and it probably was not worth looking at yet.

He hugged the others as well. Leon and Sue headed up to the house, while Pipo and Audrey walked toward the workshop. They all turned when they heard the crunch of tires on gravel again. A second black Toyota pickup trundled up the drive and parked behind Pipo's 1981 Ford truck, popularly known as "the Silver Wraith." Out popped the lanky figure of Charles, grinning widely.

"Family reunion," Leon said. He had heard nothing about his brothers' plans to come home that weekend, so it was a surprising development.

They found Xavier and Philip on the porch, already into the Cuba

Libres. Lilly was in the kitchen tending several pots on the stove.

"Seems like we have a few things to talk about," said Philip.

Leon and Sue looked at each other.

"You have no idea," said Leon, settling into one of the rocking chairs.

His brothers were lounging on the swing. Philip was in another rocking chair. Caca Lacka, the half-Labrador, half–Australian shepherd mix, occupied her usual perch in one of the Adirondack chairs.

"What's everybody doing home?" said Leon.

"Time to compare notes," said Xavier.

"And we know something's happening but we don't know what it is," said Charles, paraphrasing one of the Bob Dylan songs they were all raised on.

Just then, Pipo came trudging up the stairs with Audrey on his back.

"Pipo and me are hungry," she said. She had sometime ago appointed herself his official spokesperson and translator.

So they all went in and grabbed a plate of chicken and corn, then came back out on the porch and gathered around the picnic table.

Leon started the family conference by saying, "I think we might have found something pretty significant up in map quadrant 23. Actually, Audrey was the first to see it when we were up there looking at evidence of a village site downstream from the find."

Audrey and Sue joined in telling the details, and Audrey was praised by all.

Leon slid a photograph to the center of the table. "This is the best shot we could get of the carvings on the underside of the rock. I tried to enhance it on the computer so you can make out the figures better."

Charles and Xavier bent over the photo while Pipo came around and looked over their shoulders. Lilly was looking at it upside down.

"We don't know what this row of symbols means," said Leon, pointing to the right side of the photo, "but we think this is someone's hand holding an ear of corn."

Lilly squinted and spun the photo around so she could see it better.

She smiled. "I don't think that's an ear of corn, son. You should recognize what it is." She held the photo up so they could all see it. "That is a cacao pod. See the lobes there?" She pointed. "It has been cut open about halfway down, exposing the central core with the beans still held together inside. Anyone who harvests beans would recognize that. They cut the pods like that, then dump the beans out to ferment before they're dried."

The rest of the family knew exactly what she was talking about, having seen her pictures of harvesting in southern Mexico.

"This puts the connection even farther south than we thought," said Sue. "Cacao grows only within fifteen degrees of the equator, right?"

Lilly nodded.

"This changes how we're going to have to think about this thing," Leon said. "But getting back to our story, on the walk out, Audrey spotted this weird plane." He described the plane. "I just thought it was a weird coincidence to find it that close to our site. I don't believe in coincidence, so I took it up to Xavier."

"Which, as it turns out, might not have been such a great idea," Xavier said. He explained why he was taking a leave of absence from the campus, a story that was not well received by his parents.

"So what's up with you, Charles?" said Leon.

"Well, someone seems to be upset with me for requesting photos of your area from the Geostat IV satellite," said Charles.

"I know why I'm interested in that area, but why is anyone else?" Leon said. "I can't believe it's for the same reason."

"I think that's what we have to figure out if Xavier and I are going to get to the bottom of our problems," Charles said.

"You said you might have found something else up there," Leon said.

"A satellite. A satellite that's not supposed to be there and that no one is talking about,"

Charles said. "And I think it might be one of mine."

"You mean Geostat IV?" Sue asked.

"No, a different one," Charles said.

They all knew that Charles built satellites for various government and private enterprises and that he was possessive of them. That's about all they knew because he usually couldn't tell them much. Occasionally, they saw a satellite on TV or in a magazine, and he would say, "One of mine."

"How do you know about it?" asked Xavier.

"Well, I started hearing some rumors, and then I began checking for myself. It's not in any of the usual registries. I know some of the people who keep track of that sort of thing for a living, and they never heard of it. One guy said he would look into it and get back to me. He never did, and when I called him back he advised me to stop checking on things that didn't concern me because it was getting him and me into trouble."

"How do you know it really exists?" asked Xavier.

"Well, I know we made it, and I know we delivered it. I started asking the people we made it for when the launch date was. I got some vague answers, which is not that unusual when it comes to launch dates. Then, when I heard the rumor, I decided to try a little experiment. I called them and said we wanted to check and possibly modify some things. And I got every excuse in the book why we couldn't. That is unusual. Actually, it's unheard of that they would not want us making sure the bird is okay."

"So you're thinking the real reason is that it's not on the ground anymore," said Leon.

"Right," said Charles. "And then I picked up an ID signal with my own equipment—just once, and real faint. But that puts the bird out there," he said, pointing up.

"The middle of the air," said Leon.

They all knew that Charles had tracking equipment at his house in D.C.

"I thought that satellites were up above the air. That's what Uncle Xavier told me," Audrey chimed in.

Xavier gathered her onto his lap. "It's just a figure of speech, honey," he said.

"You think it's military?" asked Leon.

"No reason not to tell me if it's military. I have the clearances, and besides, they would want our guys in on the mission in one way or another. They always want us there to check things at the launch in case a problem comes up at the last minute. They would at least have wanted our computer guys," said Charles.

"So you want to do a little more sophisticated tracking on your own?" asked Xavier.

"That's why I asked you to meet me here," said Charles.

Xavier and Charles were looking at each other and smiling.

Philip began to catch on. "Are you talking about RARS?" he asked.

He was referring to the Rosman Astronomical Research Station, an incredible collection of radio telescopes—and now light telescopes as well—located way up in Pisgah Forest near Rosman. It had been established in 1963 as a tracking station for manned and unmanned space flights. The site was picked for several reasons. One, it was in a bowl-shaped hollow in the mountains, which helped shield it from radiation of various kinds. Two, no power lines—which tend to emit radio frequency noise—were nearby. Three, little or no commercial air traffic passed overhead.

In its day, it had been quite an operation, running 24/7 and employing three shifts of NASA technicians, plus a load of support staff from Rosman and Brevard—about two hundred people in all. It was an important part of the communications network all through the Mercury, Gemini, and Apollo years.

By the early 1980s, the site was no longer needed by NASA, which turned it over to the Department of Defense, which wanted it for intelligence-gathering purposes. Actually, some people thought the DOD was doing stuff it did not want NASA civilian techno-nerds knowing about, so it played the national defense card and commandeered the site. During that time, most of the locals were laid off and a whole lot less traffic went to and from the site, which started some folk tales.

By 1995, the Department of Defense mission, whatever it really consisted of, was pretty well done, and the department decided the site was surplus. At that time, the DOD showed the magnanimous side that people so seldom witnessed in its character. It resolved to present the station—complete with forty-five buildings, giant radio telescope dishes, miles of chain-link fence, generators, and all the rest of the support stuff—to the National Park Service.

Imagine the delight of the National Park Service, which had no idea in the world what to do with this thing. Imagine the delight of the administration in Washington, which was able to get rid of an unwanted DOD asset without having to explain what it had been doing with it, while simultaneously saying to the public that it had just increased its support of the National Park Service by several hundred million dollars, the current value shown on the books for the site and all its equipment.

The park service, of course, closed the site. A few years later, it agreed to sell it to a private nonprofit group led by an astronomy buff who hated to see such an asset go to waste. Rumor had it that some of the money actually was funneled to this group by the CIA, which was not opposed to seeing the station preserved just in case it might be needed sometime in the future. Whether or not this was true, everyone seemed to be happy with the arrangement.

So now, the site existed as RARS. Various colleges and universities did research projects there. From time to time, it hosted tours for school groups.

Some years ago, Charles, early in his college career, had done an internship on a project looking for evidence of intelligent life somewhere besides earth. During his stint, he found intelligent life in that part of North Carolina but had less luck in the extraterrestrial realm. He worked with a few engineers at the station and learned about running the telescopes, especially the radio frequency equipment. Xavier had been able to ride in on his big brother's coattails a few times. Xavier soaked up that stuff like a sponge wiping up Kool-Aid.

So, given all this, Philip knew right away what they were talking about.

"What do you plan to do?" he asked Charles. "Are you going to call the people you worked with up there?"

"I don't think so," said Charles. "In the first place, I don't want them to report that I'm requesting to get some time on the dish. If I asked them to let me in and keep it secret, I'm not sure what they'd do. Even if they went along, I don't want to put them in that position. I mean, calling up after all these years and asking to steal time and asking them to keep their mouths shut about it? Not cool."

"So you're thinking black ops?" asked Xavier.

"I don't like the sound of that," said Philip.

Lilly didn't like the sound of it either, especially in front of Audrey.

"Come on and help Grandma with the dishes," she said, taking the little girl by the hand. "I don't think you and I should be around to hear what your uncles are talking about," she added as they scooted into the house. She remained in the doorway long enough to give the boys a look that said, *Watch what you're getting yourselves into.* She also gave Philip a look that said, *This isn't funny anymore. Do something.*

"Damn. The Look!" said Xavier.

All the boys laughed, as did Philip, who could not resist the long-standing joke among them.

Only Pipo refrained from merriment. He was starting to pick up a vibe in all these goings-on that was making him profoundly uneasy at a deep level. He got up from the rocker and walked to the railing of the porch to knock the ash out of his pipe.

"So you're going to be staying with us for a while?" Philip asked. The prospect of an extended visit was just the kind of good news he wanted to hear.

"Well, actually, I think we'll see if we can crash at Janie's. We'd rather not make ourselves too conspicuous just now," Charles said.

They all knew the place Charles was referring to, a little farm on Indian Cave Road not far from the former training camp of the famous fighter Jack Dempsey.

"I hear the latest thing she's into is aerial acrobatics," said Philip.

"Yeah, Lilly sees her sometimes with her ecology group," Sue added. "Should be an interesting visit."

Chapter 21
Extruded Aluminum

PHILIP ENTERED THE CONFERENCE ROOM suppressing the bad mood that always overtook him when he confronted the redesign and color choices the new owners had made. From his childhood up to about a year ago, this had been his father's office. Even though Pipo in recent years had spent little time here, Philip had always kept it as his sanctuary out of respect and admiration.

The old desk and drawing board were gone, replaced by a Formica-topped conference table. The walls had been painted a tomato soup color, which according to the new owners helped create the balance between relaxation and urgency most conducive to successful and efficient meetings. The multipane windows he remembered fondly as being slightly ajar to admit the mountain breezes had been cast aside in favor of energy-efficient double-pane expanses framed in extruded aluminum. Opening a window was not an option. The air conditioning made the room feel like a morgue.

Perhaps most irritating were the wall hangings. Photos and sketches of favorite projects had been replaced by modern posters with supposedly inspirational slogans across the bottom. One showed a sailboat regatta in high wind and seas. Across the bottom was the phrase, "Adversity Inspires." Other pictures showed rowing teams and a group of people scaling the rockface of a high mountain. They had slogans, too. It often occurred to Philip the slogans could be interchanged among the photos. In fact, specific connections between the verbiage and the art were hard to find.

Pipo never entered the room now. He had in all respects moved on.

Philip had assumed that today would be another in a series of meetings intended to teach him and the other employees the new management system. He found himself looking at his watch and growing curious why the room wasn't filling up with coworkers and instructors and audiovisual equipment.

The new CEO, Michael Palance, strode in, accompanied by the quality assurance lady, Judy Gold.

"Philip, we're not training today. Judy and I have something else we want to talk to you about," Michael said, helping himself to a seat at the head of the table.

Philip noticed that Judy was pulling the door closed at the same time.

"If this is about the puppet thing...," Philip began.

"No, it's not about 'the puppet thing,' as you call it," said Judy. "The puppets are just fine, thank you very much."

Philip immediately began a mental review of his recent actions, especially with regard to his contract. The contract called for him to stay on at the company for fourteen more months. This was turning out to be a much bigger challenge than he had figured. He had envisioned being left pretty much alone, perhaps consulting occasionally on customer histories and technical points. He had not expected the management system takeover to totally disregard the core of the business. Michael had explained that his participation in the new system was important because it would be a powerful signal to the employees remaining with the company.

"We need to talk to you about Oak Ridge," said Judy.

"Oak Ridge? Oak Ridge, Tennessee?" said Philip.

"Oak Ridge National Labs," said Michael.

"And Savannah River," said Judy.

"Savannah River?" said Philip, now really puzzled.

"Yes, Oak Ridge and Savannah River," said Michael. "We have been served by the prosecutor's office of the Ninth District Federal Court with a subpoena to turn over our files concerning all dealings with Oak Ridge National Labs and the Savannah River nuclear processing site."

"Yes, and they also had a lot of questions about you and your father and sons," Judy said. "And as with many other matters, it seems that we don't actually have any files on Oak Ridge National Labs or Savannah River," she added.

Philip was straining on this one, trying to remember any jobs the company had done at either of those sites, but he couldn't come up with anything. It had done some restorative work on a couple of fountains and other structures in the squares in Savannah, Georgia, and he even remembered doing something in one of the famous cemeteries there. But why would Athenaeum have anything to do with a nuclear power or research facility? Some kind of commemorative to the Manhattan Project?

"Our lawyers have contacted the proper authorities through the Freedom of Information Act," Michael offered. "They found that both you and your father, James, filed for permits to visit those sites."

Then it came back to him.

"Pumps," he said. "Pipo found some information on surplus equipment at those sites. This was years ago."

"Nineteen eighty-one?" Judy asked, looking at a document on her clipboard.

"Could have been. That sounds about right," said Philip.

He remembered a creepy and unsuccessful visit to Oak Ridge back when. He remembered the security. He remembered the dullness and lifelessness of the place. He remembered passing through checkpoints that measured radiation levels as he left certain rooms in the complex of buildings, and a procedure wherein he stepped on a piece of tacky paper that was supposed to pick up any dust that had stuck to the bottom of his boots.

"As I recall, we saw a couple pumps we wanted to get, just in case we ever needed to take on a job with really high volumes. I think we never did make it through all the paperwork to actually buy something there. I mean, we filled it all out with our bid and everything, but we never heard from them. When I checked back, they said it had to be signed off by several levels of management and by the regulators and who knows what else. We just forgot about it."

"Well, someone in Washington apparently did not forget about it, if that was indeed your only dealing with those facilities," said Michael.

"They are still showing you with an active account. And they say you did not file the proper yearly reports on property disposition. Looks like another loose end we need to deal with," Judy said. The sigh and the droop of her shoulders suggested that this list of loose ends was an infinite burden.

By now, Philip was used to the loose-ends implication. It was part of his contract that he had to tie up all loose ends regarding open orders, customer follow-up, and legal and financial matters.

"Annual reports? I didn't know about any stinking annual reports," he said.

"We did not sign up to do clerical work on existing contracts," said Michael. He could put on the Philadelphia lawyer hat quicker than anyone Philip had ever met.

"What do you want me to do, exactly?" Philip asked.

"Handle it," said Michael.

He plopped a thin file down on the conference table and walked out. Judy made a quick note on her clipboard, smiled at Philip, and followed her lord and master to their next port of call.

"Duplicitous pump-dick," Philip said under his breath after they left.

"Clumsy wanker," Michael said under his breath in the hallway.

Chapter 22
The Girl at the Gate

THIS WAS KAY'S THING: Each morning around seven-thirty, she pulled her old, faded red Honda CRX up to the chain-link fence in a bare, sandy spot off the road near the Savannah River plant. Then she opened her thermos of coffee, poured a cup, took a slow sip, and lit a Camel filtered cigarette. Then she pulled out a beat-up, three-subject spiral notebook, turned to the first blank page, and wrote the date at the top with a Pilot pen. Then she counted trucks until she was satisfied that no more were coming out of the gate. She parked under a live oak tree about three hundred yards down the road and sometimes drew pictures of animals in the margins for no particular reason other than that it helped pass the time and gave her hands something to do. After that, she drove to the beach and counted turtles and albatrosses. But that was a different job, one she actually got paid a little money for by a team at the university. She told her friends she was a professional counter. She even had a stuffed replica of the Count from *Sesame Street* on her dashboard.

When she began the truck-counting assignment for the ecological watch group, she had finished around eight-thirty most days. But a couple of months ago, the shipments had started to increase.

When she got home in the late afternoon, she entered the numbers into Excel spreadsheets in her computer and sometimes played with the data for much the same reason she doodled animals in her notebook. One thing she did was graph the data by date. In the case of the truck counts, the graph looked like a bumpy line for some months, then jumped sharply to a new level for about two weeks, then settled into another bumpy line at a much higher level than the first. She had sent this graph to the group and provoked an immediate response, as the members had not realized what was going on. She also did a lot of other playing around with the data, like looking for a correlation between albatross sightings and the number of trucks she counted. So far, she had found a fairly high correlation—like around 0.8—for no reason she could imagine. She kept waiting for the correlation to fall apart, but so far it had not, so she decided she would just have to add that to a fairly long list of connections observed but not understood or even completely believed. Was it pure coincidence or evidence that everything was connected at some level? She was open on the subject.

On this particular day in June, she was there as usual but observed no trucks at all. She did a quick mental check to make sure she had not forgotten some holiday, but she could think of none. The moon was in its waning quarter (she liked to check correlations with the phases of the moon), which did not suggest anything in particular. She also considered the news she had heard on the car radio on the way in but didn't come up with anything there either.

The complete absence of trucks had an unsettling effect on her. She couldn't help wondering if the beach would likewise be devoid of turtles and seabirds. As she found out later, she need not have worried about that. Plenty of both were in evidence, and if anything they seemed happier than ever.*

---

* Henrico Carr and his students discovered that the happiness of sea turtles was highly dependent on the time of year. With each yearly cycle, the turtles moved from abject depression to unthrottled joy. Their cousin the land tortoise was found to be much more emotionally stable.

Normally, she sent a monthly report of the data—together with her graphs, correlations, and other observations—to a post office box in Asheville, North Carolina. She had been asked to keep phone calls to the group to a minimum. (She did not fully understand the reason for this request but tried not to take it personally.) In this case, however, she felt the development was potentially significant enough to warrant direct contact.

She pulled out a black leather-bound address book and looked up the number.

"This is Kay," she said.

This elicited a pause on the other end. Perhaps the person was trying to place the name and voice.

"South Carolina?" the voice asked, a little edgy.

"Right," Kay said. "Something's happening down here I thought you'd want to know about right away."

She took the silence as an indication to go ahead.

"Actually," she said, "it would be more accurate to say that, for a change, nothing's happening down here. No trucks this morning."

"No trucks?" asked the voice.

"Nada," Kay said.

"Okay," said the voice. "Here's what I want you to do. Don't sit there now. Stay away from the site for a few days."

"How long?" Kay asked.

"I'll let you know," said the voice.

"Is something happening?" Kay asked.

Another moment of silence.

"Yeah, I guess you could say that," said the voice. "But listen, it's not the kind of thing you want to be talking about."

"Okay," Kay said.

"And Kay," said the voice. "Let me know if anything else weird happens."

Chapter 23

Snow Crab Legs

IT CAME TO PASS that Philip found himself in possession of a large quantity of snow crab legs. What happened was this:

He and Lilly agreed to go to a neighborhood picnic to which everyone was supposed to bring a side dish to share, as well as something to throw on the grill for themselves. Of course, because of owning the ice-cream store, ice cream was Philip and Lilly's logical choice. In order to sustain the ice cream on the way there and through lengthy conversations and through eating the rest of the meal, Philip acquired a ten-pound block of dry ice and placed that and the ice cream in a large Styrofoam box.

Philip had some experience with picnics organized around this format. His low-end estimate was that there would be enough food to feed two and a half to three times the number in attendance, especially considering that most of them were people who had time to cook but who ate little. Moreover, this particular group included a few excellent cooks. Based on these considerations, he decided not to bring any other food besides the ice cream.

Upon arriving at the picnic, held in the shelter at a nearby park, they found the neighbors in exceptionally good spirits. Philip and Lilly enjoyed themselves even more than they anticipated. The event was a welcome distraction from Philip's problems at work and from whatever his sons were mixed up in.

Philip's calculations about the food did not lead him far astray. In fact, the group included a man who was a buyer for a large chain of supermarkets in the western part of the state. This individual brought a huge quantity of snow crab legs, together with a propane-fired cooking pot to prepare them. In addition to this, he contributed prepared dishes from the experimental kitchens of the supermarket chain.

In any case, the picnickers had not only plenty of good food to eat but an abundant supply left over at the end of the feast. Everyone was offering things to other people to take home. Philip, by virtue of the dry ice and Styrofoam chest, was the best equipped to make off with the uneaten crab legs. This he did without hesitation.

The bounty of the sea for the people of the mountains, he thought as he loaded up the van to head home.

ooooo

A large quantity of snow crab legs was as good an excuse as any to have a party, which Philip and Lilly felt they were long overdue for anyway. They put together their list of invitees in the usual manner— some old friends they saw frequently, some old friends they had not seen for a while, and a few people they would like to know better.

Of course, snow crab legs by themselves would not suffice, so they prevailed upon Pipo to fire up the smoker to prepare vast quantities of meat and sausage. This he did in a manner more typical of Texas than North Carolina. His feeling was that a person had to go at least as far west as the Mississippi River to find barbecue done right. Memphis in his opinion was quite acceptable, East Texas better still.

Since the disappearance of Charles and Xavier Colebrook, the FBI had decided to do the normal things like tapping phone lines, monitoring cell phone traffic, and staking out the family home in hopes of catching some clue of the boys' whereabouts—or indeed catching any other clues about "the problem," as the missing truck of nuclear materials had been euphemistically labeled. Ira Hudson assured the agents that no court order was needed for the wiretaps, as the case fell under special counterterrorism guidelines.

Where do they get this shit? Meyers asked himself. This was another one for the notebook he kept called "How to Not Tell the Truth without Lying."

One of his junior guys had been put on house duty, which Meyers did not expect to yield much. The guy called to report "unusual activity," which turned out to be just the preparations for the party—trips to the store, Pipo's producing smoke from his equipment, things like that. Nevertheless, Meyers decided he had better let Tomblyn and Haven know about this, since little else seemed to be going on.

Later, when the guests began to arrive, Tomblyn and Haven decided to be at the stakeout in person to see what they could see. What they saw turned out to be a lot of people hanging around on the porch and in the yard and in general having a good time. The smell of the barbecue drove them crazy. Haven considered raiding the party but could think of no conceivable way to pull this off. But damn, that barbecue smelled good.

In the end, the total catch for the night was a list of license plate numbers to add to the growing knowledge base about the family's contacts. From these, the agents would derive names, which they would cross-reference against other lists they had built, and thus look for frequent or unusual connections. That's how it worked.

Through this chain of events, the duo from Washington became interested in an auto mechanic, Ian Wise, who had a garage downtown a block off Main Street. Specifically, Ian appeared on several lists, which included

(a) People who attended the party
(b) People who were phoned within two days of "the problem"
(c) People who had some technical expertise related to "the

problem" (Ian, in his army days, was certified on the type of C40J transport truck involved)

(d) People who had children on the local swim team in the years between 1985 and 2000

This, they figured, was enough to earn Mr. Wise a personal visit, which they decided to do in the time-proven way of just showing up unannounced at his place of business the next day.

The garage was a one-story blue building with three bay doors and lifts for cars. It had apparently at one time been a gas station typical of the 1950s and 1960s. Remnants of the island that had held the gas pumps were still visible as an irregularity in the pavement of the parking lot.

To the side and in back of the building was a collection of vehicles in various stages of repair—a short school bus painted green, a Volvo that Haven estimated to be vintage 1963 or thereabout, a few pickup trucks, and more modern cars as well. Where the permanent collection ended and the day visitors in for an oil change or brake job began was impossible to say.

Being downtown, Tomblyn and Haven decided to walk the few blocks from their B&B in the early morning. They saw considerable activity around the work bays as they approached. It appeared to be mostly people dropping their vehicles off and discussing the needed work with the mechanics. The man they assumed to be Ian looked over his shoulder and nodded as they arrived.

They proceeded to the office area to wait out of sight and perhaps snoop a little until the owner could come over and talk to them. Pushing open the glass door, they entered a small waiting room divided by a counter. In the building's gas station days, this would have been where customers came in to pay for gas and buy potato chips and Coke. On the back wall were shelves with the usual assortment of auto parts, new and used, and catalogs and books worn and darkened by the frequent touch of oil-covered fingers. The countertop held a cash register and a credit card reader. Pens, pencils, and an ashtray made from a piston head were scattered across a desk-sized calendar with various names and numbers in the squares for most of the days. This was clearly the scheduling system for a healthy business.

True to buildings of this type, the front and side walls were floor-to-ceiling glass. The furniture consisted of a couple of car seats up on wooden blocks and the seat from a school bus, which did not need to be elevated.

The walls were so crowded with posters and shelves of parts that it took Tomblyn a moment to spot the painting hanging beside the door that led to the work area of the garage. It was not large, the frame a rather utilitarian brushed stainless steel.

At a glance, the painting appeared to be a typical representation of Noah's Ark during the part of the story when Noah and family were loading the animals. A ship of tremendous size rested on the ground, a few diagonal braces supporting it in the unlikely event that anything of such size and geometry might begin to roll. A large gangplank set at an incline led from the ground to a gaping hatch in the side of the ship. The soon-to-be occupants were ascending the incline, forming a continuous two-by-two line trailing down a road that disappeared off the right side of the canvas. Noah and family stood on the deck overseeing the operation. An angry, boiling sky of gray clouds was a menacing presence over the landscape.

As Tomblyn approached, he noticed that the line was formed not by pairs of animals but rather by pairs of automobiles. Closest to the hatch was a pair of Honda Accords. These were followed by two Ford F-100 pickup trucks, two Volkswagen Beetles (one a convertible, one a hardtop), two MG Midgets, two 1965 Mustangs, two PT Cruisers, two Chevy Camaros, and on and on.

As Tomblyn moved closer still, it became apparent that the Ark was constructed of plates of steel joined by neat rows of rivets, rather than the planks of gopher wood described in the biblical text. It looked a lot like the *Titanic*.

Noah was wearing a traditional robe, which had fallen open to reveal a NASCAR racing uniform. On his head were a set of earphones and a microphone. He appeared to be consulting a clipboard with an anxious look while Mrs. Noah looked over his shoulder.

"It's by a local artist," said a voice behind them. Ian had entered and was now taking up his position behind the counter.

"James Colebrook?" asked Haven.

"The very one," said Ian, "although we never call him that. Everyone around here knows him as either Mr. Colebrook or Pipo."

"Interesting," said Tomblyn.

"Can I help you gentlemen with anything?" Ian asked after a moment. He could not help noticing that, unlike the rest of his customers, these guys had not arrived by car.

"How do you come to have one of Mr. Colebrook's paintings hanging in your garage? Is he a friend of yours?" asked Tomblyn.

"Oh, I've known the Colebrooks just about all my life. I went to school with Philip. He's only a couple of years older than me. And then I worked out at their plant for a while, right after they put the foundry in and started casting all kinds of stuff. Philip and I did the pouring one summer, him on one end of the ladle handles and me on the other."

"So, did Mr. Colebrook do the painting especially for you?" asked Haven.

"No, I don't think that's how it works with him. I mean, I don't know that he paints or makes things specifically for someone. I think he does it just because he wants to," said Ian. "In this case, I was out at his workshop one day. I had rebuilt the engine on a little tractor for him, and I was dropping it off. Pipo, Mr. Colebrook, was in his workshop. He had just finished this picture and was starting on another one. Anyway, I started looking at it and began laughing a little bit when I saw the cars. I told him I really liked it, and he insisted I take it with me. I don't think the paint was even completely dry on it."

"Do you have any idea what that painting would be worth if you sold it?" asked Haven.

"I don't know, but then I have no intention of selling it, so it doesn't matter," said Ian. "Are you fellows in the art business?" he asked, realizing they had gotten off on quite a tangent.

"No, we're not in the art business," said Tomblyn, taking out his wallet and showing Ian his badge. "We're here because we understand you work on C40J trucks from time to time."

Tomblyn and Haven studied his face for a reaction.

"C40J?" said Ian. "Are they still running those things? They seemed like antiques clear back when I was in the service."

"Then you haven't seen one around lately?" asked Haven.

"Not outside of a parade, I don't think," he said.

"Then no one has come by and asked you to work on one lately?" Tomblyn prompted.

Ian had to think a minute about that. "The National Forest Service up in Pisgah used to have a couple I think they inherited from the CIA or NASA. They heard I had some experience with them and had me out there a couple of times, but that's got to be seven or eight years ago at least."

"Nothing more recent—say, in the last week or so?" asked Tomblyn, keeping just enough edge in his voice to suggest he was not the kind of person who believed everything he heard.

"No, nothing like that," Ian said.

Tomblyn seemed to be searching for something else to ask, but Haven stepped in.

"Thank you, Mr. Wise. We'll get out of your way now and let you get back to work," he said. He fished a card from his shirt pocket and handed it to Ian. "If you should happen to get any calls about trucks like that, or think of anything we should know, you'll give us a call, won't you?"

"Sure, I guess so," Ian said, accepting the card and looking at it with curiosity.

Turning to leave, they paused for one last look at the painting.

"What do you think it's supposed to mean?" Haven asked Ian.

"Some people think it's asking a question. If there were a flood today, what would we bother to take with us?" Ian said. "But I don't know. I asked Pipo the same thing, and he just shrugged."

Chapter 24

The Casting

NOW CAME THE SCULPTOR'S FAVORITE PART of making a statue: the casting of the bronze.

He grinned at the man tending the crucible furnace.

"A day without molten metal . . . ," he said.

". . . is like a day without sunshine," said the furnace man, returning the grin.

He gave a quick nod of his head, which had the effect of making a dark face shield fall forward. This put it in position to protect his eyes from the bright high-temperature glow of the furnace, as well as guarding his face and neck from spatters of molten metal when the moment of truth came.

Using a metal hook, he lifted the top of the furnace to expose the crucible, flames licking the outside and molten metal with a dark and cracked layer of slag on the inside.

To the uninitiated, the foundry room seemed dark and forbidding, like something out of a medieval alchemist's laboratory. Indeed, the basics of the process had changed little in the past few hundred years. Of course, the chemistry and physics were better understood, replacing the notions of elemental spirits that had guided the ancients. But the process itself—the containment of the fire and the fusing and refining of the metal—remained much the same.

The workers wore coverings of coarse, stiff material with a reflective silver coating. A jacket of this material covered the chest, arms, and torso. It included a collar that snapped tight around the neck and a skirt that extended to mid-thigh. The operators had gauntlets of the same reflective material that allowed them to pick up the steel bars and other tools of the trade but nothing much smaller. They wore thick leather chaps over blue jeans and heavy work boots. Over the boots were spats, again of the reflective material, to deflect spatters. Last were caps or scarves tied tight around their heads, and over these dark goggles or face shields.

The floor was covered with sand, much like a child's sandbox. However, this was not the white or tan sand from a beach. It was dark gray and more powdery. This was never completely cleaned off the floor, being left there for a good reason. In the event that metal was spilled, as from a broken crucible or mold, it would tend to pool in the low places of the uneven sand mounds, instead of shooting like quicksilver across smooth concrete.

What for some might have been an unpleasant day in a dirty shop was for the sculptor the culmination of a long process.

Using the photos and measurements made at the power station, he had crafted a faithful scale model of the truck in wax, a replica a little less than three feet long. The leaders of the group had checked on this process several times and found it exciting to see the product slowly taking shape. But when it came to adding the details, the leaders found the process excruciatingly slow. (Actually, the sculptor rarely worked as fast as on this project, not generally putting himself in the position of committing to deadlines.) In the end, some negotiation was needed to move the process to completion.

When the wax model was finished, he built an oversized wooden box to hold the mold material itself. He then slowly built up the mold material around the wax model, adding wax risers to provide a place for molten metal to be poured in and excess gases to escape. Once this was to the sculptor's satisfaction and the mold material was given time to set up, the whole thing was inverted and heated in an oven to melt the wax and allow it to drip out.

And now they were ready to pour the metal into the cavity of the carefully prepared shape.

They removed the crucible from the furnace using a two-man lifting bar, then paused while a helper scraped some of the slag layer away with a metal tool. Then they sidestepped toward the mold and carefully tilted the crucible until a glowing red stream of molten metal poured into the funnel-like opening in the top of the mold. A column of hot gas and sparks came out the other hole. They continued pouring until metal backed up in both openings, then emptied the small amount of metal left in the crucible into an open sand mold so it could be easily recovered and melted down again.

They put the empty crucible down and stood back a few minutes, satisfying themselves that all was well. The mold was holding, and the casting would be sound.

After that day, they had more work breaking apart the mold, cutting off the risers, grinding, polishing, and adding the finishing details. The group had been especially specific about one thing: the license number on the rear tag of the vehicle.

ooooo

In the center of Asheville was Pack Square, dominated by an obelisk made of gray granite blocks and dedicated to the memory of Zebulon Baird Vance, an officer in the Civil War, governor of North Carolina, and United States senator for many years.

In the early part of the twentieth century, Pack Square was in all respects the center of town. Facing the square was, among other things, the shop of stonecutter W. O. Wolfe, the father of novelist Thomas Wolfe. The angel of Thomas Wolfe's most famous book, *Look Homeward, Angel*, was in fact a statue carved from beautiful white marble.

That angel sat for years in front of the shop facing Pack Square, watching the comings and goings of Asheville citizens and visitors. It had long since been moved about twenty miles south to a graveyard, where it marked the final resting place of the beloved daughter of a prosperous family.

But the obelisk remained in the middle of the square like the centerpiece of a sundial. Recently, as part of the playful mood of the revitalization of downtown Asheville, a number of bronze statures had been added—a bronze pig complete with a group of piglets, a bronze turkey in midstride followed by her chicks. And now, as of July 21, Pack Square boasted a bronze tanker truck as well.

Most people did not notice the latest addition. It seems that bronze statues have the effect of immediately seeming like they have been there forever. However, an anonymous phone call to the newspaper prompted an investigation by a junior reporter, Shirley Dawn. It took Shirley some checking around to find out who was in charge of placing statues around the city. After eventually locating the right department and the right person in the department, she was assured that no sculpture of a tanker truck was located in Pack Square. When Shirley brought a picture to back up her story, the city official took the picture and ended the interview as quickly as possible, assuring her that he would have some information soon.

So, on Thursday, a slow news day, several days after the statue's appearance, a picture was published on the front page of the Asheville paper under a headline that read, "Mystery Truck." The picture showed a couple of five-year-olds playing around the truck sculpture, the bronze barnyard animals in the background. The caption mentioned that the truck had recently appeared, though no one seemed to know from where. It referred readers to page five, but the story there contained little more information because not much more was known. It speculated that the sculpture was a pretty good nondestructive prank from the Art Department at the university. But so far, no one had admitted any involvement.

ooooo

Agent Tomblyn came downstairs at the B&B and found Haven already at their customary table by the window. Haven had grown fond of a plate of grits, bacon, and eggs every morning. Tomblyn had to agree that it beat the hell out of the complimentary watered-down juice and cardboard pastries at his usual motels.

Haven, reading a *USA Today*, gave Tomblyn a mumble to acknowledge his presence. Seeing that he was not going to get much conversation from his companion until after more of the morning ritual took place, Tomblyn cast about for something to read himself. He found a used copy of the Asheville paper on the abandoned table next to them and helped himself to the front section.

On seeing the picture, he snatched the paper closer for a better look, then ripped back to page five.

"Take a look at this," he said to Haven, pushing the paper across the table and jabbing at the picture on the front page. "Is that what I think it is?"

"Oh, Christ!" said Haven. He picked up the paper. "They're going to love this in Washington."

An hour later, they were in Pack Square with Meyers and an officer with a digital camera.

Haven read the license number off the statue into a cell phone. "C48285," he said, and waited.

He looked at Tomblyn, who was scanning the buildings surrounding the plaza where they stood. Haven glanced around himself. Hundreds of windows had a good view of them now. He guessed that whoever was behind this was probably watching the show.

"Right. That's what I thought," Haven said into the phone, and snapped it shut. "That's our truck, all right," he said.

Tomblyn and Meyers exchanged a look that said, *What next?*

"So they want us to know they have the truck. They presented us with evidence like the license plate number, for instance," said Tomblyn.

"So that means they're going to be contacting us with some kind of demand, like a ransom," said Meyers. "This could be a good thing."

"Or they could be planning some threat, and they want us to know it's for real," said Haven, less optimistic as usual.

A van was just then backing up as close as possible to the bronze work. Meanwhile, a technician unbolted it from the pavement. The plan was to take it to the nearest lab and look for any evidence that might be helpful in identifying the people who made and transported it.

"Do we wait for the lab report on this?" asked Tomblyn. They were acting on orders from Washington on bringing the statue in.

"I'm thinking this was done nearby," said Haven. "I mean, the truck can't be too far away. And why put the statue here in Asheville if it were made elsewhere? So, if we assume that's right, there can't be too many places close by with the ability to make a casting like this one. We should start checking them out."

He turned to Meyers for guidance on where this might lead.

"Well, it could be the Art Department at the university. And a small foundry is in the industrial park by the airport. We could check to see what other businesses have that sort of facility." He paused a moment. "Of course, the Athenaeum Company has a foundry for casting figures for the fountains, among other things."

"So, once again, all roads lead to the Colebrook family," said Haven. "You asked why we were interested."

"I think it's time we paid Athenaeum a visit," said Tomblyn.

The statue was apparently not as heavy as it looked. Two technicians managed to lift it into the van. The doors banged shut, and it was gone.

Chapter 25
On the Potomac

IRA HUDSON GENTLY REPLACED the phone receiver in its cradle, fighting the urge to throw it across the room. Haven had been wrong. Washington, and Hudson in particular, did not love this.

Three questions weighed on his mind:

Who were they?

What did they want?

And most importantly, what did they know?

Some time ago, an ad hoc committee had formed a study group to look into certain issues concerning what was once called "our friend the atom." This was the brainchild of the leader of a conservative think tank and a few high-ranking conservative congressmen during a boating excursion on the Potomac River one night. It started with their revisiting a well-worn theme about Arabs, oil, and United States dependence on both. As with most issues, they were in agreement that the Democrats were to blame because (a) Jimmy Carter had crashed two helicopters in the desert in the 1970s rather than invading Iran in response to the hostage crisis and (b) Democrats had blocked drilling in the most pristine parts of Alaska for years.

Several drinks later, someone remarked about how cool it would be if the yacht they were on had a nuclear engine, which turned out to be a cue for the quiet, serious-looking man at the stern to step forward and say, "If you're serious about this, there are things that could be done."

And with this simple remark, he immediately had the interest of everyone on board.

The things that could be done included expanding a study that the quiet man had undertaken on his own. What he had discovered was that nuclear technology was on a sharp and dangerous decline in this country, owing to the liberal obsession with environmental impact and cowardly fears of a meltdown, which everyone on the inside knew was totally impossible with modern safeguards. (Chernobyl? That was the Soviets, for God's sake! What was to be expected?) He had also found the system to be totally constipated. Operators were not allowed to move waste materials out of their "temporary" holding locations because every time they found a good disposal site, someone thought up a reason why they shouldn't use it.

What would he need to take the next step?

An office, a few million dollars, and security clearance so he could move freely about the locations he needed to see. Most of all, this had to be away from the public eye. Otherwise, they would be right back in the same dilemma as now.

All agreed it was important. In fact, it was a matter of national security. After all, was national security not the single most important thing they owed to their constituents? And if they didn't do it, who would?

Three years later, their little study group was way past study and well into the implementation of Teraplex Building, and Ira Hudson was the man in charge.

Chapter 26
An Important Source of Energy

THE SOUND OF WIND CHIMES around the porch announced the stirring of an afternoon breeze. The same breeze carried cigar smoke up and away from the two men, one seated in a rocking chair and the other on an old oak glider. And the same breeze ruffled the ear fluff of the spotted dog dozing in an Adirondack chair.

The two men were in a kind of conversation. Philip was talking and gesturing while his father, Pipo, reacted with nods, raised eyebrows, and contemplative draws on his stogie.

Philip outlined the conversation from work that day concerning the business transaction—or more precisely, the lack of a business transaction—at Oak Ridge. Pipo in his own way was reinforcing Philip's memory of the events that had taken place some years ago.

"And you're sure nothing else was going on there, right?" Philip said to Pipo.

Pipo held up both hands. Philip could pretty much tell when his father was fooling around or playing innocent, both of which he did plenty, but this was not one of those times.

Lilly came out to join them on the porch, making exaggerated motions of fanning away the smoke and swimming through a thick haze.

"I heard you're planning to go to Oak Ridge tomorrow," she said to Philip.

Philip and Pipo looked at her for a moment, wondering how she knew that. But then she seemed to know everything going on with her family.

They both knew her intense distrust of anything governmental in general and nuclear or military in particular.

"Don't worry," Philip said. "I'm not helping them build nuclear reactors or anything. Pipo and I tried to buy some used equipment from them years ago, and apparently we have to straighten out some kind of mix-up with the paperwork."

"Don't worry?" Lilly said. "Let's see. I have one son kicked out of school and one son out of a job. I have the FBI skulking after my granddaughter. And I have you walking around in some kind of dream world over selling the business, making Pipo here the sanest one of the bunch, which is saying a lot when you think about it. No, I'm not too worried about you going to the birthplace of the atomic bomb."

Philip and Pipo looked at each other, unable to come up with anything to add to such an acute summation of current affairs.

"I don't like you going there," she said, stating the obvious.

"Don't worry. I'll be back by tomorrow night," Philip said.

"I'm worried about what you might bring back with you," she said, getting up to leave.

She was referring to the tendency of Philip and the rest of the male members of the family to come home with unusual objects. Given this, Philip's visit to a place full of unusual objects was not good news.

Philip looked to Pipo for support, but his only response was a slight shrug.

ooooo

Philip was up early the next morning and on his way with a travel mug full of Blue Mountain coffee from Jamaica, his favorite. By nine o'clock, he was approaching the state line on Interstate 40. As he always did, he looked sharply to spot the Appalachian Trail, remembering the time he met Leon there during Leon's first thru-hike. He remembered his apprehension for the several days it took Leon and his trail friends to make it through the Great Smoky Mountains National Park, the first segment of significant length that took them away from any crossroads and put them really on their own. In fact, except for the hundred-mile wilderness in Maine, it was the longest such segment. Of course, he had little to worry about, but the imagination of parents is never more agile than when dreaming up gruesome fates that might befall their children. This even if the "child" was a robust and experienced hiker.

Philip reached Knoxville by ten o'clock. The traffic through the city could be slow, but not for long, especially at that time of day. It certainly did not warrant taking the northern bypass around the city, which added miles to the trip.

On the other side of Knoxville, the countryside looked typical of western North Carolina and East Tennessee: rugged hills, farms, run-down businesses, a few strip malls, gas stations, fast-food joints.

He spotted the small sign and the turn and came almost immediately to a checkpoint he did not remember from before, part of the post-9/11 syndrome that had grown up around such places. In spite of himself, he was a little nervous when the guards approached and asked him to produce ID and pull the car over for inspection. This he had not foreseen. He was embarrassed by the large and arbitrary collection of objects in his trunk. As he stood near the front of the car and answered the questions of one of the guards, he nervously tried to remember what was in the trunk and hoped nothing was terrorist-looking. As it turned out, the pump parts, tools, bronze casting of a frog, and set of golf clubs were deemed harmless, and he was directed to the main gate leading to the visitor center.

The visitor center was a nondescript one-story yellow-brick building that could have been built anytime in the fifties or sixties or seventies. Inside was a counter with the usual middle-aged civil-servant ladies portraying the very image of boredom and determination to adhere strictly to bureaucratic protocol. Without interest, they asked questions of the several men who had entered before him, giving Philip time to look around the room.

A couple of posters attempted to demonstrate practical applications of recent research work at Oak Ridge National Labs. Philip strained to connect this work to the original mission of the lab complex—namely, to separate enough active uranium isotope to build the first atomic bombs for the Manhattan Project in the 1940s.

Much more remarkable for Philip was the display on the wall behind the desk. This was an enlarged copy of the famous letter from Albert Einstein to Franklin Delano Roosevelt in August 1939. Philip stood fascinated by the document, which arguably launched the Manhattan Project and set in motion that whole chain of events that closed out World War II and heavily impacted the planet for the rest of the century. One letter!

Albert Einstein
Old Grove Rd.
Nassau Point
Peconic, Long Island

August 2nd, 1939

F. D. Roosevelt,
President of the United States,
White House
Washington, D.C.

Sir:
    Some recent work by E.Fermi and L. Szilard, which
has been communicated to me in manuscript, leads
me to expect that the element uranium may be turned
into a new and important source of energy in the
immediate future. Certain aspects of the situation
which has arisen seem to call for watchfulness
and, if necessary, quick action on the part of the
Administration. I believe therefore that it is my duty
to bring to your attention the following facts and
recommendations:
    In the course of the last four months it has been
made probable - through the work of Joliot in France
as well as Fermi and Szilard in America - that it may
become possible to set up a nuclear chain reaction
in a large mass of uranium, by which vast amounts of
power and large quantities of new radium-like elements
would be generated. Now it appears almost certain that
this could be achieved in the immediate future.
    This new phenomenon would also lead to the
construction of bombs, and it is conceivable - though
much less certain - that extremely powerful bombs of
a new type may thus be constructed. A single bomb of
this type, carried by boat and exploded in a port,
might very well destroy the whole port together with
some of the surrounding territory. However, such
bombs might very well prove to be too heavy for
transportation by air.

-2-

The United States has only very poor ores of uranium in moderate quantities. There is some good ore in Canada and the former Czechoslavakia, while the most important source of uranium is Belgian Congo.

In view of this situation you may think it desirable to have some permanent contact maintained between the Administration and the group of physicists working on chain reactions in America. One possible way of achieving this might be for you to entrust with this task a person who has your confidence and who could perhaps serve in an inofficial capacity. His task might comprise the following:

a) to approach Government Departments, keep them informed of the further development, and put forward recommendations for Government action, giving particular attention to the problem of securing a supply of uranium ore for the United States;

b) to speed up the experimental work, which is at present being carried on within the limits of the budgets of University laboratories, by providing funds, if such funds be required, through his contacts with private persons who are willing to make contributions for this cause, and perhaps also by obtaining the co-operation of industrial laboratories which have the necessary equipment.

I understand that Germany has actually stopped the sale of uranium from the Czechoslavakian mines which she has taken over. That she should have taken such early action might perhaps be understood on the ground that the son of the German Under-Secretary of State, von Weizsäcker is attached to the Kaiser-Wilhelm-Institut in Berlin where some of the American work on uranium is now being repeated.

                              Yours very truly,

                              Albert Einstein

Philip imagined the desperate focus that must have been the mood of this place in its heyday. A group of people working so hard toward a goal few of them understood. How could they? This was something that had never been done, something no one was sure even *could* be done.

The contrast between that mental image and the bored people behind the desk was inescapable. It was the kind of transformation he associated with the end of the world. He could not imagine the advice of a famous scientist like Einstein attracting any attention whatsoever in today's Washington.

By and by, a man in drab pants and a short-sleeved white shirt open at the collar entered the room carrying a folder. He introduced himself. To Philip, he seemed glad to be called away from his computer screen. Before Philip could explain why he had come, the man invited him back through the gates to see the surplus equipment. Philip shrugged and thought, *Why not?* He had come a long way. And in any case, he was always up for looking at some surplus equipment.

They walked though several buildings and across the parking lots that separated them and came at last to an area surrounded by a fence. The man unlocked the padlock, released the chain, and slid through the gate, which didn't seem to want to open very wide. He began looking at tags on various crates and pieces of equipment, most of which seemed to be made of steel no less then half an inch thick.

To Philip's amazement, the pumps he and Pipo had placed a bid on fifteen years earlier were still there. Being made of stainless steel, they looked much the same.

At that point, Philip felt the need to explain that what he really needed to do was clear up the problem of not having filed follow-up paperwork in each of the fourteen years that had elapsed since the original bid.

The man launched into a discourse about the possible ways of handling the delinquency, all of which involved requesting approval from several departments. Then he was brought up short by a novel idea.

"Actually, do you still want the pumps?" he asked.

"What?" said Philip, not sure where this was leading but finding the tone of the man's voice more promising than at any other point in their conversation.

"I mean, can you still use the pumps? Take them with you?" the man said. "Because if you can, that would be different. That would actually be simpler. You could just sign off here, and we could load them up for you because that is the action that has already been approved."

"And that would close out the account?" asked Philip.

"Yes, that would close out the account, and you would have to begin again if you wanted to bid on something else," he said.

They discussed the price, which of course was on the paperwork. A pretty small amount back then, it seemed downright trivial after fourteen years of inflation.

And so Philip found himself headed back east on I-40 with a pair of five-thousand-gallons-per-hour stainless-steel centrifugal pumps in the back of his car and the unexpected warm feeling of actually tying up a loose end.

The man had assured him that the billing would be taken care of as soon as he turned the paperwork over to the proper department of the company currently managing Oak Ridge. Philip had agreed but decided not to hold his breath.

Chapter 27

I n the Condo

MOST PEOPLE WERE SURPRISED to learn that the archaeologist and his family lived in a condominium in the center of the largest city in the area (not that Asheville was really all that large). Say the name Leon Colebrook to his friends and acquaintances and the picture of a bearlike man with a backpack and hiking boots came to mind. The same with his wife and daughter—the backpack and hiking boots, that is, not the bearlike part. An alternate picture might put them in an exhibition of native art, surrounded by hundreds of objects. Or perhaps they might be pictured at a demonstration of primitive tool-making techniques or talking about the meaning of ancient mythology and how it related to modern ideas.

But maybe that was the appeal of the small suite of rooms with high ceilings. It was one of Leon's strategies to control the instinct to collect objects that lived in all members of his profession. Given the small amount of space at his disposal, he had to think hard about picking something up and bringing it home.

The condo was located in a building with a view of Pack Square not four blocks from the early childhood home of Thomas Wolfe. (Was *Look Homeward, Angel* the source of Audrey's fascination with heavenly messengers?) Entering from the hallway of polished maple flooring into the main room, visitors faced a wall of windows that admitted a diffuse but plentiful light that brightened the room. Their eyes were drawn to the extremely high ceiling, probably eighteen feet or more. To the left was a study area with couches and a few books, though not as many as might be expected. On these couches, the three brothers lounged and talked. Three examples of the Colebrook family drink, Cuba Libre, sat on the table nearby.

"So what do you think is going on?" asked Leon, by way of calling the meeting to order.

"Someone is sure as hell looking for something," said Charles. "Looking with a satellite and an autonomous aircraft. That's what we know they're using. Who knows what else?"

"So you're thinking you got fingered when you started looking for your satellite and for images of this area. Leon got fingered when he found the autonomous plane. And I got fingered when Leon brought the plane to me," said Xavier.

"Except that we don't know Leon actually got fingered. Nothing has happened to him. At least not yet," said Charles.

"Actually, I think we do know that Leon got fingered," said a little voice from the next room.

Even her family never knew when Audrey was listening and when she wasn't.

"Come here to Uncle Charles," Charles said, sitting up on the couch.

The little girl came running into the room barefooted and flew into his lap.

"Now, tell us what makes you think your daddy's been fingered," he said.

"And while you're at it, tell us how you know what being fingered means," added Xavier, taking great pleasure at this development in the conversation.

"Well, we were at the place where people cook food for other people," she began.

Charles looked a little confused, but Xavier just laughed.

Sue had come into the room and was leaning against the counter with her arms crossed.

"She's talking about the Waffle House," she said. "Ever since Uncle X-Man took her there the last time he was home, that's the only restaurant she wants to go to."

"Uncle Xavier told me it's a really special place because all the people on the other side of the counter want to do is to come and cook for other people," she said, and smiled at Uncle Xavier. "He said they are the nicest people in the world."

"And Uncle X introduced her to the concept of eating waffles and sausage smothered in syrup," said Sue, also smiling at Uncle Xavier.

"And two men there were watching us," Audrey said.

"They were probably just looking at you and your mom because you're so pretty," said Charles.

The boys glanced at each other as Sue collected her daughter for bed. Audrey gave each of her uncles and her father a hug, then began negotiations on bedtime stories as she followed her mother out of the room.

"That doesn't prove anything," said Xavier after they were gone.

His brothers looked at him. They understood it didn't prove anything, but on the other hand they also knew better than to underestimate Audrey's powers of observation.

"But getting back to the point," said Xavier. "You don't have any other parts to that plane, do you?"

"No, you got what we got," Leon said, true to his habit of not being a collector of objects not of immediate use. "Why?"

"Because in the fuselage you brought me was part of an actuator made by a company in Virginia. If we had the other part of the actuator, we could see the serial number on it and maybe get those guys to tell us who they sold it to," said Xavier.

"I guess it's still up in the woods with the rest of the plane. We couldn't carry it all back with us," said Leon.

"*If* it's still there," said Charles. "It looks like someone wanted it pretty badly. They took it out of Xavier's lab, so wouldn't they go to the trouble to hike a few miles into the Smokies to retrieve the rest of it?"

"For one thing, it's quite a few miles in, and I mean quite a few miles even from a park service road. And then there's the question of how they would find it," said Leon. He was getting a little uneasy about the idea of a big hunt, government or otherwise, so close to the petroglyphs. He dreaded the chance of someone's ruining everything up there.

"So maybe we should take a little hike," said Xavier.

"All of us together?" said Charles.

"Why not? It would be like the old days. Maybe Dad would want to come along, too," said Xavier. "It would do him good. He needs to move on from Athenaeum, if you ask me."

"It would get us out from under the eye of Big Brother for a while," said Charles.

"Or it might get you under the eye of Big Brother, if you're right about the satellite being focused on this area," said Leon. He was thinking about the three of them together attracting even more attention than they already had, then leading whomever right to the spot he didn't want people tramping around on.

"Leon's right," said Xavier. "We should go different directions for the time being. Besides, you and I have some other things to take care of." He addressed this last remark to Charles.

"No one would think anything of Sue and Audrey and me going in. We do it all the time. Plus, I want to check some other things on those rocks. Ever since Mom pointed out the cacao pod in those glyphs, it got me thinking along a whole different line." Leon paused, then brought himself back to the question at hand. "Anyway, can you describe exactly what I should be looking for?" he asked

And just like that, the die was cast.

Xavier spent some time describing what the actuator might look like in any of its possible configurations. They all drank up, and Xavier and Charles headed for the elevator and into the night. From his window, Leon watched them walk down the street shiny with rain. He didn't know whether to feel like a spy or like some paranoid patient in a mental ward. He saw the lights go on in their truck a moment before it drove away from the curb. Then he saw a car pull out of a parking place a block behind them.

Shut up, he told himself.

Chapter 28
Trapeze Girl

IT WAS NEARLY DARK when the small truck pulled up beside an old farmhouse. Since no lights were on in the house, it moved farther down the driveway, which continued back to a barn that appeared to be, if anything, in better condition than the house. Bright light shone through the windows and the crack in the partly opened door, and waltz music floated onto the cool night air.

Charles squeezed through the door, followed by Xavier.

The music was much louder inside, and they blinked at the light. The barn had a perfectly clean floor of wide chestnut boards. Far above them was a complex set of steel cables and bars. Eight feet up was a net almost the size of the room. Swinging from a trapeze was a girl in a set of tights. Sitting on the bar, she shifted her weight back and forth to pump the swing to its maximum height. At the apex, she fell backward in a practiced movement, catching the bar with her knees and hanging upside down, arms dangling. After a couple of swings, she reached up, grasped the bar, released her legs, and assumed an upright hanging

position. Then, with a jackknife movement, she released the bar, made
one somersault, and fell into the center of the net, which made a graceful catch. She used the rebound to get to her feet, smiling immediately
at the boys in the doorway. She made a spongy walk to the side of the
net and, grasping the rope that formed its perimeter, flipped over once
and onto the floor, facing her visitors.

She approached Charles with open arms, and he responded in
kind. She was much shorter than he and had a pixie haircut and round,
open brown eyes. She gave Charles a warm and long embrace, laying
her cheek against his chest and closing her eyes. She opened them after
a moment and gave Xavier a wink.

"Are you hungry?" she asked.

Xavier correctly interpreted this question as an indication that she
was hungry herself. Small wonder, after her workout.

"I'll cook," he said.

The girl led the way up to the house, taking both brothers by the
hand.

"Mind if I move our truck under those trees behind the barn?"
asked Charles.

She looked at him to find the meaning behind his question, but
he just jumped into the truck and started it. She was an old friend of
the family and so was used to surprises, but this was a little odd even
by Colebrook standards.

Xavier reached in and brought out a bag of groceries. It had been
his idea not to arrive empty-handed. Charles then moved the truck,
emerging from it with a bouquet of mountain flowers, not to be out-
done by his younger brother.

The house was plain but neat and clean. Xavier approved of the
old gas stove with its white porcelain enamel and black cast iron.

"Tofu and wild mushroom stir-fry," he announced, and got to
work. He was quite accustomed to taking command of a kitchen. He
met no resistance from the owner. Janie had tasted his cooking before
and felt no need to interfere.

Charles and Janie continued through to the living room, which
was dominated by a large fireplace fashioned from squared-off river

rock. Bookshelves were built into the walls on either side, filling out that end of the room. Charles suppressed his natural inclination to go over and peruse the titles. On the other side of the room was a black pug dog named Lazlo. He regarded Charles with an indifferent, this-too-shall-pass sort of gaze. To his mistress, he gave a look that was only a little more probing. He was searching for a sign that something interesting might take place. However, seeing that this was not going to be a dog moment, he settled back down to his relaxation, his thoughts out of reach of human understanding.*

Charles noted two futons in the room, which suited their plans well, and also a large overstuffed chair. He chose the chair, while Janie flopped onto the nearer futon.

He decided to get right to the point.

"Xavier and I are hoping we can crash here with you for a few days," he said.

"Sure, as long as you want," she said, curious. "Did you guys have a falling out with the family?" Such a development was hard to imagine, since she had known the Colebrooks since she was a little girl. She and Charles had been on swim teams that Philip and Lilly coached. She and Charles had been close in their school years, though never in a romantic way. They had kept in touch, more or less, during college. Her return to the mountains was a recent development. She had started attending meetings of the ecology group Lilly belonged to.

"No, nothing like that," he said. "We just need to lie low for a few days and sort some stuff out."

She kept looking at him, a suggestion of a grin on her face. Clearly, this explanation was not nearly detailed enough.

Seeing he was not going to get off so easily, Charles proceeded to fill her in—at least about his missing satellite and the plane Leon and Xavier had found, examined, and lost.

Expecting some kind of punch line, she said, "So what does that all mean?"

---

* The technology of Henrico Carr would soon allow humans to discover that pugs were among the most intellectual of dogs. Keenly aware of the connections that existed among all living things, they were big-picture animals.

"That's the thing. We don't know. Someone seems to be looking for something, and they don't seem to want anyone to know they're looking for it. So one possibility is that we just stumbled into these things. Actually, Leon did literally stumble onto the plane. So now we're in some kind of trouble because of what we know."

"What are you going to do?" she asked.

"That's what we're trying to figure out. It seems like the only thing we can do is try to get to the bottom of what's going on," he said.

"Maybe you should just back off," she said.

"How can we back off?" he said, spreading his hands. "I'd kind of like my job back, and Xavier wants to finish school. I know how these guys think. As long as we're under any kind of cloud, the easiest and safest thing for them is to keep us out, and that's exactly what they'll do. They don't care if it's fair or not."

"So you really don't have any idea what they're looking for?" she said.

"No, but judging from the satellite location and the plane, it's somewhere out here," said Charles.

"How do you know they're even connected?" she asked. "I mean, the plane and the satellite."

"Well, they're connected by the location. Also, we're connected. I mean, Xavier and Leon and I are obviously connected."

She nodded as he talked and let the sentence hang there to see if he would say more. She was among other things a great listener.

"And there's one other thing," he said.

Her wait was paying off.

"The type of data they were collecting was . . . related," he said.

Sensing this was as far as he was prepared to go, she jumped up and rewarded him with a kiss on the cheek. She was among other things also a good trainer, one who believed in coupling rewards closely with desired behavior.

From the kitchen came an intense aroma of vegetables caramelizing. The sounds of utensils clinking together and of the knife on the chopping board were replaced by the hiss and sizzle of the cooking process. Lazlo had relocated himself there, they noticed. He and Xavier had become the best of friends as soon as Lazlo caught the scents from the large cast-iron skillet.

Xavier's five-minute warning call served as a breaking point for the conversation in the living room. Charles and Janie came into the kitchen and breathed deeply. In addition to the great smells and sounds, the skillet was a colorful palette as well. Xavier had chosen yellow and red peppers to go with the deep purple eggplant. On another burner, rice was simmering and steaming up the windows.

"How about if you set the table while I run out to the barn for my phone?" Janie said to Charles.

She slipped out the door and performed a dancer's run across the lawn.

"Everything cool?" asked Xavier.

"Yeah, everything's cool," he said, short of total conviction. He was wondering if he had told her too much.

His attention went to the skillet, where he reached in with a fork and plucked out a small cube of tofu. He dipped this in a cup of sauce that Xavier had prepared, then popped it into his mouth.

"Not bad, Ming Sigh," he said, which threw Xavier into one of his laughs. The brothers were all decent cooks, and each as he grew older had begun to specialize. Since Xavier was on an Asian kick of late, his brothers had taken to calling him Ming Sigh.

"We're ready," said Xavier, wiping his hands on a towel slung over his shoulder Emeril Lagasse–style.

Charles reached over to wipe the steam off one of the window-panes so he could see if Janie was on her way back. The lights were still on in the barn. Through the open door, he saw her in silhouette talking on a cell phone and smoking a cigarette. She was leaning against the doorjamb, her weight on one foot, the other leg raised. She broke this pose to respond to something said on the other end. She gave a little jump and gestured with her cigarette hand, sending sparks to the damp ground. After a moment, she snapped the cell phone shut and reached in to turn off the lights. Charles opened the kitchen door and watched her pick up her pace toward the house.

"Dinner ready?" she asked as she popped in.

"Oh, yeah," said Charles.

If he was wondering if she would mention the phone call, he had his answer.

Chapter 29

We Still Pray

TOMBLYN AND HAVEN enjoyed another excellent breakfast at the inn. Tomblyn had to admit that Haven was right. He was even thinking about checking out the bed-and-breakfast scene on his future assignments.

They had decided to get their own car, partly to free up Meyers and partly because, at least for some of their calls, they wanted to go incognito, and Meyers was too well known in the area.

For better or worse, they were getting used to this place. Their route took them through the central part of town, which they accomplished by going south on the street one block off Main. It was a one-way street with a traffic light on each corner. In fact, Haven had noticed a traffic light at every single intersection for many blocks. This made for maddeningly slow going.

"What's up with all the traffic lights?" he had asked the proprietor of the inn.

"Retirees," was her one-word explanation.

The answer resonated powerfully with Haven's own observations. The concentration of retirees had indeed come to his attention almost immediately.

The density of traffic lights was explained by a related phenomenon Haven had noticed. It seemed that many males held on to the aggressiveness and Type A behavior that had served them well in the business world. To this was added an extra measure of crankiness caused by the pains of old age. Behind the wheel, the result was something like an aged werewolf with slow reflexes and bad vision. Combine those creatures with the old women whose presence in their cars was detectable only by the tufts of white hair floating above the seat backs and the gnarled fingers grasping the steering wheels and the traffic lights looked like a survival ploy.

This particular morning, the traffic on Church Street had slowed to a halt. Haven got out the passenger door to see what the problem was. It turned out to be an accident. Apparently, someone going the wrong way had been T-boned by a pickup truck emerging from a side street. Both were slightly crumpled and sitting diagonally in the street, giving Haven a good view of their identical "We Still Pray" bumper stickers.

"Not that I care," he said to Tomblyn after getting back in and advising him to turn up one of the cross streets so they wouldn't have to sit there all day, "but I wonder what that means."

"We Still Pray?" Tomblyn asked.

"Did somebody tell them to stop?" Haven asked.

"Maybe it's about praying in school," said Tomblyn.

He knew they could always ask the bed-and-breakfast lady, but he was reluctant to appear even more out of place than he already did.

They were headed for the courthouse in hopes of picking up a warrant for Athenaeum. The warrant would be specifically aimed at looking for a mold or pattern or any other evidence that the truck casting had been made there. Of course, as the agents well knew, a warrant would put them in a position to learn a lot more as well.

The county courthouse was a fine example of Neoclassical architecture dating back more than a century. When they had asked how to find it back at the bed-and-breakfast, they had received a full history to boot. They were becoming accustomed to this sort of conversation. In answer to any simple question, they were likely to receive a long and meandering story that might span several generations, including details about the various descendants of the original players. This had the effect of illustrating how interconnected and complex the local landscape and inhabitants were. Sometimes, the answer to the original question would actually surface. Other times, they had to thank the speaker for the information but then redirect them to the subject at hand.

In this way, they found that the building was designed by a famous architect from Asheville. Like all such structures, it had seen its share of bizarre murder cases and had been the gathering place for local people at some critical moments in history. It had seen additions and annexes, including a jail in back. Following the sine wave of abundance and scarcity in the area, it had fallen into disrepair. In the early 1990s, it was deemed no longer a practical place to take care of county business, and a new structure was built a few blocks away, after which the original complex was left to leak and molder while the commissioners argued about its restoration or demolition. In the end, the forces of preservation prevailed. The dome was returned to its original color. The statue of Lady Justice perched atop the crest of the dome was taken down and repaired. The statue was a typical version of her holding the scales. However, in this case, she was without a blindfold. What the significance of this detail was, no one seemed to know. It was reported that Lady Justice had sustained no fewer than twenty-one bullet strikes by the time the repairs were started.

Although court proceedings were no longer held there, several county officials maintained offices in the building, including Judge Bliss, with whom they had made an appointment.

They ascended the short flight of stairs, pulled open the huge brass-covered doors, and made their way into the relative coolness of the vestibule. An old-fashioned plaque indicated that the judge's office was in the south wing down a short hallway.

They entered through a door of oak and frosted glass to find a secretary in a small waiting room outside the judge's office proper. She showed them in and told them the judge was down the hall and would join them shortly.

They found their surroundings much as they expected. It could have been a law office out of the forties or fifties, complete with rows of books, a small conference table, and a large desk at one end.

Behind the desk hung a single oil painting illuminated by light from the window.

The scene was of a brick apartment building several stories high overlooking a city street. Several of the windows were open. Out of a second-story window, a man in a white undershirt inclined slightly forward, watching something on the street below. He was smoking a cigarette, his eyes squinting to avoid the smoke. The bright blue dress of a woman walking on the sidewalk below drew the eye of the viewer, as well as that of the man in the window. The painter's point of view was from across the street and slightly higher, perhaps a third-story window. A few autos parked on the street suggested the late 1950s.

Haven approached the painting slowly, taking it in stride by stride. He finally leaned across the desk to get a better view. It was only after this closer examination that he identified the man in the window. The smoker was without question Abraham Lincoln.

"It's by a local artist," said the judge.

They were not sure exactly when he had entered the room behind them. They did their best to turn slowly and not show their embarrassment at being taken by surprise.

"Yes, we seem to be running into Mr. Colebrook's work all over town," said Haven.

"It's not just this town you'll see it in either," said the judge. "He is really quite well known in certain art and history circles."

The men introduced themselves and sat at the table to get to the business at hand.

"We could probably go in there and ask to see their foundry area, but in case they don't want to cooperate, it will save time if we have a court order," Tomblyn explained.

What he didn't say was that it would add to the scare factor, as if the FBI showing up at your door weren't scary enough.

"Mr. Tomblyn, I do like to cooperate with the FBI in a reasonable execution of its investigations, but in this case I am reluctant without knowing more about the nature of the crime."

"As we've explained, Your Honor, this is a matter of national security, and we are under instructions to disclose the nature of the problem to no one. I can assure you that we do not make the request lightly," said Haven.

"It's just hard for me to understand what possible national security problem could be posed by a company that makes fountains and statues," said the judge.

"It may not be the company per se, but rather the family being involved with something it should not be involved with." This came from Tomblyn. He said it by way of sharing as much information as possible with the judge, but more so to gauge his reaction.

The judge did not answer immediately. He pushed back from the table and looked up at the painting.

"Was it a gift from Mr. Colebrook?" Haven asked.

The judge looked at him for a moment before answering, trying to decide if he should take offense or not.

"No, Mr. Haven, not a gift. I actually purchased the painting at auction. That's something I don't do on a regular basis—buying paintings, that is. In this case, I had gone to a fundraising auction with my wife, and the bid was going to a fellow from out of town, a person who collects artifacts related to Lincoln. As you probably know, just south of here is the home of Carl Sandburg, who among other things wrote the definitive biography of Lincoln, so it just seemed wrong to let the painting go."

"So you fell in love with it right away?" asked Haven.

"Not really. To tell you the truth, I thought it was pretty funny at first. But then I started to look closer and to wonder what it meant, and before long it seemed like it really belonged here," the judge said.

"And what do you think it means?" asked Haven.

"Well, sometimes I think it means that Lincoln was timeless, a great man. And sometimes I think it means that Lincoln came along at exactly the right time, that if he had been born later, like in the painting, he would have been just an ordinary guy. Hell, it probably just means that Pipo felt like painting it and then moved on."

"Moved on to what?" said Haven.

To himself, the judge had to admit that the Colebrooks in general and Pipo in particular were predictable in their unpredictability. Based on this, he could not in good conscience rule out the possibility that, intentionally or not, they could be involved in something beyond the scope of his imagination.

"I'm going to give you your warrant to search for the type of objects you mention here, but I'm going to expect you to observe the limits of the warrant. This is a family that has done a lot for the community, and I will not be part of a witch hunt that could do them any undue harm."

"Thank you, Your Honor," said Tomblyn, accepting the document and rising.

"You-all enjoy your visit here, and good luck with whatever you're trying to find."

And with one last look at the painting, they left.

ooooo

The agents were braced for at least some form of resistance at Athenaeum but encountered none. Showing up unannounced with legal warrant in hand had the desired destabilizing effect on Michael. He brought Judy to the lobby with him to meet the two visitors. He examined the papers, then handed them to her.

"Does anything in particular lead you to suspect someone at our company is involved in some illegal act?" he asked them.

"I'm afraid that the information we have at this time must be held in confidence. We do, however, need to see your foundry area," said Tomblyn.

"Of course. I understand completely," Michael said. He smiled and nodded. "I would frankly not be surprised by much after getting to know the previous owners of this establishment."

"Are you aware of anything the Colebrooks have done that we should know about?" Tomblyn asked.

Judy and Haven cleared their throats at the same time, signaling their discomfort with the direction the conversation was headed.

"Let me just say that we will be happy to cooperate with the authorities in any way we can," Judy said.

"Really," Michael said. "Anything at all."

As they were escorted through the plant, it occurred to Haven that he would not necessarily be able to recognize the foundry area. He had no idea what one looked like. Tomblyn was not similarly troubled. He figured he would know it when he saw it.

In the end, they found nothing but rough castings, black smoke from resin burning out of a mold, and a bunch of wooden patterns they could make no sense of. They left with sand in their shoes and some holes burned in their coat lapels from slag spatter when they got too close to a pour. They also left with further assurances from Michael that they could depend on him.

Chapter 30

R ARS Raid

CHARLES AND XAVIER SPENT A COUPLE OF DAYS making their preparations for RARS. A visit to the website convinced them that little had changed in terms of the physical layout of the place. That figured, since RARS basically had no serious money anymore.

The day of the raid, they picked up what few supplies they needed and refined their plan of attack. Janie was at a meeting of her environmental group, which saved them the task of explaining where they were going. They simply left a brief note.

They departed at dark and drove the black truck along the mountain roads to the observatory. Xavier and Charles could not suppress the urge to sing the theme song from *Mission Impossible*. Years ago, in a Paris hotel room on a family trip to Europe, they had made up words to the well-known instrumental:

Dut dut duda, dut dut duda
I am the black guy, I know how to build things—
Dut dut duda, dut dut duda
I am the old white guy, I'm the boss of everyone—
Dut dut duda, dut dut duda
I am the other white guy, I know how to do makeup—
Dut dut duda, dut dut duda
WHADA WA , WHA DA WA

This was usually as far as they got without laughing. Then another verse:

I am the hot girl, sometimes I get captured—
Dut dut duda, dut dut duda
WHADA WA, WHA DA WA

If no one was around to stop them, this could go on for quite a while.

They were both dressed in jeans and navy-blue long-sleeved T-shirts and dark watch caps. This was as close to nighttime commando attire as they were prepared to get. Putting charcoal on their faces seemed too ludicrous. Besides, it would be impossible to explain if they got caught.

The compound was reached by ascending some of the most tortuous curves in Pisgah National Forest. The road, however, was wider than most of the tracks in the forest. In its prime, the compound had employed several hundred people, most of whom even to this day would not talk about what they had done there.

Turning off the main road (if it could be called that), the truck crossed a bridge over a swift-flowing mountain creek. It did not emerge from the canopy of the forest for another quarter-mile or so, and when it did, the guardhouse of the compound was visible in the moonlight. They stopped the truck before it left the shadows of the woods. Charles switched off the lights, backed the truck, executed a turn, and found a place where he could pull off the road and slightly into the forest. If anyone came in behind them, they would not spot the black truck well back in the trees. He turned off the engine, and they sat for a minute looking and listening. If their presence had been noticed by anyone, they saw no sign of it. They heard only the clicks and pings of the engine cooling and the sounds of the night insects.

When they could put off action no longer, they slipped quietly out of the truck and shut the doors. Each had a small backpack with a few tools and a laptop computer.

They advanced through the shadows of the trees, pausing from time to time to look and listen. They approached a chain-link fence. Xavier started moving toward the main entrance gate, which was standing open, but Charles restrained him with a hand on his shoulder. He pointed to his left instead, to a gate just big enough to walk through. That area was much more poorly lit.

They found the gate unlocked, just as Charles had expected. Entering did require that they move out of the shadows and into the light, at least for a moment. They paused and waited, attuned to any sign of life. At length, they nodded to each other and moved out at a speed calculated to smoothly deliver them to the other side without being frantic. In the distance, a dog barked, a sound they found somehow reassuring.*

Inside the gate, they moved to the right and plunged into the shadow of the first building like diving into a pool of ink. That vantage point allowed them to remain virtually invisible while getting their first look at the main building, their target for the night. No artificial lights were to be seen anywhere. A cloud moved in front of the moon and plunged the whole place into darkness complete and primeval.

As their vision adjusted, they looked down into the natural bowl of the compound. They could barely make out the road curving down the hillside. Just then, the cloud glided away and the moon shed its light on the most prominent structure in the whole place, the enormous thirty-meter radio telescope dish. The structure was an eerie milky white, otherworldly in form and color and sheer size, a device

---

* The research group led by Henrico Carr actually established that, although night barking by dogs was a way to send up an alarm, it was often a form of reassurance, like sentries checking in from their lonely outposts.

not designed to deal with anything of this earth.

The huge dish was pointed almost straight up to the heavens, so that its inside surface was barely visible. Above the dish, supported by a structure that was almost invisible, was a metal cylinder. Located at the focal point of the parabola formed by the dish, this contained the receiver for the reflected radio waves, as the boys knew. Underneath the dish was a heavy steel support structure forming a complex truss system anchored to massive concrete foundation blocks. At the top of the truss, supporting the dish itself, was what looked like a giant protractor, part of the mechanism that allowed the dish to be tilted almost to a vertical position.

Charles tapped Xavier on the arm and led him to look down the slope on the other side of the building. There, even closer, sat a thirty-meter dish identical to the one they had been looking at. Beside it on the roof of a cement-block building was a smaller, more agile-looking dish with a happy face painted on it.

They returned to their original vantage and looked again at the first dish. Just down the hill was a low rectangular building known, with all the imagination expected of the government, as Building One.

They had begun to make their way slowly down the hill toward Building One, still alert for any other presence, when a loud metal-on-metal screech and pop plastered them against the side of the building and into the thin sliver of shadow it provided. The sound was followed by the hum and grind of a powerful electric motor and gearbox. They looked up to see the giant dish above them begin to move in a majestic arc against the backdrop of stars and clouds populating the sky that night.

"Someone must be in the control room," Xavier whispered.

"Not necessarily," said Charles. "They have this thing hooked up for control by Internet connection. They've got people in universities all over the place writing grants and doing research without ever making a trip out here. They just sit in their offices back home and run the show and collect the data."

Although this made perfect sense, Xavier could not suppress the feeling that something was fundamentally lame about that scenario. He knew that if he were an astronomer, he would want to be hanging out in a place like this. But anyway, it was good news in terms of their mission tonight.

They relaxed a little and continued to Building One. As Charles had suspected, they had little security to worry about. They shunned the main entrance in favor of a small service door beside the loading dock.

"Watch this," Charles whispered with a grin. He took a piece of notebook paper from his pocket, inserted it under the door, and moved it back and forth. They heard the faint but distinct click of a bolt releasing. Charles reached up and opened the door a few inches. "Motion sensor," he said by way of explanation.

Xavier immediately understood. Many security systems that employ card or keypad access to enter a building use motion detectors on the inside. That way, a person does not need a card or code to leave, only to enter. Any motion will do, including a paper moving around on the floor.

They quietly let themselves into a loading bay area. Presumably, this was where large pieces of equipment and shipments of supplies were received. Since RARS was receiving next to nothing these days, the area was becoming a museum of obsolete equipment.

Through a window in the door on the other side of the room, they saw their first artificial light since entering the compound. They moved through the obstacle course of dark shapes and made it to the door without knocking anything over. The window allowed a view into a hallway dimly lit by a few fluorescent tubes. To Xavier, who had idealized his visits from several years back, the site was a bit of a letdown. After the exotic moonlit landscape outside, this could have been a hallway in any industrial office anywhere in the country. From the gray vinyl floor tiles to the pastel green walls to the drop ceiling with dirty white acoustical panels, he saw nothing to fire the imagination.

Charles removed a small Petzl light from his pocket and examined the edges of the interior door. As he suspected, he found no evidence of a security alarm. He pulled the door open a few inches and paused to listen. The boys heard no footsteps, no voices, no tapping of keystrokes on a computer, nothing but the whir of ventilation fans.

Charles pointed down the corridor to a pair of doors on the left, indicating to Xavier the next objective in their mission.

They pulled the door open enough to squeeze through, then glided down the hall. The next set of doors led to the main control room. If anyone was in the building that night, Charles knew this was the most likely place to find them. However, RARS was primarily a radio astronomy observatory. Unlike the traditional astronomers of the last several centuries, these guys had no particular reason to work at night. A few light telescopes were on the site, but they were way up on the ridge tops surrounding the bowl.

Nevertheless, it took some nerve to open the door when the moment came. Charles motioned to Xavier to go to the end of the corridor. From there, he could check out the intersecting hallway. Xavier crept up, listened, and peeked carefully around the corner. He gave Charles the thumbs-up.

Charles eased the door open a couple of inches and did a quick scan, then pulled it the rest of the way, motioning for Xavier to follow.

Xavier found this room almost as disappointing as the hallway. It looked more like a disorganized classroom than ground zero of a multimillion-dollar facility used to probe the secrets of the universe. The room had the same institutional trappings as the rest of the building—vinyl tiles, drop ceiling, and all. It was furnished with folding cafeteria tables arranged in pairs to create worktables. The mismatched collection of chairs could have been collected from abandoned offices and waiting rooms. Several computer stations were set up seemingly at random on some of the tables. Against the far wall was the only piece of equipment that looked high tech. It was a rack of electronics—probably, Xavier assumed, amplifiers and signal conditioners. The front of the rack housed a few meters and an old-fashioned oscilloscope. The mountings and patches suggested a history of changes and upgrades.

Just like Santa Claus, Charles spoke not a word but went straight to his work. He shrugged off his backpack and pulled out a thin laptop. After checking a couple of the screens that were up and running, he chose one and plugged his laptop into the computer it was attached to.

Concluding that his brother did not need his help, Xavier decided to check the room, beginning with the door on the other end. He listened there for a minute, then opened it to find a large but conventional classroom. Charles had explained to him that the compound was used extensively for educational projects including summer camps for high-school and college students. Most of the student work involved the light telescopes up on the ridge and the small radio telescope, which was tuned to the frequency given off by hydrogen. The barracks over near the second large dish and the nearby cafeteria served the camp students.

Back at the computer terminal, Charles was into the system. He had needed no passwords, just as in the days of his internship. The command program had changed little.

He checked out the list of instructions currently in the system for the number-one dish, which he intended to use. It looked like the dish was currently programmed to follow the course of some distant object in the sky, recording a span of wavelengths around the resonant frequency of nitrogen. It was following instructions from a remote location, which was good for two reasons. One, it meant that the chance of a local astronomer coming in to check the progress of his program was that much lower. Second, it meant that the program was of low-enough priority that Charles could trump it from the local control station.

Charles quickly programmed in the coordinates to position the dish. He had made time and trajectory estimates for the satellite—but they were only that, estimates. The longer they could leave the dish in position, the better their chance of catching the download they were after.

He worried that the receivers in the dish might have been switched out. The frequencies used for satellite communication were quite a bit different from the elemental frequencies of interest to most radio astronomers. The astronomers therefore had to add some specialized gear to the dish to collect their data. The government, as a stipulation for continuing its meager but important funding, insisted that the receivers for satellite frequencies stay as well. The astronomers loved to bitch about this but of course left them in place anyway.

In any case, the receivers were still there as an option on the program.

Positioning the dish was easy and also kind of cool. On a portion of the screen was a TV image of the dish itself. The operator entered the coordinates or chose a point on the map with a cursor and clicked, then watched the dish move.

Charles and Xavier knew the movement of the dish was the one thing they could not hide. They were hoping that the guards, if any were awake, would just accept the dish movement as part of an ordinary routine. Nevertheless, when the moment came, Charles looked up at Xavier, who nodded the go-ahead.

Charles made the last keystroke, then stepped back. In the side box, they saw the faint image of the dish as it began to tilt slightly and rotate toward them. The movement was not nearly as dramatic when viewed on the tiny screen.

After a few seconds, the movement of the dish stopped. Then nothing seemed to happen. They watched the monitor for a few moments before a few points began to show on the graph display, indicating they were beginning to receive a signal.

Without removing his eyes from the screen, Charles held up his hand to receive a high-five. Just as Xavier began to raise his hand to oblige, they heard the distinct sound of a heavy door opening down the hall.

They froze for an instant, then, following Charles's lead, dove behind the rack of electronic equipment. Between the rack and the wall was enough room for a person to wedge himself in and service the various instruments mounted in the displays. Bolt holes and openings from previous installations allowed them to peek out into the room.

The sound of the door was followed by footsteps. Running footsteps. Then the sound of a low voice and a high giggle. The door to the room burst open, and two bodies exploded through. The first was a girl of about nineteen or twenty with long, dark hair. She was dressed in shorts and a T-shirt that did not quite meet in the middle. The second was a boy of about the same age.

"Quit it," she said, prying his hands off her torso and trying not to laugh.

She struggled to a seat at the nearest table and tapped the keyboard of one of the computers. The boy, close behind, bent over her as she typed some commands and tried to concentrate on the screen.

"Let me check this," she said, but not too convincingly.

He stayed on her back, working his cheek next to hers from behind, putting his hand on her belly between the shirt and the shorts, then working it down. She typed a couple more commands, then arched her back, tilting her head and closing her eyes.

The boy turned her chair away from the computer screen and toward him. He pressed his mouth against hers, leaning into her and nearly rocking the chair over backwards. After a long moment, he released her, letting girl and chair rock back forward.

"This is killing my back," he moaned.

She laughed, turned toward the keyboard, and executed a quick sign-off. When she stood, he embraced her again and started exploring with his hands.

"Not here," she said, looking around the room. Her eyes fixed on the door to the darkened classroom. She turned and led him by the hand across the floor.

Behind the panel, Xavier looked at Charles.

"That should take awhile," he whispered.

Charles was not so sure. He wanted to collect signal for at least half an hour to make sure they got a good set of images. But that would be pushing things. The couple had not noticed his laptop and backpack a couple of tables away, but he guessed they would be in less of a hurry when they came back out.

They tiptoed out into the room. Charles went to the laptop to check on the data acquisition. Xavier approached the door to the classroom and listened to the progress of the romance on the other side. He nodded his approval.

Charles was pleased with what he saw on the screen. By all indications, they had several minutes of uninterrupted signal, which should be plenty.

Then they heard that frigging outside door again! This time, the footsteps were more deliberate. They dove back to their hiding place.

The door opened slowly, and a middle-aged man in the uniform of a security guard entered. In spite of the adequate lighting, he directed the beam of a long black flashlight around the room.

The boys held their breath. Charles watched through a hole in the panel no larger that a quarter-inch bolt. The beam fell on the only thing in the room that was out of place: his laptop sitting there sucking up data like a fat boy at a pizza buffet. He grimaced as the guard took a step toward it.

Just then, they heard a crash from the classroom, followed by a low curse. Charles remembered a large Plexiglas star globe that used to sit on one of the side tables in that room.

The guard looked at the classroom door and lowered his flashlight. He approached slowly, pushed the door open, and stepped through into the darkness.

They heard the girl yell something, then a lot of scurrying noises.

Charles and Xavier needed no further invitation. They scooted out. Charles grabbed the laptop, unplugged it, and headed for the door. Xavier picked up the backpack and was close on his heels.

Out in the hall, they ran silently in exaggerated strides, way up on the balls of their feet. In the shipping room, they returned the computer to the backpack and wound their way though the maze of equipment with only incidental contact.

They edged the door open and took a moment to look and listen. To the left, lights were on in a small building where they had seen none before.

"Something is up," said Charles under his breath. "I can't remember if that building is where the guards stay or quarters for visiting students."

They had already surmised that the hapless couple were college students visiting for a summer class.

They decided that a slow, I-own-this-place walk was the mode of exit that would attract the least attention, but they kept to the shadows whenever possible as they made their way toward the gate.

Xavier could not resist an occasional glance over his shoulder. More and more lights were coming on around the compound, especially near Building One. He wanted to believe that all the attention would focus on the couple in the classroom, but in his gut he could feel the place was waking up too quickly for that to be the case.

The pace accelerated as they approached the fence. It seemed like another light came on with every step they took.

Then they heard the sound they had been dreading: an engine cranking. Still a few steps from the small gate where they had entered, they both took this as the starting horn and broke into a full run, diving into the protection of the forest at the nearest possible opportunity.

Chapter 31

Unindicted Co-Conspirator

CHARLES AND XAVIER HIGHTAILED IT through the last stretch of woods and approached the black truck. It had been Charles's idea to leave it there and travel the last couple hundred yards on foot. Xavier had questioned the strategy at the time, but now it seemed like a pretty good idea because it brought them well out of range of the parking lot and streetlights. Those lights, they knew, were normally not used, so as to keep it as dark as possible for the light telescopes on the ridge. Right now, though, the place was lit up like Christmas. Adding to the festive atmosphere were a siren and a voice on a bullhorn, although they could not make out the words.

They saw a pair of headlights come from the main complex and pass the guard booth. That they expected. It would be the security guards, who undoubtedly had been sleeping peacefully a few minutes ago. What they didn't expect were the several pairs of headlights from the other direction, coming off the main road towards the complex.

As they arrived at the truck, Charles grabbed Xavier's arm and turned him toward the sight. Instinctively, they ducked, though they had little chance of being seen in the darkness well back in the woods. They counted three sets of headlights—Jeeps or maybe Humvees, it was hard to tell. They were traveling fast for such a path. What was easy to pick out was the silhouette of helmeted figures seated in the vehicles. Someone had called in the troops!

Charles and Xavier looked at each other and mouthed simultaneously, "What the hell?"

As the military convoy and the security Jeep raced toward each other on the narrow approach road, the boys thought a head-on collision was inevitable. Then came a screeching of brakes and the sound of voices yelling as the vehicles stopped a hundred feet apart. A terse shouting of orders was followed by the sounds of soldiers bailing over the sides of their rides and moving into position. The opposing headlights were joined by two searchlights, all aimed at the same spot. Those lights revealed the outline of a pickup truck with a lone figure standing beside it. It was parked in front of the main gate, well away from the small one the boys had used for their entrance and escape.

Charles and Xavier looked at each other and frowned. How the hell many people were prowling around anyway?

Xavier recognized this as one of those rare and unexpected opportunities. He placed a finger to his lips and motioned for Charles to get in the truck. Charles slowly released the hand brake and put the truck in neutral. Xavier strained to push it off the bank by the road. He rocked it a couple of times before Charles jumped out and pushed on the open doorframe. Having supplied enough energy to get over the hump, he jumped back in as Xavier continued to push from behind.

They gathered speed as the truck hit the gravel road. To Xavier, the crunching of the tires seemed deafening. After a few feet, the road dipped to a significant down slope, and Xavier vaulted into the bed, rolled toward the cab, and raised his head to see if anyone was following. By now, the scene was blurred through the trees and the mist of the night. The good part was that the lights still seemed focused on the same spot. No one was giving chase.

As he was about to turn toward the cab, a light of a different color caught his eye—a small yellow and red spark near the pickup at the center of the spotlights, followed by what looked like a burst from a Roman candle. That was followed by a loud report like a gunshot, which was in turn followed by angry yelling.

They rolled on down the hill in silence. When the wheels hit pavement, Charles turned the key, put the truck in second gear, and eased the clutch out, allowing the momentum of the vehicle to smoothly start the engine.

After another half-mile, he pulled to the side of the road and let Xavier climb into the cab.

"What the hell was that?" he asked when they were back under way.

"I don't know, but whoever that guy is, we owe him one," Xavier said, and let go with one of his laughs.

ooooo

Back at the entrance to the observatory, no one was ready to declare a break in the tension quite yet.

What had happened when the alarm went off was this: A guard named Robert was watching TV. One of the worst-kept secrets at the observatory full of radio telescopes was that the personnel stole satellite TV signals. The rationale was that they had to monitor and record them, so they could then remove them as background from the signals they were getting, in case they interfered with observations of the Crab Dip Nebula or something.

Anyway, they let Robert get the signal down at the guardroom, too. On this particular night, he was watching a rerun of *The Silence of the Lambs*, so he was pretty creeped out when the alarm went off. Another guard, Chester, was in the back room asleep and was not due to come on for another two hours.

The alarm was loud. Even Chester could not sleep through it.

Robert was getting his boots on and looking for his belt with the gun and flashlight when Chester staggered out in his boxer shorts.

"What's going on?" he asked.

"I don't know," said Robert.

"I'd better go with you," said Chester.

"Then you better get some clothes on," said Robert.

He thought about leaving Chester behind, but they weren't supposed to do that, and anyway he didn't relish going out in the dark by himself.

"Where the hell is Lewis?" Chester asked. Lewis was the third guard.

"He called in and said he was checking something out in One," said Robert.

A second alarm went off. They both shoved over to the control panel to have a look, getting more serious about the whole situation. They knew what this meant. Occasionally, sensors malfunctioned or picked up the movement of some animal. Most of the time, they would track down the sensor, silence the alarm, and be done with it. A second alarm almost surely meant something was really going on.

"It's the one on the perimeter near the main gate," said Robert.

They were moving now, checking their belts as they blew through the door. With no discussion, they went straight for the Jeep. The obvious conclusion was that the inside alarm had been hit and someone was running for it. They jumped in with surprising agility for creatures of such size, Robert behind the wheel. He gunned the engine and pulled the headlight switch. Down the long driveway, they thought they detected some object in the road. Then, as if things weren't confusing enough, they saw headlights turning off the main road—one, two, three sets.

Partly because of the oncoming headlights and partly because of the fog, they were nearly on top of the silvery gray pickup truck before they saw it sitting diagonally across the driveway, effectively blocking any chance of going around it, even if they had wished to do so. It took an application of the brake pedal just short of a panic stop to avoid a Jeep-truck union.

Standing beside the truck was an old man with a flintlock rifle.

Normally, the sight of a gun in the hands of a stranger at midnight would have thrown the security guards into a panic, but nothing in the man's stance or the relaxed way he held the rifle suggested they had anything to fear. Just as Robert and Chester were getting out of the Jeep and squinting at the man's face, trying to read his expression, the glare of oncoming headlights reduced his image to a silhouette. The old man turned to glance over his shoulder at the new arrivals.

The Humvees spread out slightly in attack formation. Upon a terse command, the troopers took up positions in a crescent around the gray truck.

"Put the weapon down," said a voice through a bullhorn. The bullhorn was completely unnecessary, since the owner of the commanding voice was less than fifty feet from the man he was addressing. It did, however—along with the mist and the various headlights and spotlights—add to the voice-of-God effect that generally got results.

Chester began to reach for his pistol, but Robert whispered, "Not you, dummy."

His left hand in the air, the old man turned and carefully laid his rifle across the bed of the truck. Being a replica of a Kentucky long gun, it actually reached from one wall of the bed to the other. Then he stepped away and slowly turned.

"This is Captain Ryan Watts," said the man with the bullhorn. "We are U.S. Army Rangers, and we are taking you into custody for acts of terrorism against a facility of the federal government."

The Rangers waited a moment to see if the old man had anything to say. He simply continued to stand in place.

Since the man was standing with his back to the Jeep, Robert decided to approach and cuff him from behind.

"We are RARS security," he said as he approached. "Please place your hands behind you back and—."

He was interrupted by a click, a spark, and a boom. Chester had approached the truck while Robert dealt with the old man. He started to pick up the flintlock with one hand. As soon as the muzzle came off its support on the opposite wall, he let it dip because of the unexpected weight.

When his hand grabbed tighter, he brushed the hammer, which had been cocked. Apparently on a hair-trigger mechanism, it sparked the pan, which ignited the charge inside the barrel, sending a .50 caliber ball neatly through the wall of the truck bed and making a hell of a racket and display of fireworks.

This blast sent the soldiers, who had begun to relax, back into their at-ready crouches. The captain and Robert both jumped back a step, their hands going to their side arms. Only the old man remained calm and not much surprised by the commotion.

After a moment, Robert and the captain both glared at Chester, who was now holding the smoking piece with both hands.

"I know," he said. "You don't have to say anything."

Regaining his composure, Robert stepped back up and completed the handcuffing. He then positioned himself to see the captive's face. The captain did the same.

Robert and the captain made introductions, although the captain did not elaborate on what a group of Rangers was doing on the scene.

"What's your name?" the captain asked the old man.

The old man said nothing but made a backward nod of his head.

Robert understood and reached behind the captive to withdraw a wallet from the back pocket of the overalls he was wearing. He retrieved an old leather wallet barely holding together.

"Better pat him down for weapons," said the captain.

Robert began to do so and stopped when he felt an object in the old man's right front pocket.

"What's that?" he asked, sliding a hand gingerly into the pocket.

The old man continued to look forward silently.

Robert removed his hand and brought the object into the light. It was an ancient briar pipe. He snorted and slipped it back in.

Stepping back beside the captain, he flipped the wallet open. It contained a few wadded-up bills and bank slips. After some further prying, he found the driver's license he sought. Although several years out of date, it did identify the owner.

"Mr. James Colebrook?" he asked.

The old man nodded.

"Mr. Colebrook," said the captain "is anyone else out here with you?"

This led Robert and several of the soldiers to look around. Robert was getting a little tired of the captain's always being a step ahead of him.

In reply, Pipo gave a short whistle and looked toward the cab of the truck.

Up from the passenger side of the seat came the head of a yellow Labrador, looking a little startled but nonetheless ready to engage in whatever game might be afoot.

Into Pipo's mind came his favorite phrase from the Watergate investigation: "Unindicted co-conspirator."

Chapter 32

L azlo at the Keyboard

JANIE CAME IN FROM ANOTHER TRAPEZE workout in the barn wiping sweat off her face, cooling down. Charles and Xavier were up and hard at work in the living room. As in most spaces these two inhabited, a strong technological element had emerged. She saw that they had set up three computer monitors, together with a couple of boxes with wires coming out containing God knew what kind of equipment.

Where the hell does all this stuff come from? she thought. It seemed to materialize from nowhere when Charles and Xavier were around for any length of time.

She enjoyed a long shower as part of her payoff for a hard workout, slipped into a white bathrobe, and rejoined them in the living room/lab.

Charles was sitting on the floor with Lazlo the pug on his lap. Reaching on either side of the dog, he was typing on the keyboard and trying to see the screen as Lazlo attempted to lick his unprotected face.

Xavier was fiddling with the wires on one of the boxes and looking occasionally at Charles to gauge the success of his efforts.

"Okay," Charles said. "Leave it right there." And he typed some more.

Xavier got up and swooped to pluck the pug off Charles's lap.

"Hey, buddy!" he said, holding the pug in midair. He spun around and sat on the couch beside Janie.

"You guys were out late last night," she said.

She had come home about eight o'clock to find a note saying they had gone out to "take care of some things" and not to worry if they didn't make it back that night. They must have returned in the early morning because she had heard nothing by the time she went to bed around midnight. She found them sleeping in their dark clothes when she got up for her workout at seven.

"Some bagels are in the kitchen," Xavier said. "And some cream cheese and coffee."

"What are we looking at this morning?" she asked, not so easily distracted. She squinted at the image on the central computer screen.

"We're not exactly sure yet," Xavier said.

A map was on the screen. Charles was changing features and moving the view in and out, making it hard to figure out exactly what was being depicted. After Janie watched this frustrating display a few minutes, the concept of bagels blossomed fully into her consciousness. She pushed herself up from the couch and started padding toward the kitchen. Sensing food-related action, Lazlo sprang off Xavier's lap and followed with a snort.

By the time she returned with a toasted toroid and a cup of tea, the screen had settled down and the boys were sitting back and taking in the product of their work.

The image was now recognizable as a map of western North Carolina and East Tennessee. They had overlaid a road map showing major highways and superimposed the jagged outline of the border between the two states. A few bright dots were visible at seemingly random intervals on both the major highways. West of Knoxville on the extreme left of the map, the bright dots coalesced into a larger glowing splotch.

Near the border of North Carolina and Tennessee and a bit south was another point of light, slightly bolder than the ones along the highway.

Janie studied the map along with them.

"Where did you get this?" she asked.

They both pointed straight up without taking their eyes off the screen. Knowing the brothers as she did, she understood the gesture to mean outer space.

Janie concentrated on the dot almost exactly on the state border. It was just off the highway—so close that she wondered if anyone would notice it was not in fact on it. She glanced at the map, then at the brothers to gauge their reaction.

"I'm guessing radiation," said Xavier. "Probably some very specific type of radiation."

"Based on?" asked Charles.

"Based on the fact that the sensor we took out of Leon's plane is supersensitive to radiation. Also, that's Oak Ridge over there, right?" He pointed to the cluster of bright dots west of Knoxville.

"I think I have an atlas in the truck," Charles said, and started to get up.

"I keep one in the bookcase over there," Janie said.

Charles found it and turned to Tennessee.

"Yeah, that's Oak Ridge," he said. He looked back at the screen. "So what are all these dots along I-40 and I-26?"

"Do they transport that stuff on trucks?" Xavier asked.

"I think they're supposed to be limited to some low-level stuff, and they have all kinds of regulations about it," Charles said.

Working in the government, he picked up things from time to time. In this case, he vaguely remembered some DOE guys bitching about the paperwork needed to move their favorite isotopes from point A to point B.

But if Oak Ridge was point A, what was point B?

"If the stuff, whatever it is exactly, is starting out in Oak Ridge, where is it ending up?" asked Xavier.

"Or for that matter, how do we know it's starting out in Oak Ridge?" Charles said. "How do we know it's not starting out somewhere else and ending up in Oak Ridge?"

They fell silent for a while. Lazlo pressed himself into the space between Janie and Xavier on the couch and seemed to consider the matter as well.

"Port of Charleston?" Xavier asked.

No one answered, though it seemed a perfectly plausible suggestion.

At length, Charles said, "Savannah River. The Savannah River site is down that way, isn't it?"

They thought about that a minute.

"I thought they weren't processing at Savannah River anymore," said Charles.

"They're not supposed to be," said Janie with unexpected authority.

Both boys looked at her. Then they remembered that she was somewhat politically active and kept up with environmental stuff, especially certain issues close to home. They looked back at the screen.

"Jesus, that's a lot of dots," said Xavier.

They started counting. On the stretch of road covered by the map, they could see in excess of twenty dots. Twenty truckloads of material hot enough to be picked up by a satellite orbiting two-hundred miles above them.

"I wish we had another batch of data to get some idea of the time line—you know, to see the movement of the trucks," said Xavier.

"I wish we could get a wider image to see the other end of the route," said Charles.

"Can you?" asked Janie, almost afraid to hear the answer.

The boys looked at each other just before Xavier broke out in one of his famous laughs.

"I don't think that's happening real soon," he said.

Janie returned her attention to the screen.

"If all those other dots are trucks, and that's Oak Ridge over there, what's this?" she asked. She indicated a slightly larger but fuzzier point south of I-40 by a considerable distance.

They all looked.

"Where the hell is that?" Xavier asked.

They turned back to the atlas and estimated the distance south and slightly to the east of the intersection of the highway and the state line.

"That's nowhere," Janie said.

"That's not nowhere," said Charles. "That's in the Great Smoky Mountains National Park."

Charles and Xavier looked at each other, and Charles nodded to the unspoken question. Yes, that did look like the location that Leon had given him to check out some weeks ago. Only the first satellite he had plugged into had no sensitivity to this kind of radiation, only infrared.

Since they had come to such an impassable point, there was only one thing to do: eat some bagels. So the boys, together with Lazlo, went to the kitchen and got busy with the toaster.

Janie watched them go, then went to a small desk in the corner and retrieved a computer disk. She returned to Charles's computer, inserted the disk, and, as silently as possible, hit the keystrokes needed to copy the map onto the disk.

In the kitchen, the boys whispered.

"We need to let Leon know about this," said Xavier. "Did they leave yet?"

Charles pulled out his cell phone and punched in the number. He held the phone up so Xavier could listen, too. What they heard was Leon's recording saying he would be out of the office for about a week.

"On the trail again," said Xavier.

"I think that's where we need to be, too," Charles said.

Chapter 33

S hirley Dawn

SHIRLEY DAWN WAS THIN and ate a lot of candy. In fact, she ate a lot of everything, but she was still thin.

After several excursions into other majors, Shirley had decided to follow her bliss and go into journalism. She graduated in fairly short order from UNC-Asheville, having amassed a huge number of credits in subjects ranging from astronomy to art history to physical therapy.

She had many friends in diverse fields in Asheville, which was a real asset when investigating stories. She nearly always had someone she could call on for background. This also meant that she received plenty of input from friends for story ideas, some more helpful than others. Her circle included a disproportionate number of conspiracy theorists. One believed that Thomas Wolfe was a direct descendant of Jesus Christ. This friend frequently sent her xeroxed pages from history books, clippings from magazines, and pages from Wolfe's own writings, all of which, to the friend's way of thinking, supported his thesis.

She also knew a guy whose hobby was trying to start a local Bigfoot myth. He had begun with a crude set of boots with fake enlarged foot patterns for treads, then moved on to more sophisticated costumes. His problem was that he was more bigmouth than Bigfoot. Whenever he left tracks or staged an appearance or produced a video, he was so proud of his work that he couldn't contain himself. Not content with his friends as a circle of admirers, he also notified local officials and anyone else who would listen. He offered Shirley Dawn exclusive stories on his endeavors, apparently misunderstanding the implications of the word *exclusive*. Although she never published any of this crap, she did keep a folder on the guy, figuring he himself might make a good story someday, especially if he got into serious trouble.

On this particular day, her stack of mail was of moderate size. Seeing a manila envelope with the Bigfoot guy's return address, she tossed it aside on her desk for coffee-break material. Her stack also included several advertisements, a postcard from Mexico, and an oversized white envelope with her name handwritten on it in purple magic marker. The envelope bore no return address, no postage, nothing at all apart from her name, so presumably it had been hand-delivered. This got her attention enough to make her sit down, kick back with her coffee and some malt balls, and slip a letter opener under the flap.

A mysterious-looking map slid from the envelope. It depicted part of the southeastern United States, centering approximately on Asheville and also covering parts of South Carolina, Tennessee, and Georgia. It showed little detail, just some of the major roads and the state lines but no printed words or labels. A few features had been hand-labeled with a purple ballpoint pen. Asheville, I-26, and I-40 were identified.

The most curious aspect of the map was a set of yellow dots. The dots were spread along I-26 south and east of Asheville, then along I-40 westward into Tennessee, ending in a large cluster just west of Knoxville.

She checked the envelope again and found it not empty as yet. It still contained a note and a single caramel wrapped in clear plastic. The caramel she took to be a sign that whoever had sent the envelope knew her well enough to be aware of her candy addiction. The note consisted of one cryptic sentence: "Each dot on the map is a truck just like the one we made a casting of."

What am I supposed to make of that? she wondered. Though she was on the lookout for any information about the mystery casting, this did not seem like much of a clue.

Chapter 34

On the Trail Again

DESPITE ALL INTENTIONS, Leon and family did not achieve the early start they wanted. Getting up by six and on the road by seven would have put them on the trail by eight, even with a stop at the store to buy bottles of water and candy bars. This would have allowed them to reach a trail shelter easily by dark, even with a relaxed pace and some sightseeing. As it was, the time was well after nine when they pulled the truck off the road and hoisted their packs.

They had never seen so many cars there before. This was one of the busiest times of year on the trail, but the crowd was unusual even so. They also saw a sheriff's van with the K9 Division label on the side, which had to mean some kind of trouble.

Nearly an hour in, as they were taking a pause to drink and rest, they saw their first fellow hikers on the trail. These were two guys in their early twenties who looked to be thru-hikers, meaning that they intended to hike the entire length of the Appalachian Trail.

The hikers told Leon and Sue that they had seen the cops with dogs earlier that morning. They were supposedly looking for a lost hiker. Leon asked if they had seen other searchers, and they said no. This didn't sound like any other missing-person search Leon had ever heard of. Because of his familiarity with the trail, he was occasionally called in on search parties. In his experience, they tended to involve a cast of dozens at the least.

"How long ago did you guys leave Fontana Dam?" he asked.

Fontana Dam was a point south where hikers could get off the trail and provision. Most people took at least five days to hike that stretch. But these guys said they were into their fourth day and almost done.

"You must be hoofing it pretty good," Leon said with respect.

"It's a little spooky in there right now," said the one with the red bandanna. "I mean, with all the army guys and everything."

"You mean the Rangers?" asked Leon.

"I guess. Whatever. They don't say anything to you, like you're not really there."

After some more questioning, Leon learned that they had encountered the Rangers about a day out of Fontana Dam, and that the Rangers were headed north at the time. It was not unusual for hikers to come across them, or to have that kind of reaction. What was unusual, at least in Leon's experience, was to see the Rangers this far north on the trail.

Leon and family hiked on, gaining altitude for most of the morning. They stopped for lunch on a ridge top. From that point on, as they well knew, they would face a series of sawtooth climbs and descents, none awfully steep, at least by local standards, but nonetheless tiring in their relentlessness.

They stopped frequently to refill their water bottles from springs and pools in the small streams that crossed the trail. Audrey saw it as her job to work the pump that drew the water through a microfilter. Water was plentiful here, the sources well marked on trail maps. Any lengthy segments that were short on water were always a topic of discussion among experienced hikers. They would remind each other in the camps to fill up at certain points because it was going to be a long haul.

They had made good time in compensation for the late start, so they were in no hurry to hoist the packs again. Leon munched a few extra bites of trail mix during one such stop, occasionally flicking pieces of seed or cereal to the juncos, his favorite birds on the trail. They were such constant companions in this part of the woods that he thought of them as the mascots of hikers. Since they showed up at bird feeders around the houses in the nearby towns only in the winter months, most people considered them harbingers of snowfall.*

He tossed a piece of Chex cereal a few feet away, attracting three juncos at once. The first broke off a piece, the second scooped up the larger portion left on the ground, and the third sat for a moment trying to decide which of the first two to attack in hopes of forcing them to drop their treasure in defensive maneuvering. Just then, a large shadow passed over the ground, and they all scattered. Leon looked up, expecting to see a red-tailed hawk or some other bird of prey. Instead, he witnessed a small plane, a brother to the one they had found and taken to Xavier.

Audrey and Sue saw it, too. They jumped to their feet to watch it glide on, making almost no noise as it passed.

"Whoa!" they said together.

It seemed to be gaining altitude as it passed up the hill and out of sight behind the trees.

The little girl ran to Leon.

"Did you see that?" she whispered.

"Yeah, honey. I saw it, too."

"Do you think it's looking for the one we found?" she asked.

"I think it's looking for something," he said. He gathered the little girl into his lap and held her close. "But it's nothing to worry about. It doesn't have anything to do with us."

Audrey didn't seem exactly scared, but she didn't seem exactly convinced either.

---

* Accessing junco thought patterns through the use of Henrico Carr's technology would soon reveal how excited the birds became when snow fell. The males especially were conscious of their image. Nothing showed off their pearl-white underbellies and slate-gray backs like a backdrop of freshly fallen snow.

They pulled the packs on, headed out, and hiked without incident for most of the remainder of the afternoon. Every time they entered a clearing where the canopy of trees allowed them a view of the sky, they could not suppress the urge to scan for the plane, but it did not appear again.

Marked on the trail map was a symbol for a shelter at Pine Tree Gap. Leon and family found themselves there about seven o'clock on the first night of their excursion. The place was well known to them, as they had camped there several times before. The shelter was pretty basic. It was a small, three-sided building of logs cut from the forest nearby. The roof was made of sheet metal, which must have been a bitch to carry in there. The floor was pressure-treated two-by-sixes. On the open side, it extended a few feet out, forming a porch. Likewise, the roof extended out over the porch to give extra shelter from rain, at least if the wind wasn't blowing from the wrong direction. Inside the shelter was a shallow elevated loft that created additional sleeping area. The several pegs protruding from the walls provided convenient places to hang packs and dry clothes.

A few feet down the hill from the open front of the shelter was a well-used ring of fire stones. Around the fire area, several logs and sections of split tree trunks had been pulled up to form a seating area.

To the right of the shelter sat a crude but serviceable table made with a minimum of imported materials.

About two hundred yards to the left of the shelter was a privy. On this part of the trail, an outhouse was considered something of a luxury. At many shelters, campers had to pull out their spades and head into the woods.

As with all shelter sites, a good water source was located nearby. In this case, someone had made a small dam below a spring in the hillside and cemented a pipe through the dam, creating a constant flow of water into a second pool below—and providing a pleasant background sound, if campers were quiet enough to hear it.

Above the shelter was a small clearing. Many hikers chose to pitch their tents there rather than sleep in the shelter itself. Shelters were welcome refuges in the rain, but the floors made hard sleeping surfaces. Then, too, tents were protection against insects and provided a degree of privacy not found in the shelters.

They all felt the sense of relief and excitement that accompanied the end of a hard day's hike when they crested the final hill and saw the campsite and the short side trail that led to it. The absence of cooking smells suggested they were probably the initial ones there for the night.

Audrey ran ahead as usual and was the first to slip her pack off and lay it on the table outside the shelter.

Her next order of business, as with most hikers, was to jump up into the shelter and look for the logbook.

Each shelter had one of these books, usually just a spiral-bound notebook with ruled pages. Hikers customarily entered their stays into these logbooks, together with any information, observations, editorial comments, speculations, plans, theories, feelings, opinions, jokes, or anything else they might want to leave behind. It made good reading. For thru-hikers, it was a device for locating friends on the trail. Thru-hikers often met people they liked to hike with, but as people got on and off the trail at different times and for different durations, the logbooks were the best means of keeping track of these folks.

Thru-hikers also customarily adopted trail names, perhaps because hiking the Appalachian Trail seemed to have little to do with their lives in the real world. The choice of trail names was sometimes premeditated before setting off but more often was derived after some days or weeks of hiking.

The Colebrooks had never adopted separate trail names, perhaps because their time on the trail seemed a natural extension of the rest of their lives, rather than something apart. However, they were collectively known as "the Angel Band" because Audrey liked to draw a picture of an angel in the logbook whenever they stopped for the night.

Running her finger back over the list of entries, Audrey found that such worthies as Chuck Mouse, Freaky Deaky, Swan, Scrunchy, Deer Butt, and Miss Teenage America had been through over the last few days. The next name caused her to call out to her parents.

"Klondike was here!"

Klondike was huge, even to a little girl who was used to being around men of good size. The family saw Klondike so frequently on the trail that to Audrey it seemed he was a spirit of the woods, always present.

He was in fact a frequent hiker, a man of considerable and diverse skills and knowledge, and calling him a spirit of the woods was not far off base. This summer, he was mostly guiding groups on trips of anything from a day to a week. He was often subcontracted by camps and church groups and other organizations.

Leon had the good fortune to meet him when he first walked the Appalachian Trail. Leon had set out not really knowing what to expect or how far he would go. He encountered Klondike at one of the first shelters north of Springer Mountain, the southern end of the trail. At that time, Klondike was already on his fourth or fifth thru-hike, although the word *thru* was not quite accurate because Klondike never did seem to completely finish the trail end to end. That year, Leon's excursion turned into a complete six-month thru-hike. Meanwhile, Klondike got off the trail and hitchhiked into Boston, where he chose to remain and apprentice with a luthier, learning how to make and repair guitars and violins.

Hearing his daughter tell him that Klondike was in the woods added to Leon's sense of satisfaction as he released his pack and sank onto the bench at the table.

"That's great. Bring the book over here, honey, and let's have a look."

This she did with glee as her mother joined them.

They first leafed back through the pages to the last time they had been at the shelter, a few weeks ago. They easily spotted their entry thanks to the angel sketch provided by Audrey.

Leon and Sue remembered how excited they had been that day about finding the stone with the petroglyphs. They both had the same impulse to write something about it in the logbook. In a way, it seemed dishonest not to do so, like withholding important information from the brotherhood of the trail. In the end, they settled on an enigmatic quote from *Look Homeward, Angel*: "A stone, a leaf, an unfound door."

And then their own feelings: "A good day, a day to remember. Some of what was Lost"—a further private reference to Thomas Wolfe, since his original title for *Look Homeward, Angel* was "O Lost"—"has now been found."

And there as always was the sketch of an angel that Audrey used to mark her passage.

Following this, they skimmed the entries. Most were routine, such as one under June 23:

> Made almost 14 miles today. Tired and hot. Saw two black bears near Lock Creek. Now eating the last of the Snickers bars; damn it is good.
>
> Alfalfa

Snickers bars were indeed a favorite among hikers. Some other entries were as follows:

> June 24
> Randy, hope you're okay. I'll wait for you at the border house.
>
> Tree Girl

The "border house" was the hostel at the end of the Smokies.

> June 27
> Didn't sleep much last night. Mouse ran across my face. Going to be a long day.
> Farfel

The trail had basically two kinds of shelters: ones with a lot of mice and ones with a big snake living under them, which tended to keep the mouse population to a reasonable level.

Leon remembered one of the first trail survival lessons Klondike had taught him. This was to unzip all the pockets of his pack when he hung it up for the night. Although he already knew to put all his food in a bag and hoist it over a tree branch so as not to attract bears, this was a new and useful tip. Even with the food gone, the pack would retain enough scent to attract rodents. The idea was to leave the pockets open so mice could explore and get back out without gnawing holes in the fabric. This was pretty representative of the usefulness of going with the flow while on the trail, as opposed to fighting certain natural tendencies.

> June 28
> Watch out for big hornets' nest on southwest corner of
> tent area.
>
> Leapfrog

This was pretty typical of another kind of entry—one that simply passed useful information from one hiker to another.

The next entry caught Leon's eye:

> June 29
> Saw a bunch of Rangers at the campsite. They seemed to
> be looking for something. One of them was reading the log
> and taking pictures of some of the pages. They ran out when
> we came.
>
> Orion

Hikers were often spooked by Rangers, who appeared and disappeared in the forest like ghosts. This report, however, was unusual. Leon had never heard of Rangers having anything to do with the campsites. In fact, they had almost no interaction at all with hikers, which Leon had always supposed was part of their instructions.

Leon and Sue looked at each other, considering the implications of this information. They thought back to their conversation with the brothers and the speculation about whether or not they, too, were under scrutiny.

After that entry were more of the usual jottings of lonely and tired hikers as they slogged mostly south to north and approached the end of the strenuous but rewarding stretch from Fontana Dam to the Tennessee border at I-40. The only exceptions were two reported sightings of strange-looking planes flying low over the trail. Apparently, the hikers got only quick glimpses.

And then there it was, in a script surprisingly neat and ornate for someone so large, the entry from Klondike that Audrey had seen:

> July 2
> Leading a group of worthy pilgrims, five in number, into the wilderness. Left at 6:00 A.M., rolled in here at 7:00 P.M. Two fell asleep without their supper. One mending blisters on feet—not too bad. Much angst about the details of setting up tents. Destination: Jeter Mountain and back. A good group. I predict they will make it.
>
> > Klondike

Leon and Sue smiled at the note. Although short, it contained a wealth of information on and between the lines.

Obviously, it established the date he had passed through. The reference to "worthy pilgrims" let them know that he was leading a group of adults. He would have referred to children as "grasshoppers" or "hiklings." The number reference meant that he counted five heads but had not as yet seen a glimpse of personality from at least some of the group. That situation was likely to change before the trip was over. Klondike would make sure of it. The reference to the wilderness meant they had not engaged in this kind of thing before. The mention of blisters, tents, and collapsing in exhaustion conveyed the general condition of the crew. Nothing was unusual about any of those things. His prediction that they would make it was a form of personal declaration on Klondike's part. It meant that he foresaw a challenge but was determined to meet it. Declaring so was part of making it happen— perhaps, some would say, the most important part.

Leon and Sue fell asleep feeling much more secure and at peace knowing their old friend was nearby. As they drifted off, Audrey was still leafing through a book by the light of her Petzl.

Chapter 35

Lewis Carol

AS A SPECIAL REWARD, the Ranger trainees were allowed to build a campfire that night, not that any of them felt like sitting around toasting marshmallows and telling ghost stories. Hot food was an unbelievable comfort after several days with nothing but cold rations, or none at all.

They ate their meal almost in silence, not counting the snorting and slopping noises reminiscent of a crowded pig trough.

After that, they collapsed into sleeping bags—that is, all but the ones on sentry duty.

The captain was pleased with their performance and had not arranged any unpleasant surprises for them that evening. The trainees, of course, had no way of knowing this and were compelled to keep up their guard.

At that time of year, darkness fell around 9:00 P.M., so by 8:45 only dusty light remained. Ranger trainee Lewis Carol, a tough guy in spite of, or perhaps because of, his name, was lying on his back and unwinding from his surveillance exercise, watching the sky turn darker and darker, navy blue on its way to black. He saw a star or a planet, maybe Venus, centered in the sky. Other stars, more by the minute, came into view like guests showing up at a party.

His breathing began to slow and his eyes to blink, although he had resolved to remain conscious long enough to see the Milky Way appear. But then a dark silhouette as of a figure bending over him eclipsed his view, coming out of nowhere, moving with a silence and sureness that took his breath away.

Training kicked in. He rolled out from under the intruder. With one efficient and lightning-fast kick, he was out of the sleeping bag and onto his feet in a fighting crouch, simultaneously issuing a yell to alert the rest of the camp.

In an instant, three more trainees were on the scene, two behind the intruder and one behind Lewis.

This was the situation when the captain found them. In the light of the fire, he saw that his trainees had surrounded a little blond girl of perhaps five years.

Audrey was watching Lewis Carol to see what he would do, but her gaze shifted to the captain when she saw Lewis and the other trainees look his way. Everyone seemed to be waiting for the captain to decide what to do next.

"What's going on here, Private Carol?" he asked, still looking at Audrey. He was trying to read something in her expression that would give him a clue about what she was doing here and what was going on.

Before Lewis could answer, it occurred to the captain that the little girl might be some sort of decoy or diversion. "Sentries!" he shouted.

In turn, three voices answered out of the darkness.

He shouted a command that immediately brought four more trainees to his side.

"I want you men to circle out from here two hundred yards. Look for more intruders. Get the night vision equipment. Go and report back."

Then he said to Audrey, "Who is with you, little girl?"

"You mean here?" she said, looking around.

"Yes, who brought you here?" he asked.

"No one brought me here. I'm here with all of you," she said.

"Where are your mother and father?" he asked.

"Probably back at the shelter," she said.

"What's your name?" asked the captain.

"My name is Audrey Colebrook," she said. "What's yours?"

Some of the trainees turned away so as not to laugh or allow their discomfort in suppressing laughter to be seen either by the captain or his young guest.

"You don't need to worry about my name right now," he said. His instincts had thrown up all kinds of warning signals by now, so he was not inclined to give out any information.

"I'm not going to worry about your name. I just wondered what I should call you. Should I call you captain?"

He wondered for a moment if she somehow recognized the insignia and stripes on his arm, then realized she had probably just heard the others address him.

"Yes, captain will be fine," he said. "What are you doing out here in the woods at night, Miss Colebrook?"

Audrey seemed to like being called Miss Colebrook.

"I followed one of your soldier men here," she said.

She glanced at Private Carol, and one of the men muttered, "Nice work, Lewis."

"You followed one of my men here?" the captain asked. That was a good story. One of his masters of stealth detected and tracked by a five-year-old girl. "Tell me how you did that."

"We hiked all day, so we were tired, so we fell asleep real early. But I woke up because I felt someone looking at me, and I saw one of the soldier men looking at us, so I decided I would come and see why he was looking at us," she said.

That still did not explain how she had managed to find her way here. But before the captain could press the question, she spoke up again.

"Captain, I am very tired, and I want to go to sleep now."

The captain looked around quickly. He hated hesitation, especially in front of his men, but he was unsure what to do about the situation.

"Sergeant!" he shouted. The sergeant was the only other person in camp with a tent to himself. "You will install this young lady in your tent for the night. You will put your sleeping bag outside the tent flap and allow no one in or out. Understood?"

"Yes, sir," replied the sergeant, zero inflection in his voice.

At that point, the sentries returned with the news that they had seen no sign of anyone else, even using the night vision goggles. Audrey regarded the men in their buglike gear with a combination of curiosity and skepticism.

The sergeant gave her a quick wave, and she turned to follow him. She looked back at the captain and the men in night vision goggles. Then she said to Private Carol, "I really like your poems," and trundled off to bed as quietly as if she were going upstairs with Grandma.

The captain returned to his tent and got on the satellite phone. He figured that at this hour he would probably interrupt Ira Hudson at some Washington social affair, but he did not particularly care.

ooooo

The presence of the little girl in camp may well have had some influence on the quality of breakfast the next morning. She accepted the plate of scrambled eggs the sergeant handed her and ate with relish. When the recruits joined her by the fire, she did not seem in the least ill at ease about becoming the center of attention. After all, she was used to her uncles.

The captain watched this scene develop from inside his tent as he talked on the satellite phone to Hudson again.

"The thing is, we think they might be involved in the disappearance of the object you have been looking for," said the voice on the other end.

"A five-year-old girl?" said the captain. He had been pushing Hudson to let him get the child back to her parents ASAP, even arguing that this would give him an excuse to question them. So far, the Rangers had learned little by observing from a distance.

"I mean the parents," Hudson whispered with exasperation.

"Look, I've got a squad of men here who are starting to make her into the company mascot. We know exactly where the parents are, or at least where they were last night. How am I supposed to explain why we're not returning her?"

"Send someone to keep an eye on the parents. Tell the men you are keeping the little girl until you know that the parents are okay. After all, what kind of parents let a little girl wander off into the woods? And have another try at asking her questions. You've been trained in interrogation, for Christ's sake."

The click on the other end informed the captain that this was the last of the conversation.

He looked again at the little breakfast club that had formed and saw the men cracking up over something the little girl had said.

"Sergeant!" he said in his command voice.

The sergeant came double-time. The men around the fire took this also as a call back to reality for them. They began to get up and deal with plates and utensils.

"Sergeant, I want ten men in full camouflage to move to the intruder campsite to set up surveillance. I want the rest in gear and ready to deploy to another site. Before you do that, though, bring our guest up here so I can have a talk with her."

The sergeant acknowledged the orders and moved to execute them without further discussion.

He bent and whispered in Audrey's ear, and she looked over at the captain. She handed the sergeant her plate and cup and stood to walk in her deliberate way to the designated spot.

The captain was formulating the first question of his interrogation, but the little girl spoke first.

"The men like you," Audrey said. "I heard them talking outside the tent."

"Really? What did they say?" he asked in spite of himself.

"One of them said that under your gruff exterior beats the heart of a real asshole," she said in her matter-of-fact voice. Then, seeing the captain recoil, she added, "But it was the way he said it that told me he really likes you."

"Listen," the captain said, attempting to regain control of the conversation, "I want to ask you some questions."

"Okay," said Audrey.

"I want to know why you came here."

"You mean, why did we come into the forest?" Audrey asked.

Actually, the captain had intended to get around to that question a little more subtly later in the questioning. However, since they were already there, he decided he might as well see what she had to say on the subject.

"Okay, let's start there," he said. "Why did you and your parents come into the forest?"

"We come here a lot," she said. "We do all kinds of things. We walk, and we look at birds and animals. We cook our dinners. We explore and take pictures of things, and my father writes down a lot of notes on things, and my mom and I draw pictures."

"What kinds of things do you take pictures of?" he asked.

They were now getting into an area that made Audrey uncomfortable. Her mother and father had told her not to talk to anyone about the petroglyphs. They had explained that if people found out about the pictures before their meaning was explored, they might lose the chance to understand what the people who left them there wanted to say.

"My parents told me not to talk about it," she said.

"Did your parents come out here looking for something on this trip?" he asked.

"They're always looking for something," the little girl said. "My grandpa Philip says everyone is looking for something."

"What were they looking for this time?" he asked.

"It's a secret," she said. "I'm not supposed to tell anyone about it."

The captain held up a finger as a signal to wait for him. He went inside his tent and emerged a second later with a small pack. Reaching into a side pocket, he brought out a couple of pieces of caramel wrapped in clear acetate paper. They were a particular weakness of his.

He held one out to Audrey. She accepted it, unwrapped the end, and took a small bite.

"This is almost as good as the caramel my grandma makes," she said. "She has a candy store. Ice cream, too."

"Sounds like your grandma is someone I'd like to meet," the captain said.

Then he removed an envelope from the pack. He opened the clasp, took out a number of pictures, fanned them out, and selected one showing a drone in flight.

"Have you ever seen one of these?" he asked.

"Sure," she said. "One was flying around here yesterday."

If he was looking for any sign of nervousness or tension, he was disappointed. The little girl, if anything, seemed relieved. He paused to study her face. Often, people will elaborate to fill the silence, but it didn't seem that this was going to work, so he decided to shift.

"Tell me about your uncles," he said.

"You know Uncle Charles and Uncle Xavier?" she asked, greatly cheered.

"Yeah, well, let's just say I've heard of your uncles," he said. "Have you seen them out here?"

"No, they're not out here with us," she said, a little sad.

"Do you know where they are now?"

"They're checking some stuff out," she said.

"What stuff?" he said.

"I think they're like me," she said. "They want to know why people are following them around."

The captain was formulating his next question when the satellite phone buzzed.

"You can go back and finish your breakfast now," he said to Audrey.

Chapter 36

 obile Detector

THE GUYS IN THE STAKEOUT CAR were under orders to record the comings and goings at the Colebrook house, no matter how mundane, and to call in if anything of importance happened. If they spotted the missing boys, they were to follow them when they left. The broad assumption was that Charles and Xavier were off somewhere conspiring with the terrorists who stole the truck.

Noting a vehicle moving toward the house, the agent on duty checked it out through binoculars. A plumber's van pulled up the gravel drive and stopped in front of the workshop/studio. The driver's door popped open, and a man in coveralls and a dirty ball cap emerged, clipboard in hand. He looked at the house, then the workshop. He decided to go to the workshop, perhaps because he saw or heard the old man working inside.

Seeing nothing suspicious, the agent logged the arrival and settled back.

At the plumber's van, the passenger's door popped open and another man emerged, dressed in a matching set of coveralls and an even more wretched-looking ball cap. He opened a sliding side door, pulled out a toolbox, and followed his fellow plumber into the shop.

Pipo was holding the first man in a long embrace and patting him on the back.

"We owe you one, Pipo," the second plumber said.

Pipo looked up and smiled at his youngest grandson.

The boys had of course heard about Pipo's arrest and subsequent release. Even though hanging around outside an observatory in the middle of the night with a flintlock rifle seemed suspicious as hell, the authorities had a hard time defining exactly what statute the old man had breached. Also, the FBI was not too interested in explaining what a squad of Rangers was doing there, so the matter was reluctantly dropped.

Xavier had come up with the idea of borrowing an old friend's plumbing van as a cover for moving about town incognito. The friend had thrown in the coveralls and caps to complete the subterfuge. Turns out, nobody paid much attention to repairmen in coveralls, especially with ball caps pulled over their eyes.

Before Xavier could say anything else, Pipo put a finger to his lips and pointed out the window. The boys understood. Someone could be listening. Best to keep the conversation on a professional level.

Xavier wasted no more time. He set the toolbox down by a workbench at the far end of the room. From it, he removed the small component he and Leon had extracted from the drone during their autopsy in the robotics lab. He also withdrew a plastic bag that held a couple of batteries and a few other odds and ends.

Meanwhile, Charles rummaged through a set of drawers in another bench, selecting various pieces of junk and moving on. It was almost as if he had never moved away. At one point, he came across a soldering iron and held it up for Xavier to see.

"Might as well plug that baby in. We're going to need it," Xavier said.

Pipo smiled, too, at the old iron he had used to teach the boys the fine art of soldering. That and a lot of other lessons had taken them a long way.

The boys could not help growing nostalgic in the shop that had been so much a part of their childhoods. The walls were almost entirely lined with shelves and workbenches that held chaos, but not chaos. The first bench they encountered upon entering was used for woodworking now. It had been the original, all-purpose workbench that Pipo moved from his previous residence. He had told the boys it was old even when he acquired it in a trade for installing a pump in a fishpond at a house in town. Like many other functional items of that generation, it was made from the wood of the American chestnut, one of the most plentiful sources of material in the southern Appalachians until it was wiped out by blight. The top of the bench was formed of two wide planks with a thousand nicks, stains, holes, and marks of every description. At one end was a heavy steel vise with a long handle. The top of the vise had a flat tail that could be used as a light anvil. The projects this old guy had seen!

Here and there, the Colebrooks had pinned up some of the drawings used for various projects over the years. One was a sketch of a model of the Wright brothers' first airplane. They had made the model for their mother as part of a display in the window of the fudge and ice-cream shop. Another drawing depicted the moose that was the mascot of the shop—a chocolate moose, of course. It showed a ghostly outline of the creature with a skeleton of wood framing underneath, complete with dimensional notations. This had been in preparation for making a fiberglass figure used (and abused) in several ways at the business.

The boys were pleased to see that several sketches of their science fair projects from school also remained. One actual project had been too good to throw away. This was a sort of humanoid form of foam rubber. Charles had made it at the age of twelve. Xavier, eight at the time, had served as the model by lying down on a large slab of polyurethane foam cushion material while Charles traced his outline with magic marker. Charles had subsequently cut the foam with an electric carving knife. He inserted electrical wires and colored lights to demonstrate a simplified version of the circulatory system.

"Immortalized in foam," said Charles to Xavier.

Xavier looked up at the foam boy suspended from the ceiling and gave an abbreviated form of his laugh.

Pipo had come over by Xavier and was looking over his shoulder at the device from the drone, which Xavier had laid on a cleaner, more modern workbench. This was the bench they used for fine work like electronics. He pointed at the gadget by way of asking Xavier what it was.

Xavier whispered to tell him what he and Leon had observed at the university lab.

"So, since everyone seems to be looking for something that gives off this type of radiation, Charles and I decided that maybe we should, too. We came over here to try to put together some kind of mobile sensor so we might be able to do some scouting."

Pipo nodded in approval.

"What are you working on, Pipo?" Charles asked.

They walked to the rear of the shop, which Pipo had converted to a painting studio. A heavy easel was set up. Charles noticed that Pipo had also built a smaller version for Audrey to use when she visited. A bench with shallow drawers held paint, brushes, and various tools. On top of this was a large unglazed earthenware jar that held a bouquet of brushes and spatulas. The floor looked like a Jackson Pollock painting.

On the easel was a canvas of about two by one and a quarter feet. *The magic dimensions*, Charles thought.

The piece of work was in a formative stage. Pipo had started developing some background shading—dark at the bottom, lighter at the top. In the foreground were two figures sketched in faint lines with charcoal or pencil. They appeared to be two men in business suits and hats, but the outlines were rudimentary, so it was not possible to say who they would be or what they would be doing. They appeared to be standing in front of a car, but it was impossible to make out the type. Only the lines of the top and the windshield were visible so far.

"Blues Brothers?" Charles said, although he knew better than to ask Pipo about a work before he was ready.

The old man smiled the smile of the unknowable.

There came to Charles's mind something he had once heard in reference to his grandfather. It was from one man speaking to another in a barbershop when his grandfather walked by.

"He is in this world but not of this world," the man had said. Charles did not know exactly what the man intended to communicate by this description, but it stuck with him and came drifting to the surface occasionally in times such as these. *In this world but not of this world*. He thought maybe it came from the Bible.

"Do you think we need a variable power source for it?" Xavier asked.

His brother's voice brought Charles out of his reverie and back to the business at hand.

"No, I don't think so. You guys were using nine volts DC, right?" Charles said, and joined him at the bench.

Xavier located a small digital indicator they could use to monitor the output of the sensor. This Charles proceeded to mount to an aluminum panel while Xavier worked on the rest of the circuitry, soldering resisters and diodes on a piece of breadboard. They decided to mount everything in an old lunchbox and thereby make a portable and robust unit they could carry without drawing too much attention to themselves. Pipo nodded, approving their choice.

As an afterthought, they added a small speaker with the innards of a transistor radio as an amplifier, so the device could give off an audible signal if they chose.

They cast about for some way to test the unit.

"Pipo, do you have a watch with a luminous dial?" Xavier asked, remembering the experience in the university lab.

Pipo shook his head, and they all looked slowly around the premises. Scanning a room for a source of radioactivity might in most cases be an extremely foolish thing to do, but this was no ordinary room. This was the workshop. The den. The cave. The womb of remarkable things.

After a moment, Pipo raised his finger and proceeded to the

painting corner. Rummaging in one of the lower drawers, he at last withdrew a glass jar containing a bright yellow substance.

"Ah, yes," said Charles.

Pipo removed the lid and held the jar up to the sensor. The speaker and the digital display both jumped to life.

Xavier was delighted but confused.

"What the hell?"

"Uranium oxide. I remember hearing the old painters used uranium oxide as a source of yellow in their paint. Leave it to Pipo to go authentic on us," said Charles.

Pipo shrugged as if to say, *It's nothing*.

"You know, that could be it," said Xavier. "That could be the source of the radiation at Leon's site. Remember how Sue said some of the rockfaces near the one with writing looked like they had a plaster coating? When she tried to wash the dirt off, the plaster looked yellow. If that was uranium oxide, it could explain the radiation source out there."

"I guess," said Charles. "But it seems like that would take a hell of a lot of uranium." It also made him think they had no idea how big the site really was.

Xavier flipped the lunchbox/radiation detector closed and brushed the dust off the side. It was flat black with a few dents and scratches. By the method of decoupage, several magazine photographs had been lacquered onto the side: a robot, a spaceship, and a golden retriever with a lunchbox in its mouth.

They were set to go.

"We must away, Pipo," Charles said, hugging the old man again. "Thanks again for the rescue."

Xavier came over and gave him a bear hug, too.

"By the way, did they give you back your flintlock?" Xavier asked.

Pipo shook his head, then shrugged. He walked over to the bench, pulled a crossbow from the bottom shelf, and grinned.

"Can't keep a good man down," said Xavier, laughing.

The boys gave a quick look around, then headed for the van, throwing the tools in the back. They turned around and headed out of the driveway.

Back at the stakeout, the agent sat up when he saw the plumbers leaving. He noted the time in the log, then watched the van accelerate away.

Concurrent with this, he caught sight of a Mini headed toward the house.

That would be Mrs. Colebrook returning home, thought the agent. He put the glasses on the car. He saw that it was indeed Lilly Colebrook, who appeared to be alone in the vehicle. However, an odd movement attracted his attention as she passed the van, both veering slightly off onto the grass because of the narrowness of the drive. Mrs. Colebrook seemed to see something unusual in the van and nearly turned around in her seat trying to look into the window as it passed.

He moved the glasses to the passenger side of the van, where the plumber's helper slumped in the seat and pulled his cap down even farther over his eyes. Just one subtle moment, and then it was gone.

Chapter 37

S cramble

THE NEXT MORNING, Sue woke up and instinctively reached for Audrey. She slowly pushed herself up to look around. The level of light told her she had slept longer than she intended. Audrey tended to be an early riser, so Sue was not surprised to learn she was already up.

She expected to find Audrey out at the picnic table working on her scroll or throwing breadcrumbs to the birds. However, the table was empty.

She glanced up the path leading to the latrine.

She looked to the shelter and saw that Audrey's pack was not hanging beside their own larger bags. This sent a shiver down her spine, and she called out for Leon.

A quick inventory of the site confirmed that girl and backpack were gone.

No one else was in camp. They looked at each other, suddenly feeling helpless and alone in the vastness of the Smokies. Evoked into full flesh was the primal fear—the image of their child lost in a great wilderness.

Following a few more panicked moments, a dozen search plans rushed through their heads. As much as they hated to separate, it was clear that one of them needed to stay at the camp. After all, one of the most likely scenarios was that Audrey would return on her own.

In the end, they decided that Leon would actively search and Sue would abide in camp. Should either of them meet other hikers, they would immediately enlist the newcomers in the search.

Leon felt it was most likely that Audrey would stick to the trail or close to it. She had been coached on this often enough. As to direction, he chose forward, deeper into the wilderness, rather than back the way they had come. Audrey had seemed even more eager than they themselves to return to the place of their discovery.

Sue helped him get a water bottle and other essentials. He would leave his pack and travel light. They embraced for a moment but avoided each other's eyes as they parted. They could not allow themselves to entertain the worst of thoughts, even for a moment.

Then Leon was gone, disappearing down the trail. Sue doubled over with the worst feeling of emptiness she had ever experienced in her life.

ooooo

The first thing Klondike asked when he saw Leon was, "What's wrong?"

By way of answer, Leon gave him a long bear hug.

"Audrey's missing," he said upon releasing his friend.

"You mean here, in the woods?" Klondike asked.

Leon filled him in on the situation quickly and efficiently, leaving out the reason they had returned to the trail. Neither did he get into any of the strange stuff at home with his brothers. They would have plenty of time for that later.

Klondike's pilgrims began to emerge into the clearing from the tree tunnel of the trail. Klondike looked at them for a moment, switching into an organizational mode of thinking.

First out was a young Japanese couple.

"Izooke," he said, addressing them with a trail name either he or they had made up. "This is my friend Leon. We need to help him out with a problem."

These were the fittest of his pilgrims. Much to Klondike's previous consternation, they had brought a cell phone. (For no particular practical reason, seasoned hikers looked down on the practice of carrying cell phones. Possibly, they felt phones did not contribute to the otherworldliness of the trail experience. It should be noted, however, that this feeling did not run so deep as to prevent them from borrowing phones from time to time.) He explained about Audrey, gave them a description, and wrote down some notes to describe the location of the shelter that would form the nexus of their operation. He lightened their packs of all but essentials and instructed them to hike with all speed to the place where they had entered the forest, trying for a cell phone signal from time to time as they went. Leon and Klondike thought it unlikely the couple would find a signal anytime soon. In fact, Leon recalled that even at that point on the highway, phones would blink out. They figured the best chance would be one of the ridge tops near the entrance. If the Japanese couple came across the little girl, they were to take her directly to the shelter. If she was injured, one would stay with her and the other would return to the shelter or the trail exit, whichever was closer.

The couple took off almost at a run.

About that time, the other three pilgrims—a middle-aged couple and a bored-looking teenage daughter—came straggling into the clearing. They seemed the very picture of a dysfunctional family attempting to bond in the forest. This was not an entirely unique endeavor, and one that actually worked, at least to some degree, from time to time. As they approached, Klondike and Leon appraised their gaits and the general way they carried themselves. They saw no signs of serious problems that would impede their progress—no limping or uneven strides that suggested bad blisters or pulled muscles or stress fractures, no unnatural tilts of the shoulders to suggest bad backs. They looked at each other with an unspoken thought: *Good. These three are not going to be a liability.*

Klondike let them drop their packs and relax for a moment, during which he introduced Leon and explained about the missing girl. The mother turned white, easily able to dial back the clock a few years and remember how she would have felt in that situation.

"We're going to need your help," said Klondike.

The family looked intent. The daughter seemed to like being included with the adults.

They would all head to the campsite, which had been their destination in any case. Leon and Klondike would go at a faster pace while the others followed in their own good time. Leon and Klondike might split up and make some side excursions along the way, if they saw anything worth exploring off the trail.

Without further hesitation, the two experienced hikers headed out. Leon glanced over his shoulder a few moments later to confirm they were out of earshot of the others. Klondike was a few paces ahead.

"Have you noticed anything unusual out here?" Leon said.

Klondike glanced back with his wry smile and thought for a moment before answering, another habit hikers were likely to pick up on the trail.

"Let's see," he said in a tone that implied a list was about to ensue. "Could my friend be talking about Rangers farther north than usual? Could he be referring to strange objects flying overhead? Could he be talking about a bunch of black sedans at the trailhead? Everyone seems to be looking for something out here. Including you and me. As of a couple of nights ago, I would have said that you and the rest of the Angel Band were the only ones to find what you were looking for—that is, based on the journal entry. How did that go? 'A stone, a leaf, an unfound door'? By the way, I figured out that was from *Look Homeward, Angel*. But I still don't know what you were talking about. And now you've lost your angel. But I'm sure she'll turn up."

Leon let this sink in. He knew Klondike was the one person outside the family he could tell about the petroglyphs, but he wondered if it should be a story for another time. And yet his friend clearly felt he was holding something back. In fact, Klondike had kicked the door open for him to talk about the site.

They came quickly to a side trail. It was not the one where the Angel Band had made its discovery, but the intersection looked similar. Thinking that Audrey might have taken this by mistake, Leon suggested they split up. Leon would proceed back up the main trail while Klondike and company explored the side trail for a distance.

Chapter 38
Buckwheat Pancakes

THE CLOCK OF THE SEASONS does not always tick smoothly and evenly. Thus, in the heat of summer, in the first days of August, there may come a day and night so chilly and damp that they must be messengers sent ahead by autumn so that the turning of the leaves won't be such a complete surprise.

That Monday was such a day.

Xavier and Charles were in complete agreement on the subject of sweatshirts: No sweatshirt could beat a hooded sweatshirt. And then the corollary to the rule: No hooded sweatshirt could beat a maroon hooded sweatshirt with orange letters, the colors of their university.

Xavier associated the coolness of the morning with buckwheat pancakes and proceeded to bring that idea into reality.

Charles, in hooded sweatshirt and jeans, walked out to the barn/gymnasium with two cups of coffee.

Coolness or no coolness, Janie had worked up a sweat. She accepted the cup with pleasure and gave him a hug. They walked back to the house together. The aroma upon entering the kitchen was unbelievable.

"I'll be right back," she said, and headed up to her room.

They heard the sound of the shower.

On the table beside the armchair in the living room were two oval cameo portraits mounted in an antique walnut frame hinged in the middle so it could be partly opened and form a self-supporting structure. Charles picked up the pictures for a closer look. The major axis of the ellipse of each portrait was about eight inches high, the minor axis about five inches. The images were of a man and woman in middle age. The colors were deep brown and off-white. The poses were three-fourths on frontal. The dress and hairstyles suggested the Elizabethan period or thereabout. Both figures wore heavily starched and ruffled collars. The man had on a round cap that matched the cloak draped over his shoulders. The woman's hair was brushed back from her face and held in place by a jeweled comb. The paint under the yellowed varnish was cracked, suggesting great age, but Charles knew the portraits to be less than ten or fifteen years old. These were paintings of Janie's parents by his grandfather.

"I think he did those as a present for their twenty-fifth wedding anniversary," Janie said. She walked in wrapped in a short robe, drying her hair with a towel. "It's by far my favorite picture of them. Way better than all the photographs from birthday parties and holidays."

"How long after this did they break up?" Charles asked.

He realized after he said this that he might be treading on thin emotional ice, but Janie did not seem to mind.

"I don't know, maybe two or three years," she said.

Charles noticed that the figures were posed to face slightly away from each other. He had seen similar pairs of portraits by his grandfather in which the couples faced inward. He wondered if this was a random choice or if his grandfather was trying to say something, like maybe that the couple were heading in different directions. With his grandfather, he never knew for sure.

"Listen, I really want to thank you for putting up with Xavier and me staying here," he said.

She came over and gave him a hug.

"We're going to hit the trail for a while, so we'll pack our stuff and get out of your way."

"How long do you think you'll be gone?" she asked.

"We're planning for a few days, but it could be longer if things don't go well," he said. "And listen, if anyone comes and asks questions about us being here—I mean, the police or anyone like that—just tell them the truth. Your old friends came and visited for a while, and we had a good time, and then we left. You don't have to get involved with all this other stuff we've been looking into."

"Okay," she said, knowing that would be the easiest way to end the conversation. "What's Xavier making?" she asked. The smell from the kitchen was becoming hard to ignore.

"Buckwheat pancakes," Charles said. He had expected more resistance from her on the subject he so delicately broached.

"Dang," she said. "Now, that one I should keep around for a while."

They joined Xavier in the kitchen. Charles accepted a plate and took it to the table. Janie slipped her arm around Xavier's waist, whispered something in his ear, and then bit it. His head went back, and he let out one of his laughs.

ooooo

Charles was driving when they turned off the highway and followed a narrow road that led to a bridge over the river. When they reached the other side, the road was considerably rougher, though the bumps did not wake Xavier, who had fallen asleep in the passenger seat.

What woke him was a loud beep from their detector device as they rounded the bend and passed the power station. By the time he came awake enough to find the box, they were around the curve and the device had settled down again.

He looked back over his shoulder. "Must be interference from those power lines," he speculated.

"Either that or this road knocked something loose," Charles said. A couple minutes later, they parked and headed up the trail.

Charles and Xavier had not walked a mile before the old feelings took over. The sights and smells of the woods filled their senses. Then, too, the rhythm of walking had a power of its own. Leon had a theory that the walking rhythm was an important part of what some people called "the hiker's high." According to this thinking, the rhythm of walking long distances had the same effect as chanting syllables or words over and over. It was a doorway to entering a meditative state of mind. It could take you to the middle of the air.

The two had packed lightly even by their standards and made good time. At rest stops, Xavier checked the instrument they had fabricated from the sensor found on the plane. The readings were inconsistent, which they attributed to the terrain. This sensor was supposed to be flying over the mountains, not trying to look through them.

In the early afternoon, they met the Japanese couple hiking out as they were hiking in. All four put down their packs.

The man asked, "Have you seen a little girl on your walk so far?"

"We haven't seen anyone since we've been on the trail," Charles answered. "Is someone lost?" He assumed the man meant the couple's own daughter.

The man and woman began to explain the situation. Within the first few words, the boys realized exactly who they were talking about. From the couple, they got the best information they could manage about the location and distance, then looked at the map to figure out the correct shelter. Then they had nothing to do but keep walking.

Chapter 39

S oldier's Angel

AMID ALL THE COMMOTION of the morning preparations, Audrey located her pack and set up for some work on her scroll. She borrowed a clipboard from the sergeant and placed it on the flat part of a large rock near the firepit. This provided a reasonably steady desk and was about the right height if she knelt beside it.

She pulled her backpack beside her and untied the leather cord that held the top flap in place. She could tell that the soldiers had been in there because it was tied with a different knot and pulled tighter than she would have done herself. Flipping open the flap with the back of her hand, she was relieved to see the scroll had been returned to its proper place in a special pocket that seemed to have been designed specifically for this object. That was in fact exactly the case. The design and construction of her special backpack had been a joint effort between Pipo and her uncle Charles, accomplished during Charles's extended visit home last Thanksgiving. At that time, Audrey had been well into her angel scroll project, precisely the kind of activity that Pipo, Charles, and the rest of the family were prone to support.

The pack also contained several other pockets and devices, including a secret hiding place and a pleated elastic band for holding pencils and pens.

Audrey first pulled out a sepia-colored pencil about half its original length. She held this up to carefully examine the condition of the tip. The gesture itself and her facial expression would have reminded any of the family of her grandfather. She then pulled out a thin block of wood with a piece of sandpaper attached to form something like an emery board. This she used to shape the pencil tip to her satisfaction.

Then she carefully removed the scroll from its place in the pack. As was her custom, she took a few moments to review some of the previous drawings before starting on a new one. A few days ago, she had completed a drawing of an angel kneeling beside a pool of water. She was especially pleased with the rendering of a faint reflection of the angel on the surface of the water.

Seeming to arrive at some conclusion, she reached into the pack for the tarot card she used to form the frame for each new drawing. Sometimes, she sketched on scrap paper before committing a drawing to the scroll. This time, she seemed sure enough to proceed.

The drawing began with a few faint lines, almost invisible. She looked up from time to time at one of the trainees, who had collapsed in a half-sitting position against a tree, no doubt taking advantage of the few minutes when nothing was demanded of him that day.

Near his tent, the captain drank coffee from a tin cup and watched the purposeful little girl working away with a diligence beyond her years. He had exchanged several calls with Ira Hudson in Washington, all most unsatisfactory. The day was getting on toward noon, and the captain was growing restless. He didn't like what was going on here. He surveyed the camp as the men came and went on their various tasks. They didn't like it either. He could feel it, although of course none of them would say anything to him or even be caught looking his way. He thought about calling Washington and telling Hudson to forget it. He was already in this deeper than he wanted to be.

He threw out the last third of the coffee and strode over to where the little artist was working.

For this frame of the scroll, Audrey had drawn a soldier with a helmet. He seemed to be walking in a slightly crouched and alert position. His head was turned slightly to the left, as if he were responding to some sound he heard. Hovering above and slightly behind the man was an angel with wings unfolded and palms extended in a protective gesture over him.

The picture was still in its formative stages—just an outline, really—but the intent and the theme were clear enough.

This simple drawing struck the captain to his core. He felt a rush of emotion and a sudden tearing up in his eyes that he had not experienced in years. The story the guys in Washington had tried to build up in his mind about the little girl or her parents being terrorists evaporated like the summer mist. He felt in his deepest gut that no way was this group of people a threat to anyone, at least not in the way Washington had managed to fabricate.

"Sergeant!" he called.

The sergeant materialized in seconds in a scuffing of boots.

"Assemble the men and radio the outposts. We're taking this little girl back where she belongs," he said without looking up.

"Yes, sir!" the sergeant shouted, then moved out with a grin.

The captain bent down near Audrey.

"You feel like going for a walk this morning?" he said.

"Sure," she said. "We walk every day."

"Do you want to finish your drawing first?" he asked.

"No, it will take a long time to finish it the way I want it," she said.

He got the impression she felt she had been sitting still long enough.

The sergeant helped her pack her things while at the same time yelling orders to his men. For once, they actually seemed relieved to move into action.

Chapter 40

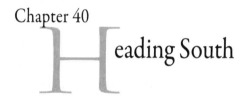 eading South

"I THINK WE SHOULD HEAD SOUTH," said Hudson's aide.

"I think the whole fucking thing is heading south," said Hudson.

Heading south, unraveling, falling apart, wheels coming off—pick a cliché. Since the truck disappeared, Hudson and company had not enjoyed a good day or night, their lives more cigarettes than sleep.

"I can't believe those Rangers are taking that girl back," said the aide.

Hudson just shook his head.

"Why don't you order them to arrest the parents when they bring her back?" the aide suggested.

Hudson did not look up.

"I know. Have them turn the little girl over to the mother, tell them they found her wandering in the woods, and arrest the father for child neglect," the aide said.

Hudson looked at him as if seeing him for the first time as the exceedingly odd and repugnant creature he was.

"In the first place, the Rangers don't arrest people. They don't charge people with crimes, certainly not civil stuff like child neglect," Hudson said. "In the second place, I don't order the Rangers to do anything. I asked the captain to do me a favor, and it sounds like he is way past doing any more favors now."

Still, the aide's idea was not without merit. Hudson liked the idea of locking the father up until they figured out what was going on with him and his freaking family. A precedent had been established in cases of terrorism. The term was *enemy combatant*, a person who could be locked up indefinitely.

They paused to stew over the latest developments. Then the phone rang with another one.

Hudson's aide listened and asked only short questions:

"What?"

"Who?"

"How long ago?"

He concluded the conversation by saying, "You just sent it?" Then he turned to Hudson. "The truck's back," he said. "They're sending an e-mail with the news story right now."

The aide pulled out his laptop and clicked away. When he found the e-mail attachment, he pulled up the picture and story. The photo showed the truck sitting in the parking lot of an Asheville establishment that showed movies and served pizza and beer. He filled Hudson in on the basic facts as he read, though Hudson seemed not to be listening.

The reporter, Shirley Dawn, had received an anonymous tip and proceeded to the parking lot with a photographer. The photo showed a side view of the truck. The marquee visible over the hood displayed the name of last night's movie, *Dr. Strangelove*.

Shortly after her arrival, a massive wrecker had removed the truck to places unknown. Shirley and the photographer were detained and questioned by two men who identified themselves as federal employees, which prevented the intrepid reporter from following the truck to find out its destination.

The published story offered little more except for Shirley Dawn's note that the truck was a perfect match for the casting that had materialized in Pack Square a few weeks earlier.

"I guess we'll hear from our guys if anything is missing," said the aide.

"I'm guessing not," said Hudson, still distracted. "But I guess this will keep our so-called FBI guys busy for a while."

"What about the FBI?" the aide said. He was back now to his original line of thinking. "They can arrest people, and we have a couple of guys on the ground pretty close to this place."

Now, that was something Hudson could not dismiss. He thought for a moment.

"That's not a bad idea," he said. "And neither was your first one."

The aide struggled to remember exactly what the first idea had been.

"Going south," Hudson filled in.

Hudson had reached a tipping point in feeling sorry for himself and disgusted with the people who kept screwing up his plans. Time to go on the warpath. Time to take things into his own hands. If you want something done right, do it yourself. Pick a cliché.

Chapter 41
Not That Complicated

THE TROOP OF RANGER TRAINEES set out that morning in a tighter formation than usual. The arrival of the little girl in their camp had at first provided a welcome relief from their training and exercises. Anything that gave them a chance to pause and catch their breath felt good at that point. But it had quickly begun to feel wrong. What was she still doing there, and why had they not immediately tried to find out where she belonged and returned her? Now they were doing so, and it felt good.

No matter how much a hiker thinks he's listening and paying attention, he is almost always surprised to meet another person. The hiker goes around a twist in the trail, and there the other person is, looking equally surprised. Such was the case when Klondike encountered the first of the advance guard.

He found it unusual that the trainees stopped and took notice of him, a mere hiker. He was about to explain his mission and try to enroll them in his search for his friend's child when the body of the troop caught up with the scouts. And there, peeking out from behind the sergeant, was the best sight he had seen all day.

Before any of them could react, Audrey sprinted for Klondike, who reached down and scooped her up in his arms.

"We've been looking for you, Miss Angel," he said as she hugged his neck. He let that soak in for a while, then looked at the military men in front of him. "I see you've found some new friends," he said.

"These are soldiers," she said by way of explanation.

Something about the way the little girl said the word evoked a feeling of pride in the men. The captain was watching this exchange from a little ways back in the column with arms crossed. Not far below the surface at all times during the training maneuvers was a basic question: Were the men behaving in an effective military manner? For a time, he had been unable to make sense of the present situation. But now he knew they were doing the right thing.

Klondike scanned the men until he came to the captain. Before he could conceal it, a look of recognition crossed his face. The captain looked back straight into his eyes with his best poker face but then broke into a wide grin.

The two men walked toward each other and exchanged a strong handshake. They had met some years ago when Klondike treated one of the captain's Rangers for snakebite. Klondike was one of the few hikers to break though the barrier that separated the two groups that uneasily coexisted on the trails in the southern Appalachians.

"It seems like you have lots of friends here in the woods," the captain said to Audrey.

"My uncle says that Klondike is the spirit of the trail," she said proudly.

"Yes, I believe he just might be," the captain said. "How about if you run over to the sergeant and ask him to show you what an MRE is while I have a word with the spirit of the trail here."

The two men withdrew from the group while the sergeant knelt beside the little girl and slipped off his pack. Klondike and the captain looked at each other, not sure exactly how to start the conversation.

Klondike began, "So you're picking up little girls in the woods now?"

"Damnedest thing I ever saw," the captain said. "She came wandering into camp last night."

"Where was this?" Klondike asked.

The captain indicated approximately where their camp had been.

Klondike did the mental math needed to realize that the girl could have been back with her parents several hours ago.

"So you've been wandering around for quite some time looking for her parents," Klondike said by way of beginning a story he hoped the captain would complete.

But the captain didn't rise to the bait, saying only, "Something like that."

After another awkward moment of silence, the captain tried a different tack.

"You apparently know the little girl," he said.

Klondike nodded and said, "Since she was born."

"And the parents, too?" the captain asked.

"Yeah. I hiked most of the A.T. with her dad a few years ago." Steered by nothing more than an uneasy feeling about the whole situation, Klondike found himself reluctant to open up further.

"You know where they are now?" the captain asked.

Klondike nodded over his right shoulder, which the captain understood to mean back down the trail they were on, then left on the A.T.

"I could take her off your hands and get her back if you want," Klondike offered, perhaps too casually.

"I'm not sure," the captain said. "This is a little outside the normal range of what we do." He was clearly searching his memory for some procedural guidance.

"It's not that complicated," said Klondike. "A little kid got lost, and you brought her back to her parents."

"This case is more complicated than that, believe me," the captain said.

"I guess I'll have to believe you, since no one is telling me what's really going on here," Klondike said. It was typical of him to move quickly to the inevitable conclusion.

"Well, for now, I think you're right after all. It's not that complicated. Little kid got lost, and we got her back to her parents," the captain said.

Seeing that he was going to receive no further explanation, Klondike said, "Let's just saddle up. I'll show you the way."

The captain gave the appropriate hand signals, and the men reslung their packs. They moved out with Klondike, Audrey, and the captain in the lead.

ooooo

In late afternoon at the campsite, Sue's day of waiting finally came to an end.

At that particular moment, she was sitting cross-legged on the bench of the picnic table by the shelter. In front of her were her open journal and a tiny pen. She had thought to pass some time by writing but so far had produced only the words, "Waiting for Audrey," followed by swirls and circles in random patterns across the page. Now she sat trying to be quiet in mind and body, listening for any sound of her little girl.

Two juncos jumped and pecked in the dry leaves around the firepit. They heard the approaching party before she did, and their movement made her sit up and take notice.

Into the clearing from the southern entrance of the trail emerged a strange band of wanderers.

The instant she saw Klondike's face, she knew the news was good and came running. The next person she saw was the captain, but she had little time to wonder about him because Audrey herself came dodging by and ran into her arms.

No one said anything for a moment.

Klondike came over with his pilgrims, and Sue hugged him, too. She glanced at the trainees holding back near the edge of the campsite and gave Klondike an inquisitive look.

"It's all right," he whispered. "I'll tell you all about it."

The captain began to walk over.

"Leon's not back yet?" Klondike asked.

"He should be anytime," she said, and looked up at the captain. To him, she held out her hand and said, "Thank you for bringing my little girl back."

"Sorry we couldn't get her here sooner," he said. He glanced away at his men. "She just wandered into our camp yesterday evening." He looked back at Sue and smiled. "She made quite an impression on the troops."

"Yes, she does that," Sue said. She was clearly sensing more to the story.

The awkward silence that followed did not last long.

"Daddy!" Audrey yelled, and went running to the opposite end of the clearing.

Leon Colebrook was indeed there. He had entered from the other direction and come up short looking at the odd sight—campground, wife, daughter, other hikers, Rangers.

The human mind is good at putting together stories based on little real information. Give a person a snapshot and he can write a novel about it. Throw in a little history, some preconceived ideas and attitudes, and he thinks he knows everything.

But even with this capacity for invention, Leon was having trouble making these particular puzzle pieces fit together.

The little girl launched herself into his arms and buried her face in his neck. Leon walked across the clearing to the others with her so attached.

"You'd think I was the one who was lost," he said, shaking Klondike's hand and putting his arm around Sue.

Chapter 42

The Senator

THE SENATOR FROM NORTH CAROLINA had a particularly pleasant walk to work that morning in our nation's capital.

The door to his suite of offices was open when he got there, just as he liked it. This open-door policy had begun mostly as a symbolic gesture, but it turned out to be practical, too, as it allowed the staff to be more in touch with who was coming and going down the halls.

He was greeted by the head receptionist, just as he had been every day since his arrival in D.C. As he sat at his desk, another aide brought him a cup of coffee. He started his computer, quickly checked the day's schedule, and looked around for the usual stack of mail. Seeing none, he was about to call and ask about it when a third aide came through the door with the mail bundle in his hand.

This aide was a thin young man named Jonathan, perhaps the most eager of all the political science majors the senator had employed over the years. The mail bundle was about average in thickness for a weekday morning. However, an unusual envelope was in the stack. For one thing, the envelope was odd in size and shape. It measured about twelve inches square, which made it stick out from the other, more conventional pieces of mail. It also had a little heft to it, as the aide had found when he picked it up. Most remarkable were the color and feel of the material it was made of, apparently some kind of parchment.

"Good morning, senator," Jonathan said, nodding and approaching the desk. He had the bulk of the mail in one hand and the unusual envelope in the other. "I wasn't sure what to do with this," he said. He placed the other mail on the edge of the desk and turned the larger envelope so the senator could read the name on the return address. "It's been through security like everything else, but I thought maybe we should have them take another look at it. Feel the weight."

The senator took the envelope, slipped on a pair of reading glasses, and smiled broadly when he read the return address:

> James Colebrook
> Hendersonville, NC

He laughed as he reached for a letter opener.

"Believe me, Jonathan. We have absolutely nothing to fear from this gentleman. He's a very old friend of mine."

Jonathan looked relieved and a little uncertain as to whether he should leave or hang around. The senator noticed this.

"Pull up a chair," he said to the young aide. "Let's see what's on Pipo's mind these days."

"Pipo?" the aide asked. He readily pulled up a chair as suggested.

"I guess they don't teach too much art or engineering in the courses you take," the senator said.

He directed the young man's attention to a painting on the wall of his office.

Jonathan had been in and out of the office hundreds of times and had seen the painting without really looking at it. It was a scene on a golf course, and since he had little interest in the sport, he had paid it little mind. He assumed it was one of the noteworthy North Carolina courses, and that the players were some famous pros he had no clue about.

"Take a good look at the guys in that painting. I know they teach history in your course of study," the senator said.

Jonathan approached the painting now in earnest. He stared and strained and then smiled.

"Is that who I think it is?" he said.

He looked back at the senator, who was smiling with delight and nodding.

"I know that's Robert E. Lee, and that's Stonewall Jackson," Jonathan said, pointing. "I know I've seen pictures of these other two also, but I'm not sure."

"Stuart and Early," the senator supplied.

Indeed, the painting depicted Robert E. Lee, Stonewall Jackson, Jeb Stuart, and Jubal Early. All were dressed in modern golfing garb, Stuart being the most colorful. Stuart was behind the wheel of one golf cart and Lee behind the wheel of another. Jackson sat beside Lee, beer in hand, cigar in mouth, deep in contemplation. Lee seemed to be adding up the score on the card in front of him and not liking what he saw. Stuart was in a much more buoyant mood as he watched his partner, Early, lining up a difficult shot. Early had choked down on a nine iron to deal with a white pine tree directly in front of him. The ball was on a steep bank, forcing him into a stance that bordered on contortion. Meanwhile, the branch of a holly bush was nearly sticking up his butt.

Jonathan studied the painting awhile longer, then said, "So what's your interpretation? Does Early make the shot?"

The senator thought for a moment. "Based on history and on how far the ball is below his feet, I would guess not. I think the shot is pretty close to impossible. I would say the point of the painting is that he is attempting it with a dutiful attitude. If he doesn't make a complete follow-through, he doesn't even have a chance. So he is going to step up and swing, and no matter what the flight of the ball or the luck of the bounce, no one can accuse him of holding back."

This was the longest analysis the senator had ever given the painting. He knew perfectly well there was an equal chance it was intended to mean none of these things.

"Anyway, the man who painted that picture is the same one who wrote this letter, or whatever is inside this envelope," the senator said, getting back on focus.

He slid a letter opener under the flap of the package. From the envelope, he withdrew a letter a few pages in length, handwritten on the same thick paper, and also a map printed on conventional copy paper.

The aide sat and waited respectfully as the senator read and at one point held up the map for closer examination. The senator's face reflected a more and more serious mood. Twice, he flipped back to reread a particular section.

At length, the senator put down the papers and removed his reading glasses. He sat and thought for a moment, then got up from the desk.

"You'll need to cancel any appointments I have for the rest of the morning," he said.

Jonathan looked at the letter lying on the desk, but the senator scooped up the pages and slipped them into a briefcase before the young aide could see much.

Chapter 43

Riobamba

TOMBLYN AND HAVEN were seated at what had become their usual table in the breakfast room of the inn. Outside, the sky was noncommittal, as was often the case in the mountains. They found it hard to tell if the overcast of the morning sky was just normal condensation that would burn off by ten o'clock or if it held a more substantial load of moisture that would make itself known later in the afternoon.

The front door of the inn opened, and Meyers from the local FBI office entered. He exchanged a few words with the owner, who was carrying a plate of eggs and toast out from the kitchen. She smiled and nodded toward the table by the large bay window.

Tomblyn and Haven looked up from their papers as he approached, then glanced around to see if anyone else was paying attention. Apart from a young couple trying to get some oatmeal inside a three-year-old boy, they had the room to themselves.

It occurred to Tomblyn that Meyers was in an especially good mood that morning. Meyers pulled out a chair, sat down to join them, flipped the cup in front of him to an upright position, and poured himself some coffee from their carafe.

At the same time, he produced a fat envelope from his coat pocket and laid it on the table.

"Interesting test results," he said.

Tomblyn and Haven waited while Meyers took a sip of coffee.

"Remember the partial shoe print we got from the truck when we brought it in?" he asked.

He opened the envelope and unfolded a report that included photos, graphs, and analysis. One of the photographs showed a partial but distinct print of a shoe with a worn tread. The impression of the tread was smeared, making it appear that the person's foot had slipped a little from left to right. On the right edge of the tread was a ridge of dark brown material that was raised enough for a decent sample to be scraped off. This discovery had been made by one of Meyers's men, who sent the sample to the forensic lab outside Washington. Tomblyn had made sure it was treated as a priority.

"Turns out it's mostly chocolate," Meyers continued.

"Wait a minute," Tomblyn said. "What about tread identification from the imprint itself?"

"Too smeared," Meyers said. "They couldn't tell anything, not even the size, since the print didn't go all the way back to the heel. But the chocolate could be a breakthrough."

"That may not be of much use, since you can get chocolate anywhere. Someone drops a candy bar, then someone else steps on it. It could even have happened after the truck was parked in Asheville. That was a very public place," Tomblyn said.

Haven grimaced at the last remark, remembering the phone call they had placed to Washington.

"Turns out," said Meyers, "not all chocolate is created equal." He unfolded the report and began reading from an underlined paragraph. " 'Chocolate is primarily a mixture of cocoa solids, cocoa butter, sugar, milk products, lecithin, and other emulsifiers. The specific taste of different chocolates is determined by the ratio of these constituents as well as the trace compounds within the cocoa itself. For instance, they all have different amounts of theobromine.' "

"Theobromine," said Tomblyn. "Isn't that the stuff that makes chocolate poison to dogs?"*

"Yeah, I think so. Anyway, each chocolate has an individual and highly distinct chemical signature, making it possible with a high degree of certainty to identify the source of chocolate from the analysis of even trace amounts," Meyers said.

"And I suppose the lab has some kind of database of the chemical signatures of the hundreds of kinds of chocolate made in the world," said Haven.

"It does, at least for the major brands," said Meyers. "This one was on the list. The analysts identified the chocolate as a high-quality brand called Riobamba."

"Presumably, if we send them a sample of chocolate—for example, from the shop of a family of suspects—they could confirm we have a match," Haven said.

"The problem is, that still wouldn't tie us to the Colebrook family for sure, assuming the test shows a positive match," said Tomblyn. He picked up the first page of the report and looked again at the photo of the print. "You've seen what that place is like," he said. "How many thousands of customers do they have?"

Indeed, their "investigation" had taken them back to the shop several times in the course of the last week.

"It gets better," said Meyers. "This was not pure chocolate. It was a blend of raw chocolate, two kinds of sugar, shortening, butter, cream, and vanilla. In other words, it was a fudge mixture." He waited a moment for that to sink in. "And it gets even better," he said. "The components of the fudge were not completely blended."

---

* Henrico Carr noticed, through an accident with a large bar of Swiss chocolate, that theobromine enhanced the feelings of attachment dogs held toward humans. Dogs also considered chocolate to be a health food. Nutritionists' recommendations to the contrary were thus shown to be bullshit.

"You mean it's a low-quality product?" Tomblyn asked.

"No, he means it was not yet completely cooked and blended together," Haven broke in. "You remember the guy stirring that big pot in the store? That's where all that stuff gets blended together."

"And that also means the print couldn't have come from just any customer who happened to buy some of the product, since they don't let customers enter the kitchen. It came from someone who works at the shop and handles the ingredients before they're finished," Tomblyn said.

They all sat back.

"So I guess we'll be needing a list of everyone who works at the Chocolate Moose," said Meyers.

"I don't think we need any more lists of suspects," said Tomblyn. "How many more connections do we need to pick these guys up?"

"Which guys specifically? You mean the whole family?" asked Haven.

"I mean Mr. Philip Colebrook and all three of those freaking boys," said Tomblyn.

"What have you got, and what exactly would you do with them if you picked them up?" asked Meyers. Until now, this had seemed to him like a bit of a game, the big guys from Washington coming down and chasing around after a local family. He figured they would spin their wheels for a while and the real bad guys would surface somewhere else, if they really existed. Then the big guys would return to the make-believe world of Washington, and everyone would have some good stories to tell, both here and there.

"What we have is this," said Tomblyn. He leaned forward, ticking off his list of incriminating facts on his fingers. "One, the truck disappears not far from here. Two, the plane sent to look for the truck picks up pictures of none other than oldest son Leon and family at the crash site—a crash that, by the way, has not been explained. Three, middle son Charles goes snooping around for satellite data that just happens to focus on the area where the truck disappeared. Four, Leon shows up on campus bringing youngest son Xavier a chunk of the same crashed plane. And as soon as we start checking up on Charles and Xavier, they disappear. Nobody knows where the hell they are, although I remind you of the break-in at the RARS site, formerly run by the CIA. And let's not forget who was arrested after discharging a firearm—their grandfather James Colebrook—while the two young men who did the break-in escaped."

This was the first time Meyers felt he was totally in the loop, even if Tomblyn was talking out of desperation.

"Well, now, that last point is reaching a little," said Meyers. "The old man didn't really shoot the gun himself. It was one of the security guards. And it was a flintlock rifle, not exactly a weapon of mass destruction."

"That's not the point. The point is that he was there conveniently getting in the way while his grandsons were trying to escape," said Tomblyn.

"You think it was his grandsons," Meyers corrected. He didn't want to push this point—or any other point, for that matter—too far.

"And then we have to consider the tie-in with Oak Ridge National Labs," Haven said.

"What tie-in with Oak Ridge?" Meyers asked. This was definitely something he should have been in on.

"Athenaeum showed up on a list of companies doing business over there," Tomblyn said.

"Athenaeum? What could they possibly have to do with Oak Ridge?" Meyers said. He suddenly realized that they were in a public place and that he had probably said that louder than he should have. When he took a quick glance around, the lady at the desk looked down at some papers.

Tomblyn smiled knowingly and said in a voice not much above a whisper, "You might well ask. And not only that, the names on the approved passes were none other than James and Philip Colebrook."

They sat for a moment, trying to put the pieces of the puzzle together.

"And now this," Tomblyn concluded. "This puts them with the truck, either at the scene of the crime or sometime thereafter. This is too much. These guys are up to something."

"Well, that brings up the second part of my question. What would we do with them if we did pick them up?" Meyers asked. He was getting over his skepticism of the family's involvement and was on to matters of strategy.

"We could question them and find out what's going on here," said Tomblyn. "Plus, we'd have them under lock and key for a while, so they couldn't get on with whatever is up."

Meyers thought about this.

"We have a saying around here," he said. "If you're walking down a road and see a turtle sitting on top of a fencepost, you might not know exactly what's going on, but one thing you know for sure: He didn't get there by himself."

"Meaning?" asked Tomblyn.

"Meaning," said Meyers, "that if the Colebrooks are involved in this thing—"

"If?" said Tomblyn.

"Okay, assuming they're involved in this, I don't see them doing it on their own. There must be someone farther up the line organizing this stuff, or dreaming it up in the first place. Except for a few rare occasions, the Colebrooks don't tend to get mixed up in politics, and I certainly don't see them as terrorists. I think we should sit tight, keep them under surveillance, and follow them to whoever got them into this," Meyers said.

They were all three silent.

"Consider another possibility," said Haven.

The other two looked at him, a little impatient with his dramatic pause.

"We squeeze the tube a little and see where the toothpaste starts squirting out," he said.

"You mean, go on the offensive," said Tomblyn. This idea held instant appeal.

"I don't know if I would go so far as to call it the offensive, but at least we could put some pressure on them, take the initiative away, and make them react to us. Throw them a little off balance," said Haven.

"What exactly do you have in mind?" asked Meyers.

Haven looked around the room once more and leaned into the center of the table. The others did, too, creating a real FBI football huddle. Haven might as well have been drawing pass patterns in the dirt.

Sheila, the owner of the inn, observed this as covertly as she could from the front desk. She didn't need to hear a word they said to know they were up to no good. She picked up the portable phone and punched in a number as she walked into the back room.

Meanwhile, Pipo's unlikely portrait of Gandhi smiled on.

Chapter 44

The Last of the Tyrannosaurs

"OH, SNAP!" Lilly said under her breath. "This is the last of the milk chocolate tyrannosaurs."

She removed the dinosaur sucker from the tray, now empty except for a dark chocolate triceratops. She wrapped the object and slipped it into a small paper bag. This she handed to a boy of perhaps four years, barely able to reach up to the countertop. She smiled at him and his mother, rang up the transaction on the cash register, and thanked them as they left the store.

That was the start of what would be another busy day.

Leon's idea of buying dinosaur molds had been a good one. Her idea of placing the chocolate dinosaurs and bears on the lowest shelf, in easy view of the youngest customers, was brilliant. They constituted some of the fastest-moving items in the shop. The workers had noticed a clear pattern. Little boys favored the tyrannosaurs at least three to one. Little girls leaned toward the brontosauruses by a similar margin. Fewer wanted to eat the triceratops, their protective armor plates apparently serving them as well in their chocolate reincarnations as they had in real life sixty million years ago.*

There being no other customers in the shop, Lilly walked into the kitchen and dropped several pieces of milk chocolate into the machine that melted, stirred, and tempered it.

The radio was tuned to 88.7, the Asheville station that played an eclectic collection of music. A piece by a local singer-songwriter ended, and the BBC news came on the air. Following an account of the death toll in various U.S./British operations overseas came a report concerning a missing truck full of radioactive material.

"The White House press secretary was pounded with questions concerning the rumor reported late last night," said the BBC announcer.

Voice of a well-known national reporter: "Any comment from the White House on the report of the missing isotopes?"

Voice of the press secretary: "As you know, all such materials are handled according to strict guidelines by the DOE, the DOD, and their contractors. It would be inappropriate to discuss details of security."

Voice of another reporter: "Has the president been notified that a truck is missing?"

Nervous laugh, followed by the chiding, sarcastic tone of the press secretary: "The president is not in the habit of following the movements of every truck operated by the Department of Energy."

Voice of a third reporter: "We have a report from a source close to the secretary of the Department of Energy that a truck was missing but subsequently turned up. Can you comment on that?"

Voice of the press secretary, firm and quick: "I think I've already answered that question. Now, let's please move on."

Lilly listened to this with a new perspective since taking Body Language 101. She hoped some members of the Sisterhood were listening as well, so they could talk about it later. She reflected that

---

* Henrico Carr of course never had the opportunity to read the thought patterns of triceratops, but he did experiment with a couple of armadillos. He found their thoughts an odd mixture of mammalian and reptilian characteristics, suggesting highly cynical and paranoid creatures that would not make very good company.

the BBC editors were pretty good. Playing such a nondenial denial let listeners form their own inescapable conclusion that the government once again had screwed something up and was making matters worse by talking every which way but straight.

She was looking for the clear plastic dinosaur molds when the phone rang. A girl with dark brown hair came out of the back with the portable. Lilly raised her eyebrows to ask who was on the other end. The dark-haired girl just gave her a serious look and handed her the phone.

Lilly said a brief hello. As she listened, she walked to the far side of the kitchen and turned toward the wall. The person on the other end apparently had a lot to say. Lilly stood there listening for a long time, only occasionally interjecting a word. The dark-haired girl watched from the door to the back room, trying to read the lay of the land. Lilly turned slowly on her heel, surveying the store and nodding to the dark-haired girl by way of reassurance. She asked a question and received a long response. She continued her turn until she faced the front door.

In the Chocolate Moose, the arrangement of glass panels in the front window and the entrance corridor conspired to produce an odd set of reflections. From Lilly's vantage point, the windows reflected an image from far down the street, which allowed her to observe the approach of the FBI agents when they were still over a block away.

Lilly said into the phone, "Thanks. Gotta go." She waited for a quick response and said goodbye.

She told the dark-haired girl she needed to go out for a while and instructed her to hold down the fort. She scooted back to the office, picked up a couple of things, and left through the back door into the alley.

About the time the alley door was closing, Tomblyn and Haven opened the front door of the shop. During their walk from the B&B, the fire to make something happen had cooled. In fact, Tomblyn had to fight with himself to keep it alive at all. Haven had never been particularly fired up. And to Meyers, it all felt downright wrong, and he refused to be part of the exercise. After all, he still had to live with these people when this was over.

Tomblyn and Haven recognized the dark-haired girl in the hooded sweatshirt from previous visits.

"Would you like a sample of fudge?" she asked, holding a tray of small, dark cubes out to them.

This seemed to disarm Tomblyn even further.

Haven actually reached out and took one.

Tomblyn attempted to get back to business. He withdrew his badge from the inside breast pocket of his jacket. This was one of his favorite moves, as it also allowed him to flash a glimpse of the pistol clipped into a holster on his belt.

"I am Agent Tomblyn with the FBI. We would like to have a few words with Lilly Colebrook. Is she here?"

Judging from the girl's face, the presentation had the desired intimidating effect. However, she said, "Lilly's not here right now. She just stepped out."

"Do you know where she went or when she'll be back?" Tomblyn asked.

"No, I'm not sure," the girl said. She had been trained to take the extra step to satisfy customers, but she was having trouble with this one. "Would you like to wait for her or leave a message?" she asked.

Tomblyn turned to Haven for help, but Haven had already begun wandering down the row of cases and perusing the chocolates and other creations. Sensing Tomblyn's eyes on him, he said without looking back, "Does she have a cell phone?"

"I think we have the number back in the office," the girl said, happy to have something to offer these guys after all. "I'll go back and look."

"I'll go with you," Tomblyn said. He didn't like the idea of letting the girl out of his sight just then.

Haven continued his inspection tour of the cases while they were in the back. They returned a moment later, Tomblyn with a small notebook in which he was jotting the number.

"Let's give this a try," he said. He took his cell phone and punched in the number.

"She almost never answers her cell phone," the girl said, then looked down, realizing she might have shared that fact before.

When Lilly failed to pick up, Tomblyn looked totally deflated.

"Well, I guess we'll come back later," he said. "Tell her we were here looking for her."

The girl nodded.

Haven was still engrossed in the chocolate cases.

"Can I get you anything while you're here?" the girl asked.

She and Tomblyn both moved toward Haven at the far case.

Haven looked up at her. "Do you have any other chocolate dinosaurs?" he asked.

"No," said the girl. "We were just getting ready to make some more T. rexes. All we have right now are the triceratops."

Chapter 45
I nto the Black Helicopter

THE CALL THEY RECEIVED later that day brought Tomblyn and Haven back to the private part of the airport from whence they had started. They had made the decision to call Meyers, too, although their orders did not specifically say to do so. The orders did suggest that they leave the suits behind and dress in something appropriate for tramping around the woods.

When they entered the lounge of the private jetport, they found that Meyers was already there, and in the company of another man. This man was burly and had on his face the look of someone not amused by much in life.

At that moment, what the man appeared to be most unamused about was the mural of the Wright brothers that had welcomed the agents when they first came through the lounge.

As they approached, Tomblyn and Haven heard the man saying to

Meyers, "I don't get it. What a jackass thing to do. I mean, what kind of a jackass would take the time to paint something like that? What kind of a jackass would even think of painting something like that? It's disrespectful."

"The artist's name is James R. Colebrook," said Haven.

They had walked up behind Meyers and the other man at midrant. The man turned and looked, clearly considering them an unwanted intrusion.

"Mr. Hudson, these are Agents Tomblyn and Haven," Meyers said. "Gentlemen, this is Ira Hudson."

Tomblyn decided not to explain that they already knew each other all too well.

The introductions did nothing to improve Hudson's mood. Since Tomblyn and Haven had been dispatched to the scene, things had gone from bad to worse, while the number of solid answers to important questions had remained about the same—namely, damn few. Over the phone, Hudson had made it clear he held the agents responsible, and that he was not interested in considering if that was a fair assessment. FBI agents were supposed to straighten stuff like this out. As one of the big-picture guys, which Ira Hudson considered himself to be, he felt the FBI was one of the tools intended for his use. If things went wrong, he had only to put the FBI on the case and somehow matters would be straightened out. If the FBI didn't accomplish that, it was their fault. That's what they were there for.

"I take it you don't approve of Mr. Colebrook's work," said Haven, nodding toward the painting.

"I'm thinking I don't approve of any Colebrook work, or any of the Colebrooks," Hudson answered. "And I'm thinking it's about time we did something about them."

"Mr. Hudson, as we've discussed, we are keeping the entire Colebrook family under surveillance," Tomblyn began.

"Unless you have an agent dressed up as a crow or a black bear, I don't see how you can have them all under surveillance. Three of them are out in the Great Smoky Mountains National Park," Hudson said.

Haven looked at Tomblyn.

"Yes, we are aware that Leon Colebrook and his family are hiking," Tomblyn said.

"And I suppose you know where his two brothers are at this moment," Hudson said. Putting people on the defensive was one of Hudson's strong points, a talent that served him well in his work in Washington.

"We are aware that Charles and Xavier Colebrook have been off the radar for a week or so. That is one of the reasons for extra surveillance. We have reason to suspect they have returned to this area, so we are waiting for some sign of them to surface," Tomblyn said. "Meanwhile, we are keeping a close watch on Philip and James Colebrook."

"Yes, I heard all about that," Hudson said. "You managed to arrest an old man with a flintlock rifle. Very good work." With that, he turned toward the door to the runway area and said, "Let's get going."

Waves of heat rose from the tarmac as they emerged from the building. Haven would have normally stopped for a moment to take in the vista of the mountains. But the sight of three black helicopters sitting on the runway brought him up short. As soon as they approached, the pilots fired up the engines, and the blades started cutting the air.

Haven knew little about aircraft, but these seemed to be of a size that could carry several people each. He was also struck by the total absence of markings. They bore no numbers, no insignia, no names, just a uniform dull black finish on metal skin. *Creepy* was the word that sprang to mind. Tomblyn shot a glance back over his shoulder at Haven, clearly thinking the same thing.

Ira Hudson motioned them to the nearest aircraft. With their heads bent, as all people do when approaching helicopters, they mounted the single step and found seats in the back. The pilot immediately pulled up and away. They were followed in short order by the other two and were soon flying in formation westward over the ridge top. Their aircraft took the point position, while the others took the flanks.

Chapter 46

A Shadow on the Heart

THE OLD MAN FELT THE PRESENCE OF DEATH all around him, like a troupe of stinking monkeys in a banana grove.

The rhythm of his steps was a constant as he walked. The length of the strides changed with the pitch of the terrain—shorter as the path ascended, longer when it dropped back to level, or as level as anything ever was in the southern Appalachians. But the rhythm itself was steady as a metronome.

The walking stick seemed to have a life of its own, jumping here and there, side to side, sometimes pushing against the ground, sometimes probing a mud puddle, sometimes setting up for a pulling motion to get uphill. The stick occasionally jumped from hand to hand depending on some unseen sense of where its services were needed most.

At that particular moment, the path was winding slowly upward and spiraling left. It seemed to be the bed of an old service road no longer in use. This slight upward tilt of a trail was the configuration most favored by long-distance hikers with heavy packs. On an upward slope, hikers tended to lean forward, which secured the packs against their backs and resulted in less bouncing and less stress on the shoulder straps.

But on this day, it didn't much matter. James Colebrook had only a small day pack with some water, a little lunch, and a bag of dog bones.

The bones were for his two companions, currently trotting in point position twenty yards in front. The gray spotted dog broke into a loping half-run and advanced as far as the bend in the path, allowing her to see well ahead. She glanced back at Pipo, jaw in the dog-grin position, tongue hanging to one side, ears relaxed. This was her way of giving the all-clear sign. She chose to wait at the bend for the man and the little black dog, rather than trotting back and resuming formation.

Experienced hikers know better than to think too much about a climb, or especially how much climb they have left. Better to stay in the moment and let the earth pass beneath them. However, every climb contains a moment when the hiker realizes he has indeed made significant progress. When Pipo and the black dog reached the switchback in the trail where the gray dog, Caca Lacka, waited, he could see through an opening in the trees a vista back in the direction from which they had come. He saw into the river valley and across it to the next ridge line, almost at eye level now. It was then he realized that he had climbed, step by patient step, to the shoulder of the mountain he was on. Though the top was not in view, it was not far away.

As he turned back to the business of the trail, he found the two dogs in what he thought of as the twin-sphinx position. They were trying their best to look demure, well behaved, and intensely expectant. He had to admit it was a pretty good performance. He reached into one of the side pockets of the pack, took out a dog biscuit, broke it in half, and held the two pieces aloft. The twin sphinxes immediately sat up, and he dropped the biscuit pieces into open mouths. He always enjoyed the crunching sound that followed.

The thundering paws and gaping jaws of the dogs of the Pisgah, he thought.

In town, the furnace of summer was stoked to full blast. Out here in the woods, and with some little elevation achieved, the heat was much less oppressive, although the climb, steady as it was, had produced a lather of sweat.

Several switchbacks and creek crossings later, he spied a cross up ahead by the trail. This was not a religious icon, but rather a horizontal board nailed to a vertical post. The horizontal board bore the name of the trail that ran along the ridge line. It struck him that the cross was the simplest object easily picked out in this forest as having been made by man.

That was food for thought: the simplest shape clearly identifiable as man-made. Pipo felt organized religion was based on some fundamental truths, but that these truths had long since been buried under a whole lot of misdirected stuff.

But that was too much philosophy for such a day as this. The real message of this particular cross was that they had reached the top of the ridge where the Coon Tree Loop met the Bennett Gap Ridge Trail. That meant the climbing was essentially over. From here on, the walk would coast on level ground or follow a gentle descent to the river valley.

This was a good time to pause and drink some water, and to decide whether to turn right and complete the loop or turn left and hike out to Rattlesnake Rock. Although Pipo had seen many rattlesnakes in the mountains, he had never encountered one at Rattlesnake Rock. What he had found there was a great view across the valley to the stone face of Looking Glass Rock. This time of day, it would be catching a glancing blow from the sunlight and would probably be living up to its name, thanks to the watery glaze provided by the springs above it.

Not enough energy, the old man thought, and turned to the right, the shorter of the two choices.

Soon after approaching a marker indicating the return part of the loop that would take them back down into the valley, he heard a racket in the branches just above his head and instinctively ducked. Looking up, he saw a sight he had never witnessed before: two male pileated woodpeckers in a fight. These were huge birds with long, pointed beaks. He had seen such birds demolish small trees in their quest for bugs under the bark. He imagined that two of them fighting could turn into quite a saber duel. In this case, they remained in flight, one chasing the other and trying to position itself for a blow. They swept down the hillside in that formation and out of sight.

The local Indian religion held that anytime a human being encountered an animal, the event held some significance. Although not an Indian, Pipo was the unofficial shaman of his family. He took it upon himself to diagnose the significance of such encounters. His grandsons used to approach him with stories about finding a frog or turtle, or seeing a deer at the edge of the forest at dawn. He would come up with explanations of how those encounters fit into their lives and why the animals had been sent to meet with them. This habit added much to the richness and texture of their lives and kept a larger perspective on their world.

But an explanation did not come so easily this time. Here were two gigantic, dangerous-looking birds fighting and flying at breakneck speed. Why had this thing been revealed to him? Why this image of reckless danger?

While in this reverie, he became conscious of a sound in the distance coming closer. A machine sound, a beating and roaring. A helicopter. No, helicopters, plural. He hurried along the path to a place where the canopy opened enough to bring more of the sky into view. There as the sound intensified came three black helicopters completely void of markings. They flew over moderately low and continued in a beeline west by northwest, like the birds that had foreshadowed their coming.

The birds and the helicopters gave Pipo a bad feeling indeed, and the strong urge to return to home and family. He had set out on this walk to clear his head and think, but he didn't like what he was thinking now.

Chapter 47

Flying in Formation

In the black helicopter, the agents had donned headsets and microphones so they could communicate with each other. But in fact, they said little.

Meyers had of course been in helicopters before, especially in search-and-rescue missions in the area. But those had little in common with the machine he found himself in at the moment. This one was fast, and he found the turning and banking disconcerting.

They continued in a predominantly westward direction, flying over a succession of ridge lines and valleys. Rivers, roads, farms, and houses passed underneath, but the predominant feature was the deep green of the forest.

Meyers knew the region well, but he still found it difficult to locate landmarks from the air, especially at high speed. He did pick up Mount Pisgah, identifiable by its broadcasting tower. Circling that mountain, he saw the Blue Ridge Parkway on a high flank. A little later, he thought he might have spotted the silver dome of the courthouse in Sylva, sister to the one in downtown Hendersonville. After that, his mind and eyes picked out little to anchor his mental map.

After less than thirty minutes of flying, the craft slowed, then took up a hovering position over a long, thin lake. As it pivoted, Meyers made out a long dam on one end. Recognition flashed. It was Fontana. He recalled coming here by road in 2001. After 9/11, the whole country had been on alert. All kinds of precautions were taken at all kinds of structures considered potential terrorist targets. In its wisdom, some group in Washington had decided that Fontana Dam fit the profile and dispatched Meyers's group, together with the Forest Service, to secure it. The normal route for A.T. hikers was to walk across the dam, rather than tramping around the whole lake, so it came as quite a surprise when they were stopped from doing so. In fact, it became an issue for some north-to-south thru-hikers. Fontana Dam was the southern point of the portion of trail that ran through the Smokies. As hikers had nowhere to get provisions on a stretch that took at least several days to negotiate, they reached the dam expecting to be within a few hundred yards of rest, relaxation, and food. Circumnavigating the lake added a day, so people often ran out of food, in addition to being worn out. Once this became apparent, Meyers had left directions with his men to offer whatever assistance was necessary to the hikers, but to be firm about no one crossing the dam itself.

The formation of helicopters paused only a moment over the lake, perhaps for the pilots to check their bearings, and then sprang forward again. Meyers attempted to follow signs of the A.T. but soon lost track because of the canopy of trees. By all accounts, this was as rugged a stretch of trail as hikers would encounter until reaching Vermont and New Hampshire. The scenery of forest, mountainsides, and streams was broken only by occasional balds and rock outcroppings.

By and by, they slowed dramatically. The two wing helicopters surged by the lead aircraft, then pulled up and turned to face back at it, hovering over a clearing where several people stood looking up at them.

The agents' aircraft crept slowly up behind the small crowd and began to settle in for a landing. This was obviously a well-rehearsed maneuver. Judging from the glee and expectation on his face, Ira Hudson was enjoying it immensely. This was one of the "cool" things that had convinced him about overwhelming anything on the ground by means of shock and awe. The basic idea was that the two helicopters would distract the crowd, allowing the third to land unnoticed. It didn't work, at least for long. By the time the agents' doors opened, all eyes were on them. Hudson motioned for them to exit first, so they stepped out, still not quite sure what it was they would be called upon to do.

As one of the people on the ground, Leon Colebrook had no doubt that something strange was going on. Being surrounded by three black helicopters had that effect on a man. Sue looked back to check on the other two birds, which had just landed behind them in the clearing. That no one emerged from them made them seem even more mysterious and intimidating.

Hudson followed the agents out and nodded to the shelter, which was far enough away from the helicopters to allow civilized conversation. Leon and Sue were there, along with Klondike and the other hikers. Audrey was standing in front of her mother, who had a hand on each shoulder, as if reluctant to break physical contact with the little girl. The captain detached himself from the squad of Rangers and joined them in watching the group approach from the chopper. Even from a distance, he was pretty sure he recognized the burly man in the back.

While walking, Agent Tomblyn studied the hikers and picked out Leon and family from their photos. He nudged Haven and nodded toward them. Haven nodded back, confirming that, yes, those were the people—not too much of a surprise, since they knew the family had headed into the woods.

When they reached the shelter, the agents looked back at Ira Hudson, still not sure what they were expected to do but becoming more and more uneasy with the prospects.

"Good morning, captain," Hudson said. He had elbowed his way in front of the agents and was taking charge.

The tone of his voice made it clear that he and the captain knew each other. The hikers looked at the captain, who had moments ago been playing the role of Good Samaritan.

"And good morning to you, Mr. Colebrook," Hudson said to Leon.

Leon stepped forward to shake Hudson's hand and allow him to introduce himself. But Hudson declined the handshake and let the silence hang, presumably giving Leon a chance to say something stupid or incriminating.

"Have we met before, Mr. . . . ?" Leon asked.

"No, I don't believe we have met, at least not in person. But I do know quite a lot about you, and about your family, and about what you have been up to," Hudson said.

If Hudson had designed these remarks for intimidation, he was off the mark. The result was more confusion and curiosity.

"And your name?" Leon asked.

"You don't have to worry so much about who I am as about who these gentlemen are," Hudson said. "You see, they are from the FBI, and they are here to arrest you."

Leon had decided he could no longer be surprised, but hearing those words set him back. Sue physically recoiled, pulling Audrey with her. She looked at the captain, who would not meet her eye. His role had shifted in an instant to Judas Iscariot.

Klondike put his hands on his hips. The agents looked at him, thinking they had better keep and eye on him. The mother and father in Klondike's family of campers seemed taken aback by this turn of events, trying to figure out if they were in trouble by association. However, their daughter for the first time in the excursion showed signs of genuine interest. Finally, something she could tell her friends. She took out her camera and started snapping pictures of the black helicopters and the confrontation unfolding in front of her. Hudson instinctively turned away.

"You're going to arrest us?" Leon asked.

"What would you arrest us for?" Sue asked. This was too much for one day.

"Not you," said Ira Hudson. "Just Mr. Leon here. For now. We'll talk about the charges when we get him back to Asheville."

Leon looked at the agents to see if this was true. Meyers gave Hudson an irritated look. They had not even discussed the particulars ahead of time.

One of the Ranger trainees trotted up and whispered in the captain's ear. The captain looked toward the end of the clearing where the trail led north. Standing there were two hikers, young men, speaking to a couple of his trainees. The captain gave a quick hand signal, and the Rangers pointed the hikers to the group. They walked across the clearing slowly, taking in the scene.

The FBI men watched them approach. Presently, Tomblyn recognized them from their photographs. "Charles and Xavier Colebrook, I presume," he said under his breath.

Leon and Sue turned and saw it was so. Audrey pulled away from her mother and ran to meet her uncles.

A look of glee came over Ira Hudson's face. "I love family reunions. I guess we can turn this into a triple play," he said.

After stopping to hug Audrey and hand her a present from Xavier's pack, the brothers strolled into the odd assembly as if it were the most natural scene in the world, something they might do on most any summer morning.

"Arrest all three of them and bring them on our bird," Hudson said.

He turned and walked back toward the helicopter. Giving an order and walking away before any discussion or clarification was a technique he had found highly effective in his years of management by force and intimidation.

"What exactly are you arresting us for?" Xavier asked.

Klondike's young hiker snapped more pictures. This was getting good.

Meyers looked at Tomblyn and Haven, neither of whom seemed inclined to address the question.

"I don't think we need to call it an arrest at this time," Meyers said. "Let's just say we need you to come with us to answer questions about the disappearance of some important government property."

"Where are you taking them?" Sue asked.

"No farther than Asheville, Mrs. Colebrook. Would you like us to arrange for you and your daughter to be transported out as well?" Meyers said.

Klondike stepped up. "That won't be necessary. They can walk out with us. We'll make sure they're okay."

Sue and Leon looked at each other, trying to read Klondike's reason for suggesting this. They weren't sure, but they knew Klondike well enough to go along with his plan.

Sue said, "Yes, that will be fine. I'm sure this will all be straightened out by the time we get back."

The agents allowed the Colebrooks to say their goodbyes—or in the case of Charles and Xavier, their hellos and goodbyes. Audrey seemed the least upset by the whole scene. As far as she was concerned, she was looking forward to a couple more days of walking in the woods.

When the copters pushed off with the brothers, they left the campsite ringing with silence. The captain gave the order for his men to prepare to leave. The past day had been enough deviation from the prescribed training and testing.

To Sue, he said he was sorry about the boys but that he was sure everything would work out because they seemed like good people.

To Klondike, he simply nodded and said, "Next time."

A moment later, the squad disappeared into the woods like ghosts.

The others looked around. No one was left but campers now, just as it should be at a campsite. They decided they might as well leave at once, so they started to gather their things and put their packs in order. Sue picked up her notebook and looked at the last entry. Although it had been written less than an hour ago, she thought she would require several pages to catch her account up to the present.

Audrey was already set to go, not having taken anything out of her pack. She had an unusual object in her hands and was turning it over, trying to figure out what it was. She walked over and handed it to Klondike.

"What's this?" he asked, turning it over as well.

"It's a present from Uncle Xavier," she said. "He said to give it to you in case he and Uncle Charles had to leave with the helicopters or the army men."

Klondike looked at it some more. Sue came up as well.

"Did Uncle Xavier say what it does?" she asked.

"No, but it looks like something he made. It looks like a lunchbox with some extra stuff on it," she said.

It was of course the detector the boys had put together to make use of the sensor from the plane. Audrey was right in saying it looked like something Xavier would make. The family had often discussed how each object designed and built by a person carried with it, in some sense, his or her signature. That applied no matter how simple or utilitarian the object, or whether it was meant to be art or a form of self-expression. Pipo used to laugh at students when they said they were struggling to express themselves. According to him, as long as they were making anything, they couldn't help expressing themselves. "An elephant might as well try to leave chicken tracks," he liked to say in those days.

"Can I flip the switch?" Audrey asked.

"We don't know what it does. It might be dangerous," Klondike said to her.

"Xavier would never have given it to her if it were dangerous," Sue said. Then to Audrey, she added, "Since Uncle Xavier gave it to you, it's okay, but usually it's not good to play with things you don't understand."

As they all watched, Audrey flipped the switch, and the number on the indicator jumped to forty-five.

"Forty-five what?" Sue asked.

"I guess we'll have to ask Xavier when we see him. For now, I'm guessing this little box is something he didn't want on his person when he was picked up by our newfound friends," Klondike said.

Seeing that the others were ready, he swung his own pack on and headed for the northbound trail. They all followed, Audrey falling in with the teenage daughter and beginning a barrage of questions.

Chapter 48

Decision to Indict

AGENT TOMBLYN considered himself reasonably advanced in the art and science of interrogation. The problem was that he was under strict orders not to ask any questions that would disclose a truck full of radioactive materials had disappeared because, officially, that had never happened.

The problem the brothers Colebrook had was not much different. They wanted to get out of trouble, or at least to understand how they had gotten into trouble in the first place, preferably without revealing anything about the find that Leon and family had made.

This made for some circular conversations.

Agent Tomblyn: "How did you come to have part of an expensive government plane in your lab at school?"

Xavier: "That's what we do at the lab. We work on planes."

Tomblyn: "I mean, how did you get that particular piece of that particular plane?"

Xavier: "My brother brought it to me to see what it was."

Tomblyn: "How did your brother get it?"

Xavier: "You mean, how did my brother get part of the plane?"

Tomblyn: "Yes, how did your brother get part of the plane?"

Xavier: "I don't know. I guess he found it."

Tomblyn: "Found it in the woods somewhere?"

Xavier: "I don't know where. I'm pretty sure the thing had a GPS chip in it, so the guys who were flying it would know exactly where it was."

Tomblyn: "What was your brother doing in the woods?"

Xavier: "Hiking, I guess. He does a lot of hiking."

Tomblyn: "Was he looking for something?"

Xavier: "My father says that everybody is looking for something."

The brothers were held together in a cell. They were not made to wear orange jumpsuits, although Xavier confided that he had always admired them and would not mind wearing one.

Their lawyer made an appearance and spoke briefly with the boys. The Colebrook family was quickly becoming a full-time job for him between this incident and dealing with the arrest of the grandfather, James. The boys trusted him, at least to an extent. Leon had not disclosed the nature of his find, so the lawyer was left with the feeling, quite correct, that something more was going on than met the eye.

The next day, Philip and Pipo were deposited in the cell as well.

"Sorry we didn't get up to see you boys yesterday," Philip said. "They picked me and Pipo up and talked to us most of the day and into last night."

"What did they do," asked Xavier, "go out to the house and throw you in handcuffs?"

"No, they seemed to want to make it as public as they possibly could," Philip answered. "We were down on Main Street having a couple bowls of gumbo for lunch at the Cajun Cellar, and they stomped right in before we finished. No consideration at all. The new guys out at Athenaeum were only too happy to tell them where we were."

"Damn," said Leon, thinking how good a bowl of that gumbo

would taste right about now.

"We wanted to bring you guys a big bag of sweet potato chips, but that was not to be," Philip said.

Pipo shrugged as if to say, *Oh, well,* then sat on the bench and took a short charcoal pencil from his pocket. He began to examine the graffiti left on the walls by previous inmates.

ooooo

The agents sat around a table in the conference room of the local FBI offices. The walls were posted with the usual materials. A whiteboard took up most of one side of the room. On this, Agent Tomblyn was attempting to make a diagram that would clarify the web of family activities and movements that would in some way account for the disappearance and subsequent reappearance of the truck full of classified materials. He was having a hard time of it.

He had to account for many things. Leon with the plane on the trail, Leon with the plane at the university, and Xavier with the plane, taking the damn thing apart. Charles getting satellite data and making inquires about the special classified satellite, which he had no legitimate business doing. Then Charles and Xavier disappearing, probably breaking into the RARS observatory, getting away, and disappearing again because their grandfather James, a.k.a. Pipo, got in the way of the guards with his flintlock rifle. (An attempt to trace the weapon had revealed that Pipo made it himself. Although it was not clear if this broke any laws, they had started calling the gun an "improvised explosive device" because that sounded more dangerous.) Agent Tomblyn also had to account for Charles and Xavier's reappearance and their attempt to hook up with their brother pretty close to where the plane had come down. And the revelation that the older Colebrooks had visited Oak Ridge and Savannah River. Finally came the most conclusive physical evidence link of all: the Riobamba.

"Riobamba?" asked Ira Hudson. "What the hell is that?"

Much to the disgust of the others, Hudson had decided to stay instead of returning to his lair in Washington. He wanted to get this incident behind him before it blew up any larger, and besides, the truth was that he had quite enjoyed the helicopter ride yesterday. It was the most fun he had experienced in years, and it reinforced his self-image as a man of action and intrigue. To him, it was what being in power in Washington was all about: Doing what you wanted, and using the latest resources to do it.

"Riobamba is the brand of cooking chocolate used at the Chocolate Moose. We found a trace of it on the step of the stolen truck, which definitely ties store employees to it," Meyers explained.

"Employees or owners," Tomblyn corrected. "Someone in the back room or the kitchen. It's the only explanation."

"But the problem remains," said Haven. "None of this adds up to anything in particular, certainly not enough to build a successful legal case. And it doesn't lead us to any organization outside the family. I mean, you can't have a terrorist organization composed of just one family."

Hudson looked at him and thought that this was exactly why these guys were in regular FBI jobs and he was one of the masters of the game. He liked the sound of that: a terrorist organization composed of just one family.

This had nothing to do with crime and conviction and punishment. It had everything to do with the program and preventing any ridiculous public scandal from getting in the way. Since he was losing the attempt to keep this thing under wraps, the next best ploy could be misdirection. A big, messy, scandalous piece of misdirection.

"I want you to file an indictment now," he said.

This took the others aback.

"File an indictment on whom exactly?" Meyers asked.

"File it on all of them, the whole family—father, grandfather, and all three sons," Hudson said, warming to the idea. This would make some great headlines. Three generations of terrorists caught. It would be all the press talked about for weeks. And wait until they got a load of the family. All those weird paintings, satellites, spy planes, fountains, and all the other stuff. Why had he not thought of this before?

"And what exactly are we going to charge them with?" Tomblyn asked.

"Let's see," Hudson said. He really wanted to get this right for the maximum impact. "Charge them with conspiracy to commit acts of terrorism against the United States of America. I like the sound of that."

Chapter 49

A Family Connection

A FEW OF THE BODY LANGUAGE STUDENTS were lounging in the professor's office. Since this was the summer session, everyone was a little more relaxed than usual. They flipped on the TV while taking a lunch break. As always, they were on the lookout for material for class.

The newscasters themselves were usually not good sources, since they had pretty much deadened their connection to what they were reading. However, the sound bites and footage from officials and the general public were often rich veins to be mined. (They couldn't watch the president's press secretary every day.)

The professor sat back with a cheese sandwich, a bottle of chocolate milk, and the controller and flipped through a few channels until she found a news program on one of the slightly liberal national cable channels. A man with brown skin and remarkably Caucasian nose and lips was reading from a script.

"Ah, the black-white guy," one of the girls said.

"No!" another said. "It's the white-black guy."

This had in fact been an ongoing argument in the class for a while.

The black-white guy read, "And now a breaking story about an unlikely terrorist cell in an unlikely place: a small town in western North Carolina."

During this announcement, the ticker running across the bottom of the screen read, "Terror level elevated to Orange." Like most Americans, no one in the class remembered what this meant, but orange sounded kind of dangerous.

The scene on the TV shifted to a crowd outside a building they all recognized immediately as being in downtown Asheville. Someone reached up and pressed the record button on the tape machine.

Several men in suits were in the shot. One had stepped in front of the others and was attempting to answer—actually, attempting to not answer—questions from a reporter. The presence of the TV camera seemed to make him nervous. The spokesman raised his hands as if to calm the crowd. As he began to speak, a microphone was shoved toward his mouth.

"This morning, we have filed papers asking for the indictment of several individuals in connection with suspected terrorist activities over the past months in this area," he said.

Someone off-camera shouted a question: "Is it true that all the men being indicted are members of the same family?"

The spokesman looked back at the other men in suits but seemed to get no guidance from them.

"A family connection is involved. That is all I am able to say at this time."

The man pushed through the crowd and, along with his fellows, ducked into a car and drove off.

ooooo

That evening in Washington, the senator from North Carolina sat in his office with his aides and watched the same news clip being replayed for the hundredth time.

" 'A family connection is involved,' " he snorted, quoting the official. "Are they members of the same family? 'A family connection is involved.' Where do these guys get this stuff?"

He never had bought into the convoluted Washington-speak that people around him employed to obfuscate, misdirect, redirect, or otherwise skate around issues they wanted to control. This was the subject of frequent lectures to his young aides. Indeed, the current instance was looking like it might be the beginning of another such lesson when he caught sight of the last person to enter the car. He was a burly man who swung his wide shoulders into the seat like a boxer ducking under the rope to enter the ring.

"Wait a minute!" he said. "I know that guy. What the hell is he doing there?"

No answer was forthcoming, not from the aides or the news channel, which moved on to the next story.

"We're following this one," the senator said to his aides.

They understood what this meant. It meant that they would collect for him all new stories, printed or otherwise, and stay ahead of the curve on any developments.

The fact that an action like this was taking place in his home state would have been enough for the senator to give these instructions. But the appearance of Ira Hudson, general aide and adviser to the vice president, ducking into the car really grabbed his attention.

Why has Hudson appeared on my radar twice within the last few weeks? he asked himself. *First, he's escorting a witness to a congressional hearing that he doesn't have any obvious connection to, and now this. Coincidence?*

The senator was not the kind of man who believed in coincidence.

Chapter 50

S pin Doctor

THE STEPS OF THE COURTHOUSE had been crowded by people and reporters for quite some time.

As foreseen by Ira Hudson, consummate spin doctor, the national press had indeed picked up the story and was immersed in the intrigue found and fabricated about the family. The FBI investigators had felt some restraint in drawing conclusions, at least until Hudson arrived on the scene and forced their hand. Members of the press, on the other hand, felt no such burden of proof and let their imaginations run wild.

Their speculations wove themselves into three or four popular conspiracy theories, drawn largely along political lines—or, more accurately, along the lines of the basic world views that guided political thinking.

One theory held that the incident was the tip of an iceberg hiding a widespread satanic cult. Of course, this was based on the old "Religious Series" of paintings by Pipo. The press dug up footage from years ago and also went back and interviewed some of the leaders of the religious protest.

"We seen what he was. He was not stopped then, and now it's come to this. He has bred a den of terrorists, and we best not let them go this time," said a man in a polyester suit holding a Bible.

Another theory tried to connect the family to a grass-roots survivalist antigovernment movement complete with leaders willing to claim the Colebrooks were operatives of their organization. For them, the pending case was one more example of Big Brother keeping God-fearing Americans and true patriots under his thumb. They talked of breaking the family members out of jail if they were convicted, then starting a "Free America" colony complete with its own nuclear reactor somewhere in the mountains of western North Carolina or East Tennessee.

The theory that was the favorite of the Colebrooks tied them to the Illuminati conspiracy—or even better, to the JAMs (Justified Ancients of Mumu), the sworn longtime enemies of the Illuminati. This theory involved a lot of numerology, along with finding pyramids and golden ratio rectangles hidden in Pipo's paintings. Interestingly enough, Pipo had never done any paintings of pyramids, although he had made many truncated pyramids as foundation pieces for statues. On every occasion, he had used the same angles as in the Great Pyramid of Cheops. But none of the fanatics picked up on that point.

Whichever conspiracy theory a person favored, ample evidence could be found in the careers and writings of the family, and especially in the artwork of James Colebrook. Several art historians were turning Colebrook interpretation into an industry, making the rounds of the talk shows and writing books on the subject.

When the Colebrooks finally arrived at the courthouse, they did so in an old green Chevy van. As they stepped out one by one, the crowd was treated to a sight rarely seen: all the Colebrook men in suits and ties. Up to this point, that had happened only at weddings and funerals.

They straightened their ties while the van was driven away by a friend who had agreed to be their chauffeur for the day. Then, led by their attorney, they marched single file up the steps and through the crowd. Reporters shouted questions and shoved microphones in their direction, but they simply smiled, nodded, and walked on through. If the reporters were looking for any evidence of guilt or worry, they were sorely misguided.

One astute reporter scanned the traffic to see if the women of the family were arriving in a separate car. He was disappointed in this search, as the family had agreed it would be better to keep their faces, especially Audrey's, away from the cameras as much as possible.

Instead, Audrey, Sue, and Lilly sat in Leon and Sue's condo a few blocks away.

"There they are!" Audrey shouted when she saw her father and uncles and grandfather on the screen.

She was sitting cross-legged on a beanbag chair front and center before the TV screen. She looked back and beamed at her mother and grandmother and the two men seated on the sofa. Unlike her relatives, these visitors looked to Audrey like they were used to wearing suits. One had a large, worn leather briefcase that was never out of sight or reach.

The visitors smiled back at the little girl and nodded, finding it impossible to resist the festive feeling of the day.

The man with the briefcase reached down and began to undo the worn brass clasp on the side. "Senator, maybe we should go over the testimony one more time," he said.

The senator put a restraining hand on his arm. "No need for that, Walt. You have done an excellent job of preparing everyone and organizing the documents. Let's relax and enjoy the moment."

Chapter 51
Potato Eaters II

THE COURTROOM, QUITE HIGH UP in the Justice Building, was accessible by a pair of narrow stairways and an elevator of ancient design and construction. In any case, it was a highly defensible position. Once the court officers and bailiffs made it clear that no nonsense would be tolerated, the network people contented themselves with waiting and receiving brief reports from the handful of local reporters who were allowed to attend the legal proceedings.

The Colebrooks' counselor looked down the table at his collection of defendants, trying to decide just what kind of impression they would make on a person unfamiliar with the family. Beside him sat Philip, a man in his late fifties who exuded an expansively good mood, considering he was accused of federal crimes. Beside Philip sat the boys in order of descending age. They were still called "the boys" even though they were young men now. The oldest, Leon, sat with an ironic smile on his broad face, looking straight ahead. The second son, Charles, tallest of the three, seemed to be having a good time also, shooting glances around the room as if seeking out someone in the crowd. He whispered something to Xavier, who leaned forward and stifled a laugh with his hand. On the end was their grandfather James. His suit was of an older cut and heavier material than the rest. He had a small leather-bound notebook open on the table and was sketching something in it with a soft lead pencil. The lawyer could not quite make out what he was drawing, but he thought he saw two rabbit ears and a cigarette.

They are what they are and who they are, thought the lawyer. *No use worrying about impressions at this point.*

A door in the back of the courtroom opened, and all rose as a judge in black robes entered and swiftly took his seat behind the bench.

"The Honorable Judge Rather," the bailiff announced.

As in, "I'd Rather have any other judge in the world," thought the prosecutor, who had been drafted into this particular exercise in American jurisprudence. The federal attorney had assigned this case to one of the youngest and most ambitious members of his office. The attorney had considered it a stroke of luck to be working with real FBI agents and (on the sly) an important Washington insider with connections to the White House.

He got an inkling that the job might have been sent from somewhere besides heaven when he and the other principals were first called into the judge's chamber.

"Oh, shit," Agent Tomblyn had muttered under his breath. He was looking at a small painting hung by the conference table adjacent to the judge's office.

The scene was of a card table in a smoky bar. Since the type of neighborhood bar depicted changed little with the years, it was difficult to place the time precisely, but the 1960s or 1970s were a reasonable bet. Vincent Van Gogh and Edgar Allen Poe were playing euchre against two men in ball caps. Van Gogh, his ear bandaged, was looking back over his shoulder, apparently at the painter. The viewer could see his cards, which are low numbers distributed poorly among the suits. He held a small pipe in his teeth, and his straw hat rested on the table next to an ashtray. On his face was a look of surprised misery. Only his eyes shone through with intense, unearthly blue light. Poe looked pale and unwell but strangely confident. Agent Meyers gleaned from this that he was holding better cards and was probably bidding Van Gogh and himself into an impossible position. At the bar, a roughly dressed man dipped a French fry into a pool of ketchup on his plate. This presumably was the basis for the title of the painting, *Potato Eaters II*.

The interview with the judge had not gone as well as they hoped. Only Hudson was unperturbed.

Back in the courtroom, the judge asked for a formal reading of the charges.

The prosecutor stood and read all the stuff about the defendants being accused of conspiring to commit acts of terrorism against the people of the United States of America. This was followed by a request to consider the suspects as enemy combatants and therefore subject to a whole different kind of court action and burden of proof. Basically, it meant that they could be held indefinitely while the government decided what to do with them.

The indictment, which was supposed to be a straightforward document, was full of damning phrases like "immediate threat to the republic" and "flagrant disregard of public safety." Under the direction of Ira Hudson, it was after all less a legal document than an instrument of propaganda. Hudson didn't even have a particular interest in the outcome of the trial. What he envisioned was a drawn-out court battle and a focal point for the media. The longer and messier, the better. If the Colebrooks were found guilty, fine. If they were acquitted, that would be fodder for the talk shows, too. Liberals letting terrorists go, and all that.

After the indictment was read in its entirety, the judge asked the defense attorney how the defendants wished to plead. The attorney, of course, responded that they pleaded not guilty.

The prosecutor then opened his case with a recounting of the events surrounding the disappearance of the truck. This truck was characterized as bearing a routine shipment of "research materials" between two government laboratories.

The prosecutor continued with the various circumstantial ties made to the family—always, of course, presenting the facts in the most uncomplimentary terms possible. The discovery of the plane by Leon and family was a theft of valuable government property. Xavier's dismantlement and testing of the same was willful destruction of valuable government property. The discharge of the flintlock rifle and the subsequent arrest of James amounted to a thwarted attempt to attack a government facility—a facility that, by the way, was home to several innocent students at the time. The prosecutor also had a good time with the Riobamba evidence and even included a deposition of a well-known chocolate expert from Chicago.

The proceedings went uncommonly quickly, since the attorney for the defense declined to object to any statements or evidence. Nor did he bother to challenge the deposition on the chocolate source.

At first, the prosecutor thought this was evidence that the Colebrooks had retained themselves one dumb lawyer. But as time went on, he began to suspect the opposing attorney was simply anxious to get through this part of the proceedings and on to his defense.

It was beginning to look like this was not destined to be as drawn out as Hudson hoped.

Chapter 52
Strangelove

"As our first witness, Your Honor, I would like to call Mrs. Lillian M. Colebrook to the stand," the attorney for the defense announced.

This caused quite a stir among the spectators in the courtroom, and no less among the Colebrook men seated at the defense table. All but Pipo turned to look, first at their attorney, who had not mentioned this particular detail of strategy, then toward the door, as if to confirm that it was not some other Mrs. Lillian M. Colebrook who was being called to the stand.

Of course, it was their Lilly. She wore a flowered dress that Philip thought made a good display of the curve of her hip. A murmur of approval also came from those in the crowd who were accustomed to seeing her only in her candy-making uniform at the shop.

The boys quickly resettled themselves into their seats. This was taking them back to their boyhood, Mom showing up and making everything all right.

The swearing-in was quickly dispatched, and Miss Lilly, as most people called her, took her seat.

The lawyer for the defense began, "Mrs. Colebrook, you understand that by law you are not required to appear before this court today to give testimony that concerns charges made against your husband."

"Yes, I do understand," she said.

"And Mrs. Colebrook, for the sake of full disclosure, please describe to the court any special compensation or arrangements that have been made on your behalf that might act as an encouragement for you to come forth with certain facts that have a bearing on this case."

"I was assured of full immunity in return for sharing information," she said, her expression deadpan.

This caused another stir in the courtroom and brought the prosecutor to his feet.

"Your Honor, I am not aware of any agreement of immunity with regard to Mrs. Colebrook or anyone else associated with this case."

The judge simply raised his eyebrows at the defense attorney.

The attorney returned to the defense table and removed two thick envelopes from his briefcase. One of these he dropped off at the prosecutor's table, and the other he brought to the judge.

"Your Honor, I apologize for not bringing this forward before, but the fact is, as you will note from the date on the document, the agreement was not finalized until last night."

"Would the prosecution like a recess to give them the opportunity to review this document?" the judge asked.

"Your Honor, I suggest we continue here for a few moments, during which time we will describe the nature of the document. If at that time the prosecution wishes to request a recess, we will happily agree."

The judge looked at the prosecutor.

The prosecutor had opened his envelope and was hastily examining the document inside. He flipped to the back to see the signatures and titles. This seemed to freeze him for a moment. Then he stood.

"The prosecution agrees to continue, but we wish to make it clear that we may well move to strike this testimony if we fail to authenticate the document after very careful examination." This last part he directed to the defense with emphasis suggesting he would go over everything with a fine-tooth comb.

The judge nodded to the defense. "The court likewise reserves the right to withdraw acceptance upon careful examination of the document," he said.

The attorney nodded and withdrew a copy of the same document from his briefcase.

"As the court may be aware, an ongoing investigation is presently being conducted in Washington by the Congress of the United States concerning an unauthorized nuclear project. Allegedly, this project is being run in secret by certain members of several branches of the government, together with some people from private industry. According to witnesses, the project is aimed at building nuclear power plants that are more efficient and cost effective than the older generation of plants. Of course, nothing is intrinsically wrong with such objectives. What has precipitated the investigation is that no appropriation has been made and no oversight has been stipulated for the project. Moreover, evidence indicates that, in the interest of saving time and money, the safeguards normally employed in this type of high-risk project are being circumvented or even completely ignored. This allegedly includes everything from the precautions taken in handling and transporting radioactive materials to the proper review and testing of the design elements for the reactor vessels themselves. Moreover, little or no attention is being given to the disposal of spent elements that will remain dangerously radioactive for several thousands of years."

At this point, the judge cleared his throat, which was the signal to let the defense attorney know he best not wander too far afield with the lecture.

"In any case, this congressional committee—this joint committee formed by the Senate and the House of Representatives—has granted immunity to Mrs. Colebrook in exchange for her testimony and in exchange for certain data and information that have come into her possession with respect to the inquiry. As it happens, Your Honor, this information has a direct bearing on the case before us today as well, and it is in that capacity that I have called Mrs. Colebrook to testify."

The attorney paused to let his words sink in. Considerable commotion overtook the room, so much so that the judge had to gavel the crowd back into order. The prosecutor attempted to confer with the FBI agents, but they were of no help. Hudson sat in the crowd of spectators with folded arms.

The defense attorney allowed a moment of silence before he dropped the document back into his briefcase and approached the witness stand, where Lilly sat patiently waiting for him to work his way through the preliminaries.

"Mrs. Colebrook, is it true that you are a member of an organization that has an interest in championing certain social and ecological causes?"

"That's right, but it is not a very organized organization," Lilly said. "It began as a group of friends and neighbors and mothers, and then we started having more formal meetings and activities." She seemed to exhibit a certain relief in finally getting down to what she had come to the courtroom to say.

"And the name of this organization?" the lawyer continued.

"It's called the Sisterhood of the Ancient Mountains—SAM for short," she said. She sometimes felt embarrassed about the name, even thinking it might distract from their work's being taken seriously. However, following the counsel of the attorney and members of the group, she gave no indication of that feeling in her answer. "Just lay it out there and dare anyone to snicker," one of the sisters had counseled.

"And the size of this organization? How many members do you currently have on your roster?" the attorney asked.

"I'm not sure we have a roster, officially. It's not like you have to pay dues or go through some kind of initiation or anything. But on a more or less regular basis, we usually have twenty to thirty people show up."

Tomblyn glanced over his shoulder and noticed a row of women smiling and giving Lilly various signs of encouragement. When he saw his landlady from the inn, he realized with a start that he and Haven had been under the surveillance of the Sisterhood for some time.

"And the purpose of this, uh, organization or Sisterhood?"

"You could say health and well-being—that is, on a fundamental basis for the community. Certain trends in the environment and culture we think represent a long-term threat to our families and communities, so we decided to see what we could do about those."

"What about funding? Where do you get the money to conduct your projects and activities?" he asked.

"We are completely self-funded. We decided early on to not accept donations from any industry or governmental group, or even from any other environmental organization. That way, we can do what we want when we want to do it, and not have to answer to anyone. We don't ever have to file reports to make anything public until we decide to," she said.

"And you were saying that one of the objectives of the organization is to promote a clean and healthy environment?" he asked.

"That is correct. We have several activities in that area. We monitor legislation and how our representatives vote on issues related to the environment. We also do some hands-on projects like measuring and publishing data that relates to the health of the environment," she said.

"Now, in addition to those projects, do you also monitor certain activities that relate to industrial and governmental waste products?" he asked.

"We have on occasion done projects that follow the whole cycle of waste disposal. One of the things we are interested in is getting a clear picture of what is happening that might have long-term effects. That could involve counting the number of trucks leaving some industry or government site. Sometimes, it might involve following those trucks to see exactly where they end up. After doing this, we compare the information to data in the public domain, like air-quality and water-quality permits, to see if they match," Lilly explained.

"And is this activity confined to the immediate area here in the city and county?" the attorney asked.

"When we started several years ago, we were pretty focused on our immediate area. Then, as we got some members from farther away, we expanded throughout western North Carolina. But our region is not isolated, so what happens here may affect some other place. Actually, not *may*—it *does* affect what happens elsewhere. And it works the other way around, too. Sometimes, we look at what ends up here and follow it back to where it came from in the first place. So, anyway, it ends up being all interrelated, and so you can't really draw any hard boundaries around the scope of what we are into. Everything is related."

"Now, I would like to turn to a particular project operated under the name Strangelove by your group," he said.

That name drew some whispers from the crowd.

"That was a name one of the girls came up with. She called anything having to do with nuclear energy Strangelove—you know, after the movie *Dr. Strangelove*, which apparently made a big impression on her when she was young. A few years ago, one of our members found out what kind of truck was used to transport nuclear materials, and that prompted her to find out what sort of precautions were taken and what sort of paperwork was filed with emergency response teams along the route, that sort of thing. Well, at one of our meetings, another member mentioned that she had seen a couple of those trucks, and some of the members thought that was unusual because no nuclear plants are in our area, and we couldn't think of a reason for those trucks to be there unless they were just transporting material through the region. Not much came of it at that meeting, except that she raised the question and also showed all the members a picture of the truck. By the next meeting a month later, almost everyone had seen one of those things on the highway. We decided to do what we call one of our full-circle studies. Where did it come from? Where did it go? Who shipped it? Who received it? What was it? How much? What sort of impact might it have? Did it agree with the documentation on it? We have found out through experience that when documentation does not agree with reality, someone is usually trying to pull something."

Lilly paused.

"Mrs. Colebrook, outline for us what you found in this full-circle study, please," the attorney prompted.

"Well, we found the answers to some of these questions, but not all of them. We found that the material was coming from the Savannah River nuclear processing site. We found that it was being taken to Oak Ridge National Laboratories in Tennessee. As to how much, we didn't find that out exactly, but we did learn, judging from the number of trucks, that it was a lot. And by a lot, I mean it built up over the period of our observations to several trucks per day."

"And these are not pickup trucks we're talking about here," the attorney threw in.

"No, we're not talking about small trucks. These trucks can carry several tons a load. They are about the size of a cement truck—not shaped like that, but about that size and weight," she said.

"And so members of your organization began to keep track of these trucks," the lawyer prompted.

"Yes. After we made the determination that they were coming from the Savannah River site, one of our members began sitting near the gate each morning and counting the number of trucks that left," she said.

At this point, the attorney strolled back to his table and removed a beat-up spiral-bound notebook from his briefcase. He thumbed through it seemingly with great interest as he brought it across the room and handed it to Lilly.

"Mrs. Colebrook, do you recognize this notebook?"

"This is the notebook our member used to record the number of trucks leaving the Savannah River site," she said after a brief look.

The lawyer returned to his briefcase and pulled out a single sheet of paper from a manila folder. This he also handed to the witness.

"And Mrs. Colebrook, do you recognize this document?" he asked.

"That is a graph our member prepared that summarizes the information in the notebook," she said. "It shows the number of trucks counted each day."

The prosecutor rose to object to the introduction of this unknown exhibit, but the defense stayed him with a gesture of his hand and produced copies for both him and the judge.

Returning to his witness, he asked, "Mrs. Colebrook, can you describe the main conclusions you drew when you saw this information concerning the number of trucks graphed in this manner?"

"It shows that the number of trucks increased sharply a little over a year ago, then remained on a high plateau until June of this year, at which time they abruptly stopped, at least for a time," she said.

The lawyer let that sink in, then continued, "I believe you told us previously that one of the exercises your group did was to check the observations on material movements against the statements filed with the authorities."

"That is correct," she said.

"And what did you find when you checked these shipments against the paperwork?" he asked.

"Nothing," she said. "We didn't find any statements filed with the Department of Transportation in the three states involved."

"Maybe nothing was filed because nothing potentially harmful was being carried in the trucks," the lawyer argued.

"That was what some of us thought at first. So we checked that theory out a couple of ways. First, we had a girl just walk up to one of the trucks when it was at a rest stop to see if she would draw any reaction. As soon as she got within twenty feet, the driver jumped out and kept her from coming any closer. She's pretty cute, this girl, so she started talking to the driver and asking questions, and he ended up telling her that the stuff inside was really dangerous, and he could lose his special license if he let anyone get hurt around it," she said.

"And was that your only evidence?" the attorney asked.

"No. We also checked out one of the trucks with a Geiger counter," she said. "A member borrowed it from the university, and some of the girls took it and tracked down a truck on the highway and kept passing it. They held the Geiger counter out the window when they passed the truck. And sure enough, they got a reading every time they went by." She couldn't help smiling when she thought about the old

Volvo speeding after the truck.

"So you established that massive quantities of radioactive materials were traveling between Savannah River and Oak Ridge, and that the usual paper trail accompanying such shipments was not filed," the attorney summarized.

"That's right," said Lilly.

"And did you develop a theory as to what was going on?" asked the attorney.

"A lot of theories circulated within the group. But not long after we obtained this information, we started seeing news stories about a possible unauthorized program, so we thought it might have something to do with that," she said.

"And what action did you take at that time?" he asked.

"We sent a letter to the Nuclear Regulatory Commission with an earlier version of this graph," she said. "But we saw on the news that the officials just continued to say nothing was going on. Actually, not only did they say nothing was going on, they said nothing could be going on because of all the safeguards they had in place, that every ounce of every isotope was accounted for at all times, and things like that," Lilly said.

"And I believe that brings us to this point on the graph," the lawyer said. He retrieved the graph from Lilly and pointed to the right side of the paper, where the line fell abruptly. He showed this to Lilly, then walked to where the judge and then the prosecutor could see. "This point corresponds to June the twenty-third of this year," he continued. "At that point, the number of trucks of the type you were counting dropped to zero."

"Yes," she said.

"Can you account for this? Can you explain why they would all of a sudden stop shipping the material on that date?" he asked.

"Because on the evening of the day before, June the twenty-second, we borrowed one of the trucks and hid it where they couldn't find it," Lilly announced.

Chapter 53

On the Courthouse Steps

Outside the courthouse, the crowd had multiplied several fold. Reporters from all types of media were in attendance by now. A festival atmosphere gripped the downtown as word of the revelations spread.

The first notables out of the courtroom were the FBI agents. Having become uncommonly stoic, the agents from Washington allowed the head of the local office to act as spokesman.

At the bottom of the courthouse steps, a number of microphones were raised in his direction. TV cameras pressed in.

One of the reporters shouted a question: "How do you feel about the latest developments in this case?"

"We are always happy when a matter like this can be resolved with clarity and without any further danger to the community," Meyers answered. He made a motion as if to go, but the crowd did not part for him.

"What is your next move in the case? Will you be following up on the new information that came to light in the courtroom?" another reporter shouted.

"Clearly, we will be taking a new direction from this point," Meyers said.

This time, the agents made a forceful exit amid a wave of shouted questions and confusion. Meyers opened the door of the black car at the curb and allowed his fellow agents to enter before him. The reporters—all except for one—gave up on the idea of getting further response and began to cast about for their next target.

The local newspaper reporter, Shirley Dawn, shouted into the lull, "What do you think of the Colebrook family?"

This seemed to take Meyers off-guard. He looked at the young lady who asked the question.

"I think they are a truly remarkable family, I really do," he said. "And I wish them all the best."

"Thank you," the reporter said.

Meyers held her eye for a moment, then ducked into the car, which promptly drove away from the scene.

ooooo

The senator could not have been more pleased. He had entered the courtroom with an aide and taken a seat in the back just as Lilly was called to the stand. All eyes being on Lilly, he had gone unnoticed.

His first order of business was to scan the courtroom. As he suspected, he spotted the hulking form of Ira Hudson near the back on the opposite side. He leaned close to his aide and nodded toward Hudson. At length, the aide spotted him, too. The senator made a motion with his hands as if scooting the aide off the bench, and the aide complied. The aide worked his way around the room and stood directly behind Hudson. He had been well coached on what to do when the trial was over, or if Hudson decided to leave the courtroom before the proceedings were dismissed.

The senator then had nothing to do but sit back and enjoy the drama as it worked its way to its forgone conclusion. He could not help glancing over at Hudson from time to time to see how he was taking all this in. Lilly's entrance brought Hudson to the edge of his seat and wiped the arrogant smirk off his face. As her testimony unfolded, and as she dropped the bombshell about stealing the truck, Hudson looked like he had eaten some bad fish. A master at reading body language would also have noticed that he glanced around to check out the exits, a primal fight-or-flight response.

After she told of stealing the truck, Lilly fielded more questions from the defense attorney about what her group's intent was, where the truck had been hidden, how easy the theft was to pull off, how the group made the casting, and how it eventually returned the truck when she understood it was getting her family in trouble.

The cross-examination by the prosecutor was almost nonexistent. He briefly challenged the credibility of the witness, which the judge quickly put a stop to. Then he challenged the idea that Mrs. Colebrook and her group could have done everything she claimed without the knowledge of the rest of the family. That got nowhere either, as it became apparent that, yes, the scenario was entirely feasible, as the men of the family were tied up with their own interests most of the time and were too busy to worry about the details of hers.

In the end, the judge asked a simple question of the prosecution: "Would you like me to issue a ruling, counselor, or would you prefer to make a motion?"

The prosecutor conferred with the others at the table, then rose to speak. "Your Honor, the state would like to withdraw all charges against the accused."

The room went nuts, as the senator knew it would. Thus had he positioned his aide to keep track of the slippery Hudson in the mayhem.

Hudson was too savvy to be one of the first out of the courtroom. While he was not a readily recognizable figure to the general public, he knew that some in the national press might pick up on his appearance, especially if it looked like he was fleeing the scene. He elected to wait until the FBI agents and a few of the spectators left before he made his move.

When he did, the aide was close behind. The senator, already out of the courtroom and down the interior stairs, held back near the door, not wanting to be spotted himself as yet. When Hudson exited the building and was halfway down the steps outside, the senator made a quick call on his cell phone. Simultaneously, the aide waved his hands and pointed at Hudson.

"Mr. Hudson, can we have your reaction to the court proceedings?" It was Shirley Dawn from the local paper. She was followed by a local TV news camera and reporter.

Hudson was shocked to hear his name called out in this place. He froze as panic overtook his nervous system. Once his better senses gained control, he turned to see who had called him.

"Do I know you, miss?" he said, positioning for his traditional counterattack.

The reporter glanced at the aide to make sure she had the right guy. He nodded, and she turned back to Hudson. Since he had not answered her question, she didn't answer his.

"Mr. Hudson, can you comment on what interest the office of the vice president of the United States has in this trial?" she asked, getting right to the heart of the matter.

This he had not seen coming. He could not conceal the look of surprise on his face. The several cameramen now covering the scene all knew it was a shot that would be played on every news channel all day long and pulled up for weeks to come. It was that good.

"Uh, naturally, the vice president is interested in anything to do with the war on tourism. I mean the war on terrorism," said Hudson.

Now, that really was too special. All the media present knew they had just made the jump from the news channels to the late-night talk shows. This was what being a reporter was all about.

"Mr. Hudson, what do you think of the outcome of the trial?" Shirley Dawn asked.

"I have no further comment," Hudson said.

He turned his back on the group and continued down the steps, giving the TV crews their classic shot of a guilty guy retreating.

Shirley Dawn looked at the aide, smiled, and gave him the thumbs-up. They were both beaming. Then the aide motioned her toward the door of the courthouse, where the senator was now making his exit, looking calm and pleased and chatting amicably with reporters.

The local reporter rushed up in time to get close enough to the senator to join in.

Another reporter was already asking, "Senator, were you involved with granting Mrs. Colebrook immunity in this matter?"

The senator responded in his usual unhurried way. "As you know, I have been a member of the joint congressional committee charged with investigating reports of an unauthorized nuclear program. So, yes, when it came to my attention that Mrs. Colebrook might have information vital to our investigation, I was more than happy to bring that before the committee. As for immunity, I think you can see for yourself that Mrs. Colebrook is no terrorist."

Another member of the press shouted, "Senator, when you proposed that the committee offer immunity, did you know that Mrs. Colebrook's group had stolen the truck?"

The senator smiled. "To tell you the truth, at that point, we knew only that they had some information that was potentially valuable. We had no idea just what a wealth of information it would turn out to be."

"What other information have they provided you?" someone from the crowd asked.

"Well, you heard in the court proceeding about the group's log of shipments between Savannah River and Oak Ridge. I can tell you that, so far, these cannot be correlated with any known and authorized programs. That brings up questions of security and disregard of regulations, in addition to misappropriation of funds. Where did the money come from for all this work?" the senator said, raising his eyebrows.

Then Shirley Dawn spoke up. "Senator, do you find it interesting that one of the vice president's right-hand men was at this proceeding?"

The senator sought out the voice in the crowd.

"Yes," he said. "I find that very interesting indeed, and I am sure the rest of the committee will as well."

"Do you think the White House is involved in the secret program you are investigating?" Shirley Dawn said.

"We will follow the evidence wherever it leads," the senator said.

"Do you think the vice president is directly involved?" another reporter asked.

"Well, in the words of another famous congressional investigation, we will want to determine what he knew and when he knew it," the senator said.

He smiled, nodded, and proceeded down the steps.

The reporters did not have long to wait for the next leg of their story. They heard a commotion to the left and saw that the family Colebrook had emerged from the courthouse through a side door. A group was already gathering around them and shouting questions and congratulations. A girl approached Pipo with a book of his paintings, asking for him to sign it. He took it and smiled at her.

The reporters got into position while the cameramen drank in the Colebrooks, who were standing almost in a straight line and waving at friends in the crowd.

"How does it feel to be out of there?" a reporter shouted from the crowd.

The family just kept smiling and waving. Their lawyer stepped up and answered for them.

"The family feels fortunate that the matter was resolved in such a prompt and decisive manner. They have been totally vindicated of any wrongdoing and look forward to returning to their private lives."

"Leon, what about the rumor that your little girl came up missing on the trail last week, and about the big gathering up there? Did that have anything to do with the investigation?" That was Shirley Dawn, putting two and two together.

The green van pulled up to the curb below. The side door opened, and the captain of the Rangers stepped out.

"I think that man down there can fill you in on the details better than I can," Leon said.

He waved to the captain, who waved back. This had the desired effect of clearing the mob of reporters away so the family could proceed down the steps. They made their way through the crowd and started piling into the van.

Their old friend Klondike was at the wheel, and Audrey was riding shotgun. She wore an oversized baseball cap and a huge pair of aviator sunglasses.

Leon gave her a disapproving look. "I thought you were supposed to stay home until we got back."

"Klondike said it would be all right if I came incognito," she answered.

Xavier jumped in and picked up her angel scroll, which was lying on the console between the front seats.

"Let's see what you've been up to lately," he said.

He took a look, let out one of his famous laughs, and passed the scroll around for the others to see.

The latest rectangle contained a drawing of an angel holding an old-fashioned briefcase.

Chapter 54

Four Weeks Later

MOST MEMBERS OF THE SISTERHOOD of the Ancient Mountains were students or former students of Body Language 101. One of the unintended consequences of taking the class was to make watching White House press conferences pretty much a habit. On this day, when a bunch of members were meeting for lunch, they persuaded the restaurant owner to tune in the TV over the bar so they would not miss the latest installment.

The White House press secretary was just irresistible. They couldn't help watching him, especially after all the stuff that had happened so close to home. The guy broadcast every possible lying son-of-a-bitch signal known to man, and the press just kept showing up and asking questions like waves breaking over slimy rock.

The sisters had just been served their food when the camera showed the press secretary approaching the podium. As they sat back to enjoy the usual opening moves, a banner scrolled across the bottom of the screen:

VICE PRESIDENT RESIGNS

And there was their smarmy little hero taking questions before a roomful of reporters who seemed unusually determined. The bartender turned up the volume.

"The president met with the vice president last night for an extended period, and after reviewing all possible options the vice president tendered his resignation. The president has very reluctantly accepted the resignation of the man he calls one of the finest public servants he has ever had the pleasure of working with," the press secretary said. He spoke partly extemporaneously and partly from a script. Even the best among the students found it difficult to tell where one ended and the other began.

"Are you still maintaining that the president knew nothing about the project called Teraplex Building?" asked a reporter in the front row.

"The president did not authorize the project and had no direct knowledge of the project. He learned about it just as you and I did, by listening to the news and watching the proceedings of the congressional committee," the press secretary said.

"My God!" one of the sisters said. "He's still laying it out there. Conspicuously lying and taunting them to do something about it."

Another reporter asked, "Is it true that the vice president owns stock in Steam Corporation, the company building the reactors and the one benefiting the most from the monies going into the project?"

"The vice president's assets were placed in a blind trust when he entered office, so he did not have control over specific investments made within that trust," the press secretary said.

"But it is true, is it not, that the trust held in his name has invested heavily in Steam Corporation over the last few years," the same reporter said.

"As I understand it, the trust maintains a wide portfolio, so it would not be surprising to find some shares of a large company like Steam Corporation included," the press secretary answered.

Another sister said, "Interesting, staying away from the flat denial. Rough translation: 'The bastard stood to make a mint off this.'"

Back on the screen, another reporter changed the subject. "Reports have circulated that a little girl was detained by the military unit that was dispatched to look for the missing drone. Can you confirm that, and was the vice president involved?"

"I think you are taking an incident of a lost child out of context. And you are doing a disservice to the brave military men and women who put themselves in harm's way to protect your way of life," the press secretary answered, attempting to project anger into his voice and appearance.

"Excellent," one of the sisters said. "Defending the troops against a fantasy attack by ungrateful and cowardly detractors. Always guaranteed to win points with a section of the voting public."

"Was the vice president involved in the detention of the little girl?" the reporter followed up.

"Uh, the incident is under investigation, but the vice president did not authorize it or have any direct knowledge of it."

The broadcast moved to a shot of a newscaster in the studio. At first, she seemed slightly distracted watching the monitor to her side, but she quickly shifted straight ahead to the camera.

"We will now take a quick commercial break," she said. "When we return, we will talk with Ira Hudson, author of the newest Washington insider book, *Government Without Shame: The New Art of Leadership*."

ooooo

Meanwhile, at the Athenaeum Company, Philip was carrying out one last cardboard box to the Silver Wraith. He had already said goodbye to everyone—many more than once, and in different ways. All of that on top of recent events made the last walk feel anticlimactic.

He had in fact created a little going-away present of his own. Since he had been carrying out boxes of books and various personal items for the last week or so, it was no special problem to secret out a box large enough to contain the ventriloquist dummies the cleaning crew had helped him obtain from the offices of Michael and Judy. He and Pipo had quite a satisfying creative session posing and photographing the two puppets in awkward and sometimes sexually embarrassing positions. A friend printed these in the appropriate sizes, after which Philip substituted them for the photos of sailboats and mountain climbers in the motivational posters in the company hallways. Philip was particularly fond of the one that showed the male puppet lifting up the skirt of the female puppet and looking back at the camera with an open mouth. The caption read, "Exploration Brings New Discoveries."

On his last day, he was reminded of an old lesson of Pipo's: Most adults have stopped looking at their surroundings, especially in familiar places.

One of the more observant technicians noticed the pictures right away, so an underground buzz started as various workers found reasons to visit the office area. Fortunately for Philip's plan, they kept their laughter to themselves until they were back on the floor. As Philip expected, Michael, Judy, and the rest of the management team were laser-focused on their tasks and took no notice at all. Philip knew that stories of their reactions, when they finally did discover the replacements, would make their way back to him in good time. Until then, he would savor this final prank like a glass of fine wine.

On Philip's last walk to the truck, the goldfinch at the bird feeder pecked for seed, gave him a prolonged look, then turned back to the seed. Philip suspected the bird was thinking, *I knew he wouldn't last.**

He tossed the box into the back of the truck, which also contained a couple of bronze castings, two hiking poles, and several worn toolboxes. Both Pipo and the old yellow Lab looked at Philip and tried to gauge his mood as he swung into the shotgun seat.

---

* As Henrico Carr would have been able to tell him, the thoughts of the finch were much more practical in nature. The finch simply registered Philip's departure and wondered if seed would still be delivered to the feeder in a reliable manner. This was as close to sentiment as the finch was prepared to get.

He looked straight ahead for a moment, then said, "Fuck 'em if they can't take a joke."

He turned to the old man and the dog and gave them the best grin he had mustered in three years.

Pipo smiled and nodded and shoved the truck into gear. The Labrador put her head in Philip's lap and let out a sigh of relief that needed no translation by Henrico Carr's technology.

ooooo

Meanwhile, at the local FBI office, Agent Meyers read the latest order from Washington for a background check.

"You have got to be kidding me," he said to no one in particular.

A couple of his clerks looked up from their desks.

"They are requesting a background check on Mr. Charles Colebrook," he told them.

Charles had been reinstated—complete with back pay and restoration of all access—to his job in D.C. developing satellites for the government. However, according to the ways of a blind bureaucracy, a background check was needed before his security clearance could be made whole. This order came to Meyers on a standard form with all the personality of a parking ticket.

He swiveled in his chair to view his new acquisition, a bright oil painting mounted in a deeply carved gilded frame.

It was the very painting Pipo had been working on during the investigation. Pipo had offered it as a gift to Meyers following the debacle of the court proceeding. However, since FBI agents were not allowed to accept gifts, Meyers bought if from him for a hundred dollars. Perhaps the offer was Pipo's way to put the episode firmly behind them. Meyers liked to think it was his way of saying he had no hard feelings. As usual with James Colebrook, one was left to speculate.

In any case, Meyers loved the painting. It brightened his office, and not just because of the colors either.

The painting showed a beautiful blue lake in the summertime. The most prominent feature was a Boston Whaler speedboat that appeared to be ready to jump right out at the viewer. At the wheel was the Irish writer James Joyce. Behind the boat at the end of a gracefully arcing towrope was a beautiful woman on water skis with some graceful arcs of her own: Marilyn Monroe. Striking a pose and skiing well up on the wake of the boat, she was beaming one of her famous smiles. On the left side of the painting was a small sailboat. The main sail was luffed and shaking in the wind, the halyard dipped from the end of the boom into the water, and the two men aboard seemed to be arguing, judging from their gestures and the stiffness of their poses. The whole sailboat portion was only a minor part of the overall composition, so the turmoil did not materially detract from the overall feeling of fun and optimism conveyed by the balance of the painting. The size also did not allow for much detail, but Meyers could swear the two men on the sailboat were intended to be Tomblyn and Haven.

"How are you going to handle this request?" one of the clerks asked. "We have a file on the guy about two inches thick. Do we really need to interview anyone?"

Meyers turned back from the painting. He looked at the clerk and said, "We owe it to our nation to be thorough. Let's go get some ice cream."

ooooo

Meanwhile, at the Chocolate Moose, operations were in full swing. Two workers were pouring a kettle of fudge onto a marble table to the wonderment of a row of spectators. On the marble table next to it, another worker was bent over a tray of caramel apples made from the local fruit that was just coming into season. Using a squirt bottle, she drizzled strands of chocolate around the apples. Some were coated with pecans as well.

At the ice-cream counter, a line of people looked and sampled and read the names of the thirty-two flavors in the cases. Up next was a heavyset woman with three offspring ranging from about six to sixteen.

Mother to oldest child: "Do you know what you want?"

The oldest mumbled something to the mother.

Mother to blond girl behind the counter: "He wants chocolate."

Blond girl: "Would you like that in a homemade waffle cone?"

Mother to oldest: "What kind of cone do you want?"

The sixteen-year-old pointed to a display of cones.

Mother to blond girl: "He wants a cake cone."

The blond girl complied with a smile, and the process started over with the ten-year-old.

At the counter behind the cases, Lilly was occupied with a tray of molds of their latest creation. She turned the clear plastic sheet upside down, tapped on it, then flexed it slightly. Four chocolate shapes were released onto another tray. She turned them over and examined them, pleased with the results. She trimmed the slight flashing from the edges with a paring knife, then positioned them on the display tray.

When she stooped to slide the tray into the case, she found herself face to face with a small boy on the other side of the glass. He had been examining the chocolate dinosaurs and bears and seemed startled to see her.

The little boy pulled on his mother's hand and asked, "What does that say?"

His mother bent to read the sign. "Atomic Fire Truck."

They were indeed four chocolate truck replicas, the backs of which were rendered red by coating the molds with red sprinkles before the chocolate was poured in.

The mother looked at Lilly, putting her together with the recent news stories.

Lilly smiled back. "It's our new bestseller."

"Could you put one in a box and sign it for me?" the mother asked.

Lilly nodded and smiled.

"And I think he wants a dinosaur," the mother added.

Lilly looked at the little boy. "Would you like a tyrannosaur, a triceratops, or a brontosaur?"

"Tywinosaur!" he said, and grinned with excitement.

When Lilly stood, she found herself facing her youngest son, who was holding hands with Janie. They had slipped into the shop and behind the counter while she was dealing with the chocolate case.

"So," she said, "you're a couple now, huh?"

"Yes, Mother," Xavier said, rolling his eyes.

She gave them each a hug, then looked back at Xavier.

"Did you get everything straightened out with the university?" she asked.

"Well, not exactly everything," he said. "They're carrying over the scholarship and not counting any unfinished course grades against my record. But I missed too much of the fall semester to really pull anything out. So I decided to hang out with Janie for a while and maybe do some work with Dad and Pipo and pick it up again spring semester."

ooooo

And meanwhile, in downtown Asheville:

The shaman, a small brown man, stood beside a slightly taller man with glasses and an impeccable hound's-tooth jacket. When Leon and Audrey entered the room, the shaman was looking intently at a painting hanging behind the desk. He did not at first turn to greet them as his companion did.

"Henrico, thanks for coming," Leon said.

The two men regarded each other for a moment before embracing warmly.

"Good to see you, Leon," said Henrico. He then turned to Audrey. "And this must be the young artist Audrey Colebrook I have heard so much about."

"Henrico, allow me to present my daughter, Audrey Colebrook," Leon said, adopting a grand tone. "Audrey, say hello to Dr. Carr. You've heard your mom and me talk about Dr. Carr from our college days."

Audrey picked up on the formal introduction and extended her hand to Henrico.

The shaman had turned toward them and mostly watched the little girl. He stood a bit back from the group, arms crossed. The expression on his face was difficult to read.

Henrico put a hand on the shaman's shoulder. "Leon, this is the learned man I told you about, my friend and mentor, Gammy Usela."

The shaman responded with a nod. Leon wondered if he understood any English at all. Henrico had told Leon about the shaman back when they were roommates at the university. In spite of the fact that Henrico's family was wealthy and valued modern education, they had sent Henrico to live with Gammy and learn in the shamanic tradition when Henrico was twelve. Henrico had told Leon many stories from that coming-of-age year.

Although they had not spoken for a while, Henrico being immersed in his own research, Leon had contacted him about the writing on the rock. Intrigued, Henrico had agreed to bring Gammy for his first visit to the United States.

Now, even far removed from his normal surroundings, out of place in a condo in Asheville, North Carolina, Gammy still emanated a certain power and directness. Leon could fully appreciate Henrico's respect and affection for him.

The shaman looked back to the painting and said something to Henrico, presumably in his native Indian language.

"He says he finds this painting interesting," Henrico translated.

The painting showed three square-rigged wooden ships anchoring in the calm bay of a tropical island. Clearly, this was intended to be the landing of Christopher Columbus with the *Niña*, the *Pinta*, and the *Santa Maria*. The tattered sails were ablaze with the cross of the Spanish royal family. In the partial shade of palm trees on the beach, Fidel Castro and Che Guevara sat in folding chairs patiently waiting for the explorers to disembark. Stacked behind the chairs were crates of provisions, including rum and cigars, along with a cooler of glass bottles of Coca-Cola on ice. A single carbine of World War I vintage leaned against the crates. Farther to the rear amid the lush foliage of the jungle was a cacao tree heavy with pods. A single vanilla vine climbed the tree beside it.

The title of the painting was in Spanish: *Nos Estaban Esparandos*.

"That means, 'We Were Waiting,' " Audrey said.

Henrico turned and smiled at her.

"Yes, that's very good," he said.

"My great-grandfather painted that picture."

The shaman turned and regarded her then. He spoke slowly, looking her in the eye.

Henrico translated, "He says he would very much like to meet your great-grandfather someday."

"You can meet him, but he doesn't talk to anyone," Audrey said, returning the shaman's gaze.

Henrico did not translate this reply, thinking that the two old men would probably have no trouble communicating on some level, words or no words.

"Uh, Henrico, have you and Mr. Usela had a chance to study the photographs I sent?" Leon asked.

This elicited a short burst of the Indian language from the shaman.

Henrico explained, "He says it is not in the normal language. It is in a more ancient language."

"You mean the Olmec language?" Leon asked, even though he had always read that the Olmecs had no written language.

"No," Henrico said. "Older than that."

The shaman spoke a few more words, then turned back and looked at the little girl.

"They call it the language of the spoons," Henrico explained.

"Why do they call it the language of the spoons?" Audrey asked.

"We don't really know why it is called that. It is thought to be very ancient and mysterious. A figure of speech in Gammy's language translates as, 'Old as the language of the spoons.' For instance, you might say a shirt is as old as the language of the spoons if you grow tired of wearing it."

"He looks like he's as old as the language of the spoons," said the little girl, in defiance of the shaman's persistent stare.

The shaman laughed as if he understood every word.

"Does he know the meaning of the symbols?" asked Leon. "Some of them we think we recognize. For instance, this one here we think is a cacao pod."

"Everyone thought it was corn," Audrey said, "but then my grandma said it was the pod where chocolate comes from."

"Yes. Your grandmother is a smart woman," Henrico said. "That would be the original cacao, known as Criollo. The plants came from near my home in Ecuador. Very big magic in the old tradition."

He pointed to the symbol and exchanged some words with the shaman. The shaman shook his head and pointed, too.

"Gammy claims the Criollo came from Mexico, not Ecuador," Henrico explained. "But this is an old argument. Brazilians think it came from Brazil. Let's just say we know it came from Central or South America. In any case, it figures strongly in all traditional religions of the area because it can't be grown alone. It takes shade from other trees. It takes a certain kind of mite to pollinate the flowers. It takes certain kinds of bacteria and fungus to ferment. It takes sun and rain. It is not possible to grow this crop without developing a strong respect and understanding of the complexity of the natural world. Everything is connected. That's really the basis of the traditional religions."

The shaman nodded.

Audrey pointed to another symbol. "Is this an armadillo?"

"That's right, Audrey, very good," Henrico said, and translated something quickly to the shaman, who smiled.

"Uncle Xavier says an armadillo can't decide if it's a mammal or a reptile," she said.

Henrico gave her an odd look, partly of surprise and partly of amusement.

"You have no idea how close your uncle is," he said, shaking his head.

Leon broke in before Henrico had a chance to expand on the thought.

"What can Mr. Usela tell us about the overall meaning or purpose of the rock?" he asked.

Henrico conferred with the shaman. Leon got the idea that Henrico was trying to persuade the shaman to tell something the shaman was reluctant to reveal. Henrico dropped his eyes and made a gesture with his hand, and the shaman seemed to relent. He spoke at some length, gesturing with his hands.

Finally, Henrico turned to Leon. "He says the stone is meant to tell a traveler that he is on the right track, that he is almost there."

"Almost where?" asked Leon.

Another conversation ensued between Henrico and the shaman.

"Almost to the place where the world began," Henrico said.

Leon looked at him in silence.

By and by, Leon said, "In the Cherokee religion, Shining Rock is the place where the world began."

"Leon, you must know that the stone you found is much older than the Cherokee civilization," said Henrico.

"It's much older, but it could be the origin of the Cherokee creation myth!" said Leon. "Very little is known about the pre-Cherokee culture here."

"I don't think I will try to translate the word *myth* to Gammy," said Henrico.

Leon went to a bookcase and pulled down a large volume. He quickly thumbed the pages in a manner that suggested a close acquaintance with the contents.

"Here," he said, pointing to a photograph of Shining Rock. He laid the book on the desk.

The shaman barely glanced at the picture of Shining Rock, focusing instead on the photo on the page opposite. He leaned over and looked closely for a long time. Audrey went around the desk and pulled open the middle drawer to find a magnifying glass. She had planned to demonstrate how to use it, but the shaman apparently understood it well, taking it quickly from her outstretched hand. He began talking to Henrico in a lower and slower voice, occasionally pointing out details in the photo.

Henrico turned to Leon. "Where was this picture taken?"

"Not too far from here," Leon said. "It's a large piece of soapstone in the valley of the Tuckaseegee River over in Jackson County. It was found years and years ago. People call it the Judaculla Rock."

"Tamasl'kalu," said the shaman.

"Tamasl'kalu is thought by Gammy's people to be a giant who was on earth before human beings. He was the spirit who took care of the animals and later taught human beings how to align themselves with the forces of nature so they could be hunters without destroying the balance of life. He taught them also how to use plants to keep themselves healthy," explained Henrico.

"That's pretty much the same as the Cherokee tradition, right down to the name of the giant, who they call Tsul'kalu," said Leon.

The shaman said something else to Henrico.

"He says it's a door. What you call the Judaculla Rock is a door," said Henrico.

"A door to where?" asked Leon.

A conversation between the shaman and Henrico followed.

"According to tradition, it's the door the giant Tamasl'kalu used to enter this world. That's what the writing on the rock indicates, at least as much as Gammy can read. He can't read all of it. I don't think anyone can," said Henrico.

Leon and Audrey thought about that. Sue had also come into the room in time to hear the last of the conversation. Leon could not help thinking of the line from Thomas Wolfe: "A stone, a leaf, an unfound door."

At length, Leon said, "We need to understand what went on here."

Sue and Audrey nodded their heads.

"I would like to understand it, too," said Henrico.

The shaman began to speak, and Henrico translated: "He said that in order to understand this, you will need to visit him and see some things there, and also that you will need to visit the island of St. John. Some things there are above the water and some below."

And with that, they began to plan the next part of their adventure.